"Do you want to be working with?"

"Is this an attempt to lower my defenses so I'll open up about my feelings?" Genevieve asked.

"Yes. A hundred percent," Scott said.

She laughed softly. "You won't even hide it?"

"I have to do this by the book. I'll be able to tell the commissioner that I did my best, that you played with puppies, did some training work, spoke with the therapist and that your morale was boosted by the experience."

"That's the goal?"

"That, and..." Her clear gaze met his, and he read the betrayal there. He was letting her down already. "Is it ever good to see you, Gen." Shoot. He hadn't meant to come out with something quite that honest. He cleared his throat.

"It's good to see you, too, Scott." A smile flickered at her lips, and his heart gave a flip. That was supposed to have changed after six years.

Dear Reader,

Thank you so much for picking up this book! With all the reading choices you have, I'm so grateful that you chose me.

While this book is set in Amish Country like my last two miniseries, this is a stand-alone story. So this is the only story you'll read set at the K9 Training Center. If you enjoyed this book, I hope you'll consider leaving a review or telling a friend about it. Reviews really help an author in getting the word out about her books, and you wouldn't believe how grateful we are when we see those positive reviews come in!

If you'd like to see more of my books, you can find me online at patriciajohns.com. I have quite a backlist, and there are always new books coming! I'm also thrilled to hear from my readers, so feel free to reach out. You'll make my day.

If you'd like a chance at winning some signed books and knitted surprises, join my newsletter! Every month there are four winners chosen to get packages in the mail from me, and you'll never miss out on a new release.

I hope to hear from you!

Patricia

HEARTWARMING

An Amish Country Reunion

Patricia Johns

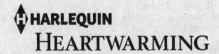

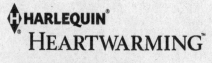

ISBN-13: 978-1-335-47582-4

An Amish Country Reunion

Recycling programs for this product may not exist in your area.

Harlequin Enterprises ULC
22 Adelaide St. West, 41st Floor
Toronto, Ontario M5H 4E3, Canada
www.Harlequin.com

Printed in U.S.A.

Patricia Johns is a *Publishers Weekly* bestselling author who writes from Alberta, Canada, where she lives with her husband and son. She writes Amish romances that will leave you yearning for a simpler life. You can find her at patriciajohns.com and on social media, where she loves to connect with her readers. Drop by her website and you might find your next read!

Books by Patricia Johns

Harlequin Heartwarming

The Butternut Amish B&B

Her Amish Country Valentine
A Single Dad in Amish Country
A Boy's Amish Christmas

Amish Country Haven

A Deputy in Amish Country
A Cowboy in Amish Country

The Second Chance Club

Their Mountain Reunion
Mountain Mistletoe Christmas
Rocky Mountain Baby
Snowbound with Her Mountain Cowboy

Love Inspired

Amish Country Matches

The Amish Matchmaking Dilemma
Their Amish Secret
The Amish Marriage Arrangement
An Amish Mother for His Child

Visit the Author Profile page
at Harlequin.com for more titles.

To my husband, who supports and encourages me with every book I write. And to our son, who is turning into a talented writer. I love you both!

CHAPTER ONE

ONLY THREE MILES to go to the Pennsylvania State Police K9 Training Center, but Trooper Genevieve Austin had stopped at a gas station just outside Strausfeld to fill up her tank and get a snack. She was putting off the humiliating moment of her arrival. The K9 Training Center, or "Puppy School" as the officers of the Pennsylvania State Police jokingly called it, was an important arm of the police, and while training dogs was the chief concern of the facility, the dogs weren't the only ones in training. It was also about correcting the bad attitudes of the officers sent there.

Using the K9 Center therapeutically was the brainchild of the previous commissioner, who'd wanted a gentler way to deal with problem officers. This involved chats with therapists, bookwork and time helping to train unruly puppies—an activity the therapists insisted was helpful in getting uncooperative officers to look deeper at their own "inner puppy." Somehow, the puppy school punishment was worse than anything else they'd cooked up before, and Genevieve was dreading it.

She grabbed a chocolate bar from the minimart display case and put it on the counter. Behind her, a woman with a little girl in tow was picking out windshield cleaning liquid. She'd been giving Genevieve some curious side-eye since she'd arrived.

"And forty dollars at pump number four, please," Genevieve said. Her black straw campaign hat was tucked under her arm. It was hot out there—only the first of June, but summer heat had rolled in. The air-conditioning in the gas station shop felt good.

The teenager working the till shot her a lopsided smile. He looked about seventeen, with a bit of acne, a company polo shirt that was two sizes too big on him, and a name tag that read Trey.

"Are you here for a movie?" he asked, lowering his voice.

"Sorry?"

"Are you acting in a movie? I know you probably can't say because they try and keep it a secret, but they do a lot of filming around here. I want to get in as an extra. Sometimes they hire locals for realistic flavor. I'm a guy with flavor." He gave her a roguish grin.

"Are you now," Genevieve said dryly.

"It looks real, you know," Trey said, gesturing at her gray uniform with black tie and the state trooper badge on the side of her sleeve. He squinted at her name pin. "Austin. Is that your character's name?"

"What makes you think I'm not the real deal—"

she made a show of looking at his name tag "—Trey?"

The teenager faltered then, and he leaned forward to look out the window. Her cruiser sat at Pump Four.

"Oh, sorry, I thought you were an actress," he said, his cheeks suddenly flaming with color. "Um—yeah, I'll just ring you up."

Genevieve knew exactly why he'd made the mistake, and he wasn't the first one to do it. She was five foot ten, a hundred and thirty pounds, and had to get her uniform pants specially made because the company that made trooper uniforms didn't make them for women with twenty-four-inch waists and legs as long as hers. She kept her long blonde hair pulled back in a low bun, and with just a touch of makeup and naturally great skin, she knew that she looked attractive. But people made assumptions. Constantly. Pretty did not equal authority in most people's minds.

Genevieve was there to be a cop, to chase down the bad guys, to make Pennsylvania roads safer, and to stand for law and order, and it was frustrating to be treated like she was less than capable because of her appearance. But it wasn't her appearance holding her back—it was Commissioner Taylor.

Genevieve took her change, put her hat back on and headed out to the cruiser. As she filled the tank, her gaze moved methodically around the parking lot. The observation was both training and habit. But this was Amish Country, and there wasn't much to see—a couple of cars passing on the road and a buggy pulled by two horses passing on the other side, the sound of hooves echoing cheerfully over the pavement. Beyond that was farmland—rolling fields of green wheat only about six inches high, by her estimate.

The gas clicked off and she returned the nozzle. Normally she'd be filling up at a cardlock, but there wasn't one close by and she'd been assured by fleet management that they'd reimburse her after her ten-day stint at the puppy school.

The woman from earlier held the gas station door open for her young daughter, who passed under her arm and out of the store. She cast Genevieve a smile.

"Good morning!" the woman called. "Honestly? I thought you were an actress, too. This spring they were filming this Amish movie for TV and Strausfeld was just crawling with actors and cameramen."

Genevieve gave her a curt nod. "I see. Well, have a good day, ma'am."

"Oh, don't call me ma'am yet!" the woman laughed. "I'm not nearly old enough for that. You know what I mean, don't you? Let us stay pretty and young for a little while, am I right?"

That was another problem with the way she looked. No one seemed to respect those professional boundaries with her—her supervisors included.

The woman opened her minivan door with her key fob and the little girl climbed in. Genevieve heaved a sigh of relief and got into her cruiser. She pulled out the chocolate bar, tore open the wrapper and took a jaw-cracking bite before throwing the car into gear and pulling out onto the road.

The PSP K9 Training Center was located on leased Amish land. For whatever reason, the Pennsylvania State Police had decided to put this puppy school in the middle of Amish country, and she kept to the speed limit as she headed down the curving road, following her GPS's directions. There was a turn coming up and an oversize stop sign indicated an intersection ahead.

She didn't blame anyone but herself for the insubordination that had landed her in puppy school. She'd lipped off to the commissioner—with witnesses. And this was her second strike.

The sign for the K9 training facility was nestled discreetly in the trees on the side of the road, and she would have missed it if it wasn't for her GPS telling her she'd arrived. She turned down the tree-lined drive toward a building that looked like it had originally been an Amish farmhouse, though a wheelchair ramp went up one side of the front verandah now, and the wall bore a large official Pennsylvania State Police sign with a crest.

There was a small parking lot, all nicely paved, and six cars, two of which were cruisers, were parked there. As she pulled into a free space, she could see several other buildings beyond and a dog obstacle course. A German shepherd, running the circuit with a handler, was jumping through tires and leaping over walls, but then shied away from a tube. The handler called him back, gave him a thorough pet and squatted down.

Genevieve looked at her watch. She was ten minutes early, which was better than late. She hated the idea of therapy, which would make up a big part of her time here, she'd been told. She didn't need to talk through her problems to identify them. She knew exactly what they were, and she had a plan that would take her away from the limitations she currently struggled against.

She heaved a sigh and then headed over to the front of the building. There was still quite a bit of farmhouse left to the setup. From the higher vantage point of the verandah, she could see past the dog run and more training ground to an actual farm next door. There was a generous garden along the side of the property, and a black Amish buggy parked beyond it.

Genevieve opened the door and stepped through. Inside, the space looked about as faceless as every other Pennsylvania State Police office. There was some basic seating, cream-colored walls and framed photos of police dogs and their handlers showing off medals. The frames looked like they'd been purchased twenty years ago.

A middle-aged woman in uniform sat at a desk, file cabinets behind her. Her gray hair was pulled back in a tight ponytail and she wore a pair of heavy-framed glasses. She looked up as Genevieve came inside.

"Ah, Trooper Austin, I believe?"

"Yes."

"Come on in," she said. "Good to see you. I've got a couple of forms for you to fill out while you're here." She passed over a clipboard.

It had some basic insurance information, a health and wellness checklist, which she zipped through, ticking the no box next to all the questions, then signed the bottom.

"Did you want to take a moment with that checklist?" the woman asked.

"Nope. I'm fine."

"Of course." She pressed her lips together. "My name is Wendy, and if you need anything while you're here, I'm your first stop. Normally, we have to keep to a tight schedule, but you're a special case, it would seem." Wendy looked at her meaningfully over the top of her glasses.

"Am I?" Genevieve asked. Even while being disciplined?

"A bit," Wendy replied, her tone prim. She didn't seem to like that fact any more than Genevieve did.

"What's different for me?" she asked.

A man came into the room from a far doorway—tall, prematurely gray and well-built—and her heart stuttered in her chest. He hadn't changed much in the last five years—except maybe he'd toughened a bit. He looked a little more dangerous to her equilibrium than he used to be.

"Scott?" she said.

"That's Sergeant Simpson to you." But his lips turned up into rueful smile. "Hey, Gen."

Scott Simpson had been her very first partner as a brand-new trooper... He'd taught her a lot. Great. Now her humiliation could be complete.

"Please tell me you're only passing through," she said.

"Sorry, I can't do that," he replied. "I'm temporarily running the K9. You're my personal problem this week."

"And you were asking what made you a special case," Wendy murmured.

She had a sergeant specially focused on her this week? How much trouble was she in?

"So what makes me so special?" she asked. She was tired of this. Make him say it. She was sick of the wink-wink-nudge-nudge answers she normally got.

"Well..." Scott cocked his head to one side. "For one, you publicly blasted the commissioner and didn't get fired on the spot. Gotta say—that's pretty special."

Scott hadn't been prepared for what he'd feel seeing Genevieve again. When they'd been stationed together, he'd nursed a rather embarrassing crush on her. But who could blame him? She was tall—almost as tall as he was—beautiful, wisecracking, hilarious and absolutely intoxicating, even in uniform with a bulletproof vest under her gray dress shirt.

"You're like a cat with nine lives," he said. "Well, you're down to eight. Actually, make that seven." This was her second write-up, after all. That had surprised him. Her first had happened back when they'd been partners. She'd directly disobeyed orders, and she'd told him personally that she wouldn't do that again. Her job had meant too much to her... So what made her so casual about her position now?

"Whatever my father has said about this," Genevieve said, "there's no need to be so careful with me, I promise you that. I'm a trooper who messed up. Put me through the regular grind."

"You might not care what your old man has to say, but the commissioner does," Scott replied. "Look, Gen, I know you hate how much clout your father has, but it's just a fact."

It was a big reason he'd steered clear of her after he'd been transferred to a different station as a new K9 officer. Her father was Constantine Austin—an incredibly wealthy man with several large corporations under him. He bought and sold businesses and politicians alike.

Genevieve handed the clipboard over to Wendy, who accepted it with a granite expression.

The last time Scott had seen Genevieve was from across a room at a Christmas party a couple of years ago. She could make an entire room turn when she walked in. She was that kind of beautiful, and it could be intimidating for a guy. All the same, he couldn't quite shake her out of his system. It had been five years, and seeing her again still tugged at that vulnerable part of his heart that had always been a little soft for her. He hadn't wanted this particular duty, but he'd been made an offer he couldn't refuse.

Scott nodded toward the door. "Let's get your bags and I'll show you your room."

Genevieve headed for the door and Scott glanced over at Wendy.

She raised her eyebrows and turned back to her desk. "I don't suppose you'd tell me what you'll get from the commissioner in exchange for working with her," she said with a small smile. "We don't normally have sergeants assigned to individual troopers. I'm curious."

"Sorry, that's on a need-to-know basis," Scott said. "But don't worry, it's under control."

"I'm not worried." She put up her hands. "But you'll be earning every penny of your paycheck this time around. That's all I'm saying."

Wendy wasn't wrong.

Scott shook his head and went to the door. A warm breeze had picked up, scented with fresh grass clippings and the tang of cattle. All of the properties surrounding the K9 Center were farms—mostly beef cattle and one egg farm that he knew of.

Scott trotted down the front steps. Genevieve

had already retrieved a small suitcase from her cruiser.

"Why are you temporarily running the K9?" she asked, walking up to him.

"Sergeant McKale's on medical leave," he replied. "She'll be back at the end of next week. You might see her."

"And then?" Genevieve asked.

"I'm a trainer. I drop back down to my usual duties."

That wasn't, at this point in time, a lie. If the other job evaporated, he would indeed go back to his usual duties. That did happen sometimes. But this opportunity had been something he hadn't been able to refuse. If he was able to prove himself, he'd be offered a position as station commander for South Kingston. It was a big step up—the kind of career high his own father could finally respect—but Scott would have to prove that he had what it took to juggle the job as well as Constantine Austin's daughter.

South Kingston was Genevieve's station and Commissioner Taylor had been concerned that whoever took over would need to be able to handle both Genevieve and Constantine Austin. But it was more than that…the commissioner was a friend of the Austin family, and he cared. He wanted to know what was eating up Genevieve, and he'd privately asked Scott to find out. A mere sergeant didn't take a personal request from the commissioner lightly. Genevieve might have connections. Scott didn't.

"What about you?" Scott asked. "What did you say to the commissioner...exactly?"

"I said he was hamstringing my career for his own political gain," she replied. "I told him if I was a man, he wouldn't have held me back, and that he was letting my father pull his strings. He denied being connected to my assignments, and I called him a liar."

Yep. Insubordination.

"What did he hold you back from?" he asked.

"A hundred things," she said, sounding frustrated. "But this time around, it was a fraud ring that was targeting seniors. We'd narrowed in on the kingpins that were running the whole thing and were going in to arrest them and take them by surprise. I'd worked this case from the very beginning, and I was benched for the final takedown. I was crushed."

"And you blamed the commissioner?"

"Taylor is in close with my father, and my father wants to keep me out of harm's way. Suddenly, I'm not getting any assignments that involve any risk whatsoever. Even when I earned a spot. I'm getting desk and traffic duty, and my partner is the biggest, beefiest cop they've got."

Scott felt a twinge of jealousy at that. He shouldn't—troopers working in partnership was simply part of successful policing. But he knew from personal experience how long hours spent together tended to form bonds, and as a trainer, Scott didn't get those opportunities anymore. Especially not with Genevieve.

"I guess it could be worse," he said.

She cast him an annoyed look. "Really? This coming from the man who's determined to climb the ladder faster than anyone in the history of the PSP? Isn't that what you used to tell me? Or has that changed?"

No, it hadn't changed. He was still hungry for promotion, but she'd pitted herself against the police commissioner. That was career suicide.

"I get the frustration, Gen. I do."

"Add to that, I just got mistaken for being an actress playing a trooper…again."

"What?" He started to laugh, but she didn't break a smile. "What do you mean?"

"I mean when people look at me in full uniform, their first thought is not that I'm a cop, it's that I'm playing a part. It's more than frustrating, it's insulting, and my father's meddling in my career is doing more harm than he thinks. He doesn't want me to be a cop, and he's making it near impossible for me to keep going."

"You're thinking of quitting?" he asked.

"I'm thinking of turning to city policing or maybe even getting a job as a cop in a different state," she replied. "I'm good at this, if everyone would just let me do it. And the Pennsylvania State Police have a strong reputation. With a decent recommendation, I could get a position elsewhere."

"The commissioner isn't likely to give that rec-ommendation at this point," he replied.

"It can be from any supervisor." She looked at him meaningfully.

Old loyalties… At one time, they'd had each other's backs for everything. But did he dare give her a recommendation without the commissioner's blessing? That would hurt *his* career, and he'd been clawing his way back from his own mistakes for the last five years, too. She wasn't wrong about the commissioner having some unfair sway over her career. Still, Scott might be able to get the man to see the benefit of her plan.

"We aren't partners anymore, Gen." He couldn't be doing her favors…

Genevieve broke off eye contact and her expression dimmed.

It stung, disappointing her—it always had.

"So why are you making me your problem this week?" she asked, turning toward her vehicle and hauling her suitcase out of the trunk. "If this isn't about old times."

"This is from the commissioner."

She dropped her case on the verandah and gave him an incredulous look. "I should have guessed. What does he want you to do?"

"He wants me to find out what's bugging you."

"I told you what's bugging me," she retorted.

"Okay, and that's fair. I can definitely pass that along. But from what he told me, this goes deeper. He's concerned that you aren't a team player—that you aren't willing to take on a supporting role for other officers."

"I've had nothing but supporting roles!"

"And if you were anyone else, you'd have been fired on the spot for your outburst."

She sighed and didn't answer.

"From what he told me, this is Commissioner Taylor giving you one last chance. This is serious, Gen. Fair or not. He told me he's hopeful but not optimistic."

Genevieve eyed him for a moment. "After all of this meddling in my career, is he going to fire me?"

"He doesn't want to."

"No, that would alienate my father, and Dad puts a good deal of money and political leverage into the PSP's coffers."

They both knew what made the state run. She could have done anything with her life. Her family's money and reputation would have catapulted her forward. But she'd chosen the one career her father had wanted for her the least.

"So you can see that this is complicated," he said.

Genevieve didn't answer and her gaze looked like it was directed inward.

"You and I are pretty much joined at the hip for the next week," Scott said. "Fair warning."

Would she mind? Would she rather have someone else assigned to her?

"And why did the commissioner choose you, Scott?" she asked quietly.

"Because I'm heading the K9 until Sergeant McKale gets back," he replied. Again, he was telling her something that was mostly true. "Anyone heading the K9 would have gotten the same assignment."

"Well, embarrassing as this is, I'm glad to see you again," Genevieve said. "Maybe we can make the best of it and it can be like old times."

And what could he say to that? It couldn't be like old times. There was no way, but he wished that for ten days it could be.

"I'll show you your room."

The upstairs of the converted farmhouse had six bedrooms that were used by troopers staying for disciplinary reasons and employees working the night shift with the dogs. The bedrooms were small, bright and clean. Three of them were furnished with army bunks and three had regular single-width army beds—nothing too lavish, but they did the trick. This wasn't supposed to be a vacation, after all. He'd assigned Genevieve to a room with a single bed. The space was smaller, but he thought she might be more comfortable.

He stood in the doorway as Genevieve dropped her small suitcase on the bed and looked around. The curtains were open and she paused at the window. From there, she could see the whole dog course, the kennels and some mock buildings that had been erected for training purposes. Past that, there was just pasture with cattle dotting the fields.

"I'm across the hall," he said.

"You're staying on site?"

"It's my turn in the duty roster," he replied. Plus, there was no family—no wife or kids—to complain about him not coming home every night. "Wendy is here Monday to Friday from seven thirty until three. And then we have dog trainers who come for shifts, and troopers who do the overnight with the puppies. The therapists come for appointments, but they don't stay on site. Your first therapy appointment is tomorrow at ten."

"A well-oiled machine," she said. "For dogs and troublesome troopers alike."

It was. And the system worked about eighty percent of the time. This was the first time he'd see it up close and personal from the managerial perspective, though.

"Do you want to come meet the dog we'll be working with?" he asked.

"Is this an attempt to lower my defenses so I'll open up about my feelings?" she asked.

"Yes. A hundred percent."

She laughed softly. "You won't even hide it?"

"I have to do this by the book. I'll be able to tell the commissioner that I did my best, that you played with puppies, did some training work, spoke with the therapist, and that your morale was boosted by the experience."

"That's the goal?"

"That and…" Her clear eyes met his and his breath caught. "Is it ever good to see you, Gen."

Shoot. He hadn't meant to come out with something quite that honest. He cleared his throat.

"It's good to see you, too, Scott." A smile flickered at her lips and his heart gave a flip.

Blast. That was supposed to have gone away over five years.

"You might want to change into something more casual, though," he added, and he sounded gruffer than he meant to. "Just trust me on that."

CHAPTER TWO

GENEVIEVE CHANGED INTO a pair of jeans and a pink V-necked T-shirt and hung her uniform in the empty wardrobe. For a moment, she stood stock-still, just breathing. Scott Simpson…of all the sergeants in all of the state police, why did he have to end up here? This disciplinary action was humiliating enough without Scott around to witness it, no matter how good it was to see him again.

He'd gone radio silent on her when he'd transferred to a new station as a K9 officer, and that had hurt. She'd thought their partnership had meant more, but he'd cut her off. She hadn't a hundred percent forgiven him for that.

Scott had aged over the last few years. Back when they'd been partners, he'd had a bit of gray, and now his hair was completely salt-and-pepper, setting off his almost black eyes. He'd also beefed up a bit since those early days—it was evident that he spent some regular time in the gym. But then, so did she. She was stronger than she looked.

She pushed her feet into a pair of Nikes and headed out of her room and into the hallway.

Downstairs, she could hear the soft rumble of Scott's voice. He seemed to be discussing a dog's ability assessment, and when she emerged into the reception area again, she heard him say, "This is his last chance, I'm afraid."

Scott handed Wendy a sheet of paper. "He won't get any more chances to train after this."

"Poor Benjie," Wendy said. "He's a sweetie."

Scott turned and saw Genevieve. He angled his head toward the door. "Let's head out then. We're working with one particular dog today. He's a bit of a special case."

Like herself, it would seem. Scott led the way through the kitchen and a mudroom with a sink, shelves and coat hooks before they emerged into the warm sunlight.

Genevieve fell into pace next to Scott, and they headed over to the obstacle course where that K9 trooper was working with his dog on the tube crawl. She noticed Scott's gaze following the dog as he started the obstacle course again. K9 troopers came out here to train their dogs and keep them sharp. She knew that much.

"How old is the dog we're working with?" she asked.

"He's a year old. At this age, if he doesn't have the skills down for K9, he won't acquire them."

"And he's…back?" she asked.

"He is. I trained this dog as a puppy and I passed him and sent him out to a handler. He's been sent back twice. He's smart, but he keeps making his own calls, and that can be lethal out there in the field."

"I can understand that," she said. "So, if he isn't ready...he goes to a home somewhere and becomes a very well-trained guard dog?"

"Nope." Scott's jaw clenched and she saw sadness in his eyes. "If Benjie can't do the job at this point, he's too well trained to be sent off to some family's home. He knows the commands to attack, and he could be deadly. If I'd cut him from the program as a pup, sure! But not anymore. If I have to cut him from the program now, it would be tough to find him a home."

"Where would he go?"

"He'd stay here. Not forever, though. We couldn't let his bad habits rub off on the other dogs. So until we could find him a home where he wouldn't be a danger to anyone, he'd have stay in a kennel a fair amount of the time."

Not even a K9 dropout. A K9 failure. The thought of the poor dog wondering what he'd done wrong...

"That's sad."

They walked across the freshly mowed lawn, its scent hitting Genevieve in the comfort spot of her brain. Beyond that lay a long, low building.

"Wait till you meet him," Scott said. "He's... lonely. That's the best way to describe him. He wants a human of his own so badly. He'll be a really sad dog if he can't stay K9. And that's my fault for not calling it sooner."

The building had large windows shaded with blinds. It looked very "state police." The door was locked and Scott punched in a code and then held the door for her to go inside first. Her sleeve brushed against his shirt as she passed him, and the faint scent of his cologne tickled memories of long hours spent together. She pushed them back.

The kennel's interior was cheerful. It had a few individual kennel spaces, two of which were occupied. She recognized a German shepherd. The other was a darker breed. A larger room, closed off with a mesh fence, contained five German shepherd puppies. Soft light illuminated some plush dog toys that were scattered around the tiled floor, and a short, plump officer sat cross-legged on the floor, playing with the puppies and rubbing their little bellies.

"Hi, Jan," Scott said. "Jan is one of our trainers."

The woman looked up with a smile. "Hi there."

"This is Genevieve. She's here for a bit over a week."

"Nice to meet you."

Jan obviously knew why Genevieve was there—there was no other reason for troopers to come for ten days at a time—but she didn't seem bothered at all.

"These are our newest litter of puppies," Scott said. "We're still trying to figure out which of them will be contenders for the K9 program. So far, they're pretty young and it's all about playing and chewing. And here—"

Scott stepped over the gate and Genevieve followed him to the occupied kennels.

"The German shepherd is Benjie," Scott said. He opened the crate door and the dog stood and shook himself. He loped out of the enclosure and came up to her side, sniffing. Genevieve rubbed the dog's head, and he licked her fingers.

"The other dog is named Konig. He's a Dutch shepherd, and he was trained in Germany. I'm told he's really good, but this dog speaks German."

"Does he?" Genevieve put her fingers flat against the bars. The Dutch shepherd looked a lot like a German shepherd, but had darker coloring—mottled dark brown and black. He sniffed her fingers and gave her a lick with his wet, velvet tongue.

"The problem is, all of his learned commands are in German, too, and we can't get the accent right."

Genevieve chuckled.

"Yeah, we're looking for a handler who can at the very least learn the German commands in the right accent."

"That's tough," she said.

"We'll find the right cop," he replied. "I'm sure of it. In the meantime, Jan will take him out for some time on the obstacle course when she's done with the puppies."

Benjie had been sniffing Genevieve this whole time. He finished his inspection at last and looked up at her with big hopeful eyes. She squatted down in front of him and rubbed his ears.

"You're a sweetie," she said softly.

Scott moved down to the end of the building then turned to face them. "Benjie, come."

His voice echoed along the corridor. Benjie jumped to his feet, slipped away from her touch, and went over to Scott.

"Sit." The dog sat. "Good boy."

Scott pulled a treat from his pocket and Benjie gobbled it up. "Wait."

Scott moved across the room to the puppies and gave them various commands, too. Benjie stayed where Scott left him, his eyes locked on Scott even when Scott ignored him.

"Try and call him," Scott said.

"Benjie." She made a kissing sound. "Come here, Benjie."

The dog's ears twitched but his attention stayed locked on Scott.

"Benjie, come," Scott said, and the dog trotted to his side, rewarded once more with a treat.

"Looks like he's doing really well," she said. "He maintained that stay like a pro."

"He's great. And he was special to me. I really got attached to this guy." Scott bent down and stroked the dog's head. "The problem is, he isn't cooperating with his handler. We need to train that out of him."

"What do you mean?" she asked. "What's he doing wrong?"

"For example, we teach the dogs to attack the proper arm in a hostage situation. This training is like a game for them. They learn which arm to grab and are rewarded for the right choice. He doesn't try to hurt me—he's aiming for the reward. But he has to go for the gun hand. Sometimes he gets it right, but other times he'll circle around and chomp me in the back of the leg to get me to release the gun or he'll put himself between me and the person acting the hostage. Effective, but not what we're training him to do. I also didn't have padding back there."

She couldn't help smiling. "Benjie, you're smart."

"He's very smart. But he can't be trying to out-think his training. At the same time, that intelligence is something we're looking for, too. It's a balance. His intelligence is why I passed him when he was a puppy. I shouldn't have, though."

"Maybe he needs more time in the training program."

Scott slowly shook his head. "He's a year old now. He's fully trained, and he's still not properly cooperating with his handler. Our human therapist said it sounds like when children refuse to cooperate with something they should be doing. Refusing to go into school, refusing to use a potty, that sort of thing. They just decide that no, they aren't doing it. Benjie's doing the same thing—he knows what he wants, and if he can't have it, he won't cooperate."

"What does he want?" she asked.

"Me." His gaze flickered toward her and some color touched his cheeks. "He bonded with me in training, and he's refusing to bond with Vincent."

"Oh…that's a problem." She could see how difficult this would be. "Poor guy."

"If he can't pass this next series of tests, he's out of the program, and it's my own fault for not pulling him earlier. His stubbornness could be really dangerous." Scott was quiet for a moment. "It's the same with officers, too, you know."

"No extra training time?" She raised her eyebrows.

"If they're sent in when they aren't ready, they can get themselves hurt," he said.

She knew what he was getting at, but if he was going to use insultingly obvious parallels, she was going to force him to say it. "Do you mean me? That wasn't a very smooth segue."

Scott had the decency to look abashed. "Sorry. But…the point stands. I've worked with you. I know that you're talented and a good officer. But it's possible that your dad, the commissioner, your supervisors…they all might have been trying to protect you from something they thought you weren't ready for."

"Of course, they are," she retorted. "But do they work that hard to protect your pretty little face, Scott? Because I'm as tough as you are."

He rolled his eyes. "I'm not picking fights."

"Good. Then don't tell me I deserve to be packed in cotton."

"It only takes one bullet, Gen. Or one collision. Maybe you've got people who don't want to attend your funeral."

This coming from the guy who'd cared so much about her that he'd never contacted her again after he'd transferred out?

"They aren't giving me the chance to prove myself, either," she countered. "They hired me, trained me, and now think I'm too precious to do the job? It's not fair. You have to see that."

"Look, I've made mistakes of my own," Scott said. "We can make the wrong call and end up in more trouble than we ever imagined."

"They wanted me to be the model for state police posters," she said.

"I'd take that as a compliment."

"I would, if they also let me do the job!"

"You're talking about that fraud case," he said.

"That's the latest example, and I guess the one that mattered the most, because I couldn't keep my mouth shut anymore. I worked on that case for months. There was no reason to hold me back, and when I got my commander to open up, he admitted that the order to keep me out of the takedown came from higher than him."

"Did the commissioner admit to it?" Scott asked.

"Not in so many words. He beat around the bush a bit, but it was clear enough. He said he had to be confident that he'd done all he could to keep his troopers safe in the line of duty. I just…saw red. I mean I deserved to be there! There was no reason why I should be kept back when an officer who was a year junior to me went along!"

"And you think it's because of your dad's undue influence over the commissioner," Scott said.

"I know so."

Scott sucked in a breath but didn't answer.

She watched his face, looking for some betrayal of his feelings, but he was keeping those locked up pretty tight.

"Scott, you used to be more open-minded than this."

"Maybe that was because I was *there*," he retorted. "I had your back. They weren't getting to you unless they went through me."

"And vice versa."

"Yeah." He smiled faintly. "I know."

They used to squabble like this in their shared cruiser, and she could feel that protectiveness emanating from him. But he didn't have a right to it anymore. He wasn't her partner, and he seemed to be on the side of the ones actively holding her back.

"So you think they did the right thing?" she asked. "Just for clarity."

"No. I think they *thought* they were doing the right thing," he replied.

Genevieve pressed her lips together, trying to contain her rising irritation. They were going in circles, and she was tired of being treated like everyone's little sister.

"You won't get your way in the police force," Scott went on. "No one does. It's a chain of command. We're stronger together, and we work as a machine. You know that."

"You also don't know what it's like to be held back," she said.

He smiled but the humor didn't reach his eyes. "Yeah, I do."

"How'd they hold you back?" she asked.

"That's a story for another day. I'm just saying, being part of the force means following orders, even if you don't like it. It's the same for all of us. Now, let's focus on Benjie, okay?"

Much like the dog, again, she realized bitterly. Not a great parallel. But fine—he didn't want to talk about that.

"What did you have in mind?" she asked.

"I want to see if he'll go after the arm with the weapon," he said. "We've been working on it."

"All right." Genevieve put her fingers into her back pocket. She'd rather discuss how Scott thought that he as a man was held back in his policing career, but if that wasn't going to happen, she might as well pitch in.

"Do you want to be the perp or the hostage?" he asked. "And before you get all huffy with me, know that if you're the perp, he may very well take a chomp out of your leg instead of going for your protected arm."

"You're toying with me now," she said with a low laugh.

"I'm more used to fending him off," Scott said, holding his hands up. "Up to you."

"I'll be the hostage."

"Sounds good." He patted his leg. "Come on, Benjie. Let's go earn a treat."

SCOTT NOTICED THE tight side-glance Genevieve gave him. Funny how little had changed over the years. But if she thought she was the only one whose career had been derailed, she was wrong. Sure, her troubles were because of her ridiculously wealthy father and his scope of influence, but when it came to the state police, an order was an order. She wasn't going to get his pity for having to follow orders.

He'd had to do the same, and her discipline—a ten-day stint at the puppy school—was a whole lot gentler than his had been. Scott had been demoted, knocked down to regular trooper, and it had taken years off his upward trajectory. He'd spent twice as long to get to this point—on the verge of achieving everything he'd been working for. He'd had to face his own father's biting disappointment— and his father was a retired army sergeant who'd started out disappointed when Scott hadn't chosen the military. *Weak*, his dad had called him. *Undisciplined. Scared of a challenge.* And his dad's judgment had only gotten sharper after the disciplinary action. Scott knew about consequences all too well.

He bent down and gave Benjie a good head rub.

"We're going to give this another try, okay, Benjie?" he said.

And Scott really hoped that Benjie picked it up this time. He was smart and he had the potential of being a really good police dog…but Scott knew what happened when a dog was pushed beyond his abilities. Scott wouldn't make that mistake again—not with a dog, and not with people. If Benjie didn't pass the next round of official tests, Scott wouldn't force him to continue.

Scott pulled a box of fake weapons out of a tall cupboard. It contained mostly rubber guns and knives. He grabbed a rubber pistol and tucked it into the back of his jeans. Then he chose a protective arm pad and led the way outside.

"Can I ask you something?" Genevieve said as they walked into the sunshine.

"Sure." He glanced down and found her blue eyes fixed on him in a way that made him feel like she was appraising him.

"Why did you cut contact with me like that?" she asked.

Shoot. That wasn't something he wanted to talk about, exactly, but he knew he'd hurt her by being so cold.

"Did you know how I ended up as your partner to begin with?" he asked.

"Just good luck?" She cast him a smile.

Scott wasn't joking around. "I was demoted."

"No…"

"Yeah."

"You never told me that."

Of course not. Like he was going to tell his rookie partner all about his mistakes? He'd had years more experience than she'd had and he'd been smarting from the demotion.

"I dated a rookie officer," he said, "and we didn't report the relationship to HR. When we broke up, she got mad and accused me of using my higher rank inappropriately. It wasn't true. You know me. But there are consequences. So I was demoted, and I had to work my way back up. So, after I was transferred to a new station as K9 again after being your partner, I... I was perhaps a little overly cautious."

"Seriously? That's it? You thought I'd cause trouble for you? We were friends!"

"I was being careful. I'm sorry. I really am."

And that was as much as he'd tell her. They *had* been friends, but Scott had also become too attached to Gen. He'd felt a whole lot more for her than he should have. Three years of working shoulder to shoulder with Genevieve had showed him a woman he'd respected and admired. He'd also been attracted to her. He hadn't been about to make the mistake of mixing work and romance again. Not that he'd thought Genevieve would have been interested in more from him, but he'd landed himself in an emotionally precarious situation, and he'd figured cutting himself out of her life would be the smartest choice. Looking at her now, he wasn't so sure.

"So, in order to appear as professional as possible, you figured you'd just never speak to me again?" She shook her head. "This does not make sense."

"I was focused on the next step," he said. Focused on getting back that lost footing, on getting his dad's words out of his head about how he was just being weak.

Scott expected her to argue, and he couldn't really take that chance. He'd hurt her feelings—that was obvious. But she couldn't know the depth of it. He needed to save at least some personal dignity.

"Come on," he said, turning around and leading the way past the obstacle course where the K9 officer was still working with his dog.

He still felt a wriggle of guilt, though. He knew he owed Gen more of an explanation than he'd given her, and her silence was deafening.

"I got into a lot of trouble with that relationship," Scott said, looking over at her. "It's not just the demotion. It's every one of my senior officers who had a really long memory. I messed up. I should have informed HR. I knew better. But that mistake held me back for a really long time."

"So that's what you meant."

"Yeah. It's also why I went overboard with professional boundaries and all that."

"Gotcha…" Her voice was soft. "I mean it still hurts, but I guess I get it. I just missed you. I wanted to hear about your life. Like…do you have anyone special right now? Someone more rank appropriate?"

"No." He felt the smile tug at his lips. "Not right now. What about you? Is there a boyfriend annoyed at you spending a week with me?"

"No, there's no boyfriend," she replied. "It's been a couple of years."

"Out of curiosity…who was the last guy you dated?" He remembered the man she'd been dating when they were partners, one of Pennsylvania's rich and famous. That was the thing with Gen. She had two lives: the one her father provided with wealthy connections and her job as a state trooper where she hobnobbed with the commoners…like him.

"He was in the petroleum business."

In other words, he was wealthy.

"How long were you together?" he asked.

"A year and a half," she said. "He proposed on a ski trip. And I…couldn't say yes."

"Ouch." He winced. "What held you back?"

The question had come out of his mouth before he could think better of it—their old comfort together slipping back between them.

"I don't know." Genevieve met his eyes, but she didn't say anything else.

Yeah, she knew, but she didn't want to say. He understood. He had a few things he'd rather she didn't know, too.

He pushed his hand into the protector and pulled

it up his arm like a sleeve, then he handed the dog treat to Genevieve.

"You ready?" he asked.

She nodded.

"Okay, Benjie," he said. "Sit. Stay."

There was a long stretch of green grass behind the obstacle course, and he headed about ten yards away from Benjie. Genevieve followed. When he stopped, he pulled out the rubber gun and held it in his protected hand.

"Now, you've got to struggle—make it what he'd see in the field," he said.

"Let's go." Genevieve matched his stare with a steely look of her own, and he grinned at her.

Benjie sat tall and alert, all of his canine attention locked on them.

Scott slipped an arm over Genevieve's shoulder, spun her around and held up the toy gun menacingly.

"You good?" he murmured in her ear.

"I'm fine." He could feel her braced against him—she knew how to combat this move. She was warm against his chest, and she smelled faintly of chocolate.

"Benjie, gun!" he said sharply.

The dog took a couple of jumps forward then stopped. Was he confused because Scott was the one both issuing the order and holding the gun? He'd practiced this with other trainers multiple times and gotten it right about half of them.

"You give him the command," Scott said.

"Benjie, gun!" she said.

Benjie lunged forward again and when Scott waved the rubber gun, he could tell Benjie was watching it, gauging his next move. Then the dog lunged and caught Scott's protected arm in his jaws, and Scott stumbled back—Benjie might not be full grown, but he was still pretty heavy. But a wave of satisfaction coursed through Scott as he let go of Genevieve and struggled to keep his balance. Benjie was doing it.

"Release," he commanded, and Benjie dropped to the ground.

"Good boy!" Genevieve said, and she bent with the treat and gave him a pet. "Well done, Benjie."

"Let's try it again," Scott said. "Benjie, sit. Stay."

They moved ten yards off again, and he readjusted the protective sleeve.

"So why didn't you marry the guy?" he asked.

Genevieve looked over at him. "What?"

"The guy who proposed," he said. "Why didn't you say yes?"

"You really want to know?" she asked.

"I wouldn't have asked otherwise. I'm curious."

"Because he wanted me to let him keep me in luxury. Dinner parties, trips to Aspen, shopping, and being the little wife on his arm."

"What a monster." Scott shot her a teasing grin. "About the luxury, I mean. You do realize that most women never get that chance? Most men, too. I mean in all my years, I've never had a wealthy woman offer to keep me in luxury—"

"He wanted me to quit, Scott." She met his gaze seriously. "And that wasn't something up for discussion. He went down on one knee and made it clear that his proposal included me quitting my job."

Ouch. That sounded...cold. Who fell in love, planned a proposal, then went out of his way to make sure she understood that it was only on his terms?

"Then you made the right call," he said quietly.

"I don't make a good trophy," she said. "I told him no. I turned down the ring, and we were over."

Dang. He was rather impressed with her. He could only imagine the look on that idiot's face when she'd let him know exactly where she stood. He was glad—she'd kept her dignity, and her spark. No one should take that.

Benjie sat alert, waiting for the command.

"So...this time, do you want to put up a fight? Give him a moving target?" Scott asked.

"A real fight?" She smiled. "Because I'm not sure you want that, Scott. I can take you."

That sounded like a challenge and he'd spent the last several years working his tail off in his job, and in the gym. He hadn't wanted to lose his edge.

"A real fight isn't a good idea. I'm still a good sixty pounds heavier than you," he pointed out.

"Fine." She turned her back to him and put her hands on her slim hips. "I'm ready."

He slid his arm over her shoulder again. She was warm and soft in his grip, and every instinct told him to gentle his touch. That was the problem with her—she affected him on a chemical level. He pulled her back against him, putting her just a little off balance. Now he was mildly nervous she would fight him in earnest, and that wasn't a fight he was willing to have. Not with her.

"Benjie, gun!" Genevieve called out, and then she pushed her weight forward, pulling him with her. She was really doing this, wasn't she?

"Gen, come on—" Scott said through gritted teeth. He was working one-armed here, holding the toy gun with the other.

Benjie came at them again, but Scott couldn't focus on the dog with Genevieve trying to position him to take him down. He knew the same moves she did, and she was looking to set him off balance and then whip his leg out from under him.

But Benjie wasn't coming for the protected arm this time around. He was circling, and Scott pivoted Genevieve, too, to keep her between him and Benjie. The K9 needed to go for the gun, not Scott's leg, but focusing on the job was getting a little harder with the soft aroma of chocolate that hovered close to Genevieve, and a sweet, floral scent in her hair—

"Benjie, gun!" Genevieve repeated.

And Benjie sat down and cocked his head to one side, wearing that look of curiosity that only a German shepherd could muster. But as Scott deflated, Gen suddenly grabbed his biceps, took a strong step forward, and he felt his own feet come off the ground. The grass spun around and then the wind punched out of his lungs as he landed flat on his back.

"Benjie, for crying out loud, *gun!*" Genevieve said.

The dog lunged at his arm and sank his teeth into the padding, snarling and tugging at his arm.

"Release," Scott said, his voice sounding strangled in his own ears, and as Benjie let go, he rolled over onto his side.

"Are you okay?" Genevieve asked, offering him her hand.

"I'm fine." But he refused the offered assistance and pushed himself back to his knees. "What was that?"

"I'm making a point," she said.

"What point?" he asked irritably, rubbing at his shoulder where he'd landed. That was going to bruise. He rose to his feet.

"Did I hurt you?" she asked, and remorse finally registering on her face.

"No, I'm fine," he lied. "So, what, you're proving you're no wimp?"

"Bingo."

He shook his head. "You have nothing to prove. I already know you're tough."

"Oh, really? What was that whole thing about me not being ready to face my actual job?"

"That was a mistake. Clearly."

Scott leaned down and gave Benjie a pet then handed him his treat. He'd earned it—eventually.

It was important to never shame a dog for doing exactly what he was being trained to do.

"You're tough," Scott continued to Genevieve. "Deceptively tough, may I add. And I'm sorry I suggested that you might need any extra protection."

"Thank you." She smiled sweetly and his heart gave a tumble. "Good. Then we're fine."

If Scott hadn't learned the hard way about these things, he'd be tempted to follow that feeling. But he did know better. He'd worked too hard to regain that lost career growth, and he finally had his chance at a big step up. There was just one problem with his upward climb. If all went well, his promised promotion would make Scott Genevieve's new boss. That was part of the challenge here. Commissioner Taylor wanted to see if Scott could work with Genevieve on a long-term basis, be her supervisor, and effectively lead her team.

Scott's relationship with Gen was going to be the deciding factor for both their futures with the Pennsylvania State Police.

CHAPTER THREE

GENEVIEVE PRETENDED NOT to notice while Scott rolled his shoulder. He'd landed hard—and that wasn't entirely her fault. He was a solidly built man and she couldn't be expected to flip him over with much delicacy. And she *could* flip him— which she'd proven. Besides, he'd deserved that one—all that talk about avoiding her funeral. What about his funeral? What about anyone else's? That was why they were well trained and worked as a team. But holding her back from doing her job wasn't fair and she stood by that. She'd been working for the force for six years now. If they didn't yet trust her to do her part, then she was on the wrong force.

While Genevieve had pointed out the gender inequality she often saw, it wasn't the only factor at play here. There were plenty of tough, effective female troopers out there. The Pennsylvania State Police was good that way. This was because her father, who donated a lot of money to police chari- ties and causes, had one teensy request that came along with his piles of money. And *that* wasn't fair.

Benjie trotted along next to Scott, looking up at him hopefully. The shepherd sensed something was off. She could see it in the way the dog's ears were perked and his tail was down. He was trying to figure it out. Poor dog. He just wanted to be a good boy.

"When is Benjie's last test?" Genevieve asked.

"End of the week," he replied.

"Wow."

"Yeah." He pressed his lips together. "I really want to do right by him. He needs to be able to do the job he's trained his whole life to do."

"So this week is the last chance for his career in K9?" she asked.

"Afraid so." Scott sighed. "I still think he's got the potential, but I have to say, I wish I'd cut him as a puppy. He'd be happier today if I had. Honestly? I need all the help I can get this week to get him into shape."

"Of course." She could see how much this mattered to him, and to Benjie.

A smile flickered at the corners of his lips. "And I can tell you this much, next time, I'm going to be the hostage and you're going to be the bad guy. Let's see how fast on your feet you are with Benjie aiming at your hamstring."

Genevieve chuckled. "Did I wound your pride, Scott?"

"A little bit." His smile faded.

"I'm sorry," she said.

He nodded a couple of times. "This isn't a competition. I'm *your* senior officer here. And you've had your second strike."

Her pulse sped up. He was pulling rank. That was reasonable, she shouldn't have been treating him like an equal—he wasn't anymore. And that second strike was embarrassing enough.

She didn't answer, her pulse thundering in her throat.

"I know it wasn't always fair for you," Scott went on. "I get it. But things weren't always fair for me, either, and I'm working my tail off to get my career back on track. And as a friend…you should do the same."

"I am," she replied. But back on track for her might mean going to a different state. "I will."

"Don't get me wrong—I'm really glad to see you again, and I really did miss you. But this next week matters for both of our careers."

That was an odd statement. "Do you want to elaborate?" she asked.

"You've got to prove yourself a team player, Gen. This is serious."

"And what does that have to do with your career?" she asked. She wasn't letting that thread go so easily.

He caught her glance, and for a moment, he didn't say anything. Then he sighed.

"There's a possible position opening up. It could be mine if I can prove myself. You're the test. They want to see me succeed in a managerial role. So… let's help each other out here. Let's use this time for its intended purpose and show the powers that be that we're both worth the effort. You're a good cop in a precarious position. I believe in you."

Well, that changed things. This wasn't about an old friendship or finding common ground.

"Okay," she said. "I'll recognize you as my SO, and we'll prove ourselves."

"Thank you."

He sounded relieved, and maybe she should be relieved, too. She couldn't treat him like the same old Scott who'd been her partner. That partner had walked out on her—she might be wise to remember that detail.

"So...how have things been for you the last few years?" Scott was trying to soften that blow, and maybe she should be grateful.

"It never was the same after you transferred out," she admitted. "They moved us to a partner rotation, so we didn't have one partner to really get to know anymore."

"I heard about that," he said.

"It was different, but I suppose it would have been different anyway. Our partnership was pretty special."

He nudged her arm with his. "I missed you, too."

Genevieve felt her face heat. She had missed him more than she should have. She'd become attached to Scott, and she'd had a tough time feeling connected to other partners afterward. That included her current partner, Roy. It made her wonder if she'd maybe slipped over the line emotionally. Other partners hadn't seemed to share quite the same connection that she and Scott had, and she'd only realized that once he'd left.

"So what's the plan while I'm here?" she asked. "Besides training Benjie?"

"You'll do your therapy sessions, and we'll talk. We'll try and get to the bottom of things."

Right. He was supposed to fix her over the next week.

"You're going to manage me," she clarified.

He shrugged. "It's my job, Gen."

Of course it was, but she had some feelings of her own that she needed to get a handle on. Scott as her SO? This wasn't going to be an easy adjustment.

Scott slowed his pace as they approached the house once more. "Why don't you take some free time? In a couple of hours, we're going to take Benjie out for another training session."

Genevieve eyed him for a moment. "Do all the insubordinate officers get this kind of free time?"

"Nope." A smile touched his lips. "I wasn't lying. You're special."

And the way he said it made it sound like maybe she, personally, was special to him. But she wouldn't let her mind go there. Scott had made it clear that he was her superior officer and he'd been tasked with sorting her out. That's all this was. Her partnership with Scott was in the past, and it had been professional. She had no other claims on the man.

"Then I'll see you in an hour or so," she said.

"Sounds good."

She'd take a walk—get some time in her own head. She had ten days of this—dogs, puppies, training, talking…and Scott.

GENEVIEVE PICKED A direction and started down the road. It was paved, with some horse droppings along the center of one lane. This was Amish Country, all right. There was something soothing about this part of the state—as if that chosen peacefulness leaked out to everyone else in the area. She could feel her tension easing from her shoulders and she picked up her pace, feeling good as she got herself moving. If she wasn't in blue jeans, she'd go for a run, but that could wait until morning.

As she crested a hill, she paused at the top to catch her breath and let her eyes wander over the landscape tumbling out beneath her. The road continued on, winding eastward, and Amish farms lined either side of it. Small fields—much smaller than regular agriculture demanded—were separated by fences, and cattle grazed in a field butted up against a crop of wheat. There were gardens in neat rows behind houses, and she could make out people, the size of ants, moving around…it was hard to tell what they were doing from there, but knowing the Amish, they were at work with some chore.

There was a young Amish woman a hundred

yards down the road who hadn't noticed Genevieve yet. She was bent over, seeming to be looking for something in the weeds around a mailbox. As Genevieve continued along the road toward her, she watched the woman straighten, turn around, and then seem to deflate. There was a sign hanging from the bottom of the mailbox, but she couldn't make it out yet.

The closer Genevieve got, she noticed that the young woman was pregnant—a small, domed belly almost hidden by a loosely tied apron. She looked up as Genevieve approached, a meek smile appearing on her face, hiding the earlier emotional turmoil. The sign on the mailbox read Jam, Honey, Preserves. She must think Genevieve was a customer.

"Hi," Genevieve said.

"Good morning." The woman gave her a polite nod but her grip on the edge of her apron was tight. "Are you here for our honey? We have a fresh batch."

"No, I'm just taking a walk," Genevieve said. "I'm from the K9 Center."

"Oh…" She nodded. "The police."

"Yeah, that's us. Are you okay? You looked like you were looking for something."

"I was just—" Color touched her cheeks. "It's okay. It doesn't matter. Have a nice day."

But it sure looked like it mattered. This young woman was upset, even if she was trying to hide it, and she'd obviously been searching for something. The woman brushed a stray hair out of her face. It had come loose from her bun, which was covered by a white *kapp*. She wiped at her cheek.

Genevieve should just carry on. The woman clearly wasn't wanting her help, but then she wiped at her face with her fingers. She was crying.

"What did you lose?" Genevieve asked. "I could help you to look."

"Are you a police officer?"

"I am. It makes me pretty good at this kind of thing. My name is Genevieve, by the way."

"I'm Alma Hertz." She gave a self-conscious nod. "But there's no crime here. It's a watch. My husband's."

"Did it come off his wrist somewhere?"

She shook her head. "No, nothing like that. But when he finds out it's gone, he's going to be very upset."

That could be a warning sign, and Genevieve put her fingers into her back pockets, trying to look more casual, less aggressive.

"What does he do when he's upset?" Genevieve softened her tone. "Are you worried about him… lashing out?"

"What?" Alma squinted then shook her head. "No! Nothing like that. He'll just be sad. It belonged to his great-grandfather, and even though it's worth a lot, he'd never sell it."

"What's it worth?" Genevieve asked.

"I don't know exactly. It's got a leather band and a gold-colored face. It's a Lange & Söhne watch."

"What was it doing out here?" Genevieve asked.

"This is just a…a hope…" Alma puffed out a wistful breath. "I'd hoped that if someone had accidentally taken it, they might have put it in the mailbox…or something. You know, to return it anonymously."

That sounded like an awfully wild hope. "What happened? When did you notice it was missing?"

"I can't involve police in this." Alma shook her head, and tears misted her eyes.

"The thing is, I might have some ideas of where you can look for it," Genevieve said. "I could just give you advice—unofficially."

"Are you allowed to do that?"

"Of course."

"Oh…well…" Alma seemed to be battling with herself, and finally she sighed. "Here's what happened. I had some friends come over to help me finish a quilt I'm making for my sister-in-law. She just had another baby. Anyway, that's not the point. They were here to help finish the quilt, and the watch was laying on the counter. My husband had taken it out to check that it was still keeping time. It wasn't, and he was considering getting it fixed. We were talking about how we'd pay for it. We don't use watches here, but since it was a family heirloom, and my husband never wore it, it was okay."

"So your friends saw the watch," Genevieve prompted.

"*Yah*. They spotted it, and they asked about it.

We don't tell anyone about it. It's…it's considered boasting to do that. They wanted to look closer, but I told them the watch was my husband's and that he wouldn't want us to touch it. So they left it alone."

"Did you mention that it was worth a great deal?" Genevieve asked.

"I think I did!" Color suffused Alma's cheeks. "It was boastful of me, and I probably deserve this now! But I wasn't thinking—just being open and honest. You know how it is with good friends. You don't have to watch yourself so much."

"When did you notice it was missing?" Genevieve asked.

"My friends got in their buggies and left when the work was over, and that was yesterday afternoon. I noticed last night that it was gone, and I prayed until late that it would be returned. And I was hoping…" She looked toward the mailbox once more. "I was hoping that whoever took it would feel guilty and bring it back. But it doesn't look like that happened, does it?"

"How many friends were here?" Genevieve asked.

"Four. My four oldest and dearest friends! I can't believe that one of them would steal from us!"

"Was anyone else in the house?"

"Just me…"

"Do you have other children?" Sometimes kids made off with valuable items just to play with them.

"This is our first." She put a hand on her belly.

"So you and your four friends were the only people in the house. Did your husband come home before you noticed it missing?"

"No, he came home afterward. And no one else came over or stepped foot inside."

"So it's definitely one of your friends," Genevieve concluded.

Alma pressed her lips together and she looked furtively toward the house. "That's what I was afraid of."

"Why don't you ask them?"

Alma rubbed a hand over the side of her belly. "If I ask them all together, whoever did it will be terribly embarrassed and never give it back," she said. "She'd be known as a thief ever after! If I ask them one by one, they'll know I suspect them, and they'll be offended. If one of them thought I'd done something like that, I'd be deeply hurt. However I approach this, it will end friendships."

"I can see that…" Genevieve murmured.

"What should I do?" Alma looked at her hopefully.

"Well…" Genevieve thought for a moment. "Whoever did this isn't your friend. We can agree on that, right? A friend doesn't come into your home and steal an item that is precious to your husband. And to you."

"True…" Alma shrugged weakly.

"So that is probably a friendship you shouldn't worry over."

"But why would *anyone* take it?" Alma asked. "That's what I don't understand!"

There were lots of motivations for theft. "I'm not sure, but the money aspect does leap to mind. If it's worth so much, it could be sold. The person who took it might be hard up financially."

"Maybe..." Alma said. "But none of those four friends is struggling that way."

"Could she be hiding financial worries?"

Alma was silent, frowning.

"I'll tell you what," Genevieve said. "I'll check out the local pawn shops and places like that and see if a Lange & Söhne watch has moved through any of them. And if it hasn't arrived yet, it probably will come through soon—if money was the motivation."

"That makes sense," Alma said. "Would you do that for me?"

"I'd be happy to." Genevieve smiled. "I just need to know what it looks like." She pulled out her phone and ran an image search for the watch brand. Then she showed the photo on her phone to Alma.

"It looks like that one. Yes, almost exactly like that one."

Genevieve took a closer look. There was a similar watch on display in a museum, and it was said to be worth a shocking amount of money. This was no simple family heirloom. This was an incredibly valuable antique.

"Okay, this helps me a lot," Genevieve said. "I'll let you know what I find out."

"Thank you so much! You're like an angel coming through here!" Alma reached out and grabbed her hand. "I hope it isn't too much for you."

"I have time on my hands." Genevieve squeezed her hand back. "Trust me, this will be fine. It's no trouble."

Besides, Scott was willing to be flexible with her time here, and Genevieve needed the distraction. The top brass wanted to fix Genevieve, but her solution was clear in her mind: transfer out. Find a position where her father's arm wasn't long enough to reach. So while she was here at the puppy school, finding a stolen watch for this lady would be an excellent use of her time. Nothing wasted.

SCOTT LEANED AGAINST the fence, watching as Jan took Benjie through the obstacle course. Benjie climbed the stairs in two bounds then launched through a simulated window, hit the ground running and did a stretch of hurdles made of chain-link fences, wood fences, stone barriers and brick walls. He was fast, smart, and powerful.

Jan called him back and pulled out his rope and ball to play with him. Rewards could be food, or play, or whatever the dog enjoyed most. Benjie would do just about anything for a good tug game. He was well-trained. He was a good dog! He just needed to start trusting his handler's orders.

But Scott's mind wasn't on the dog training alone. Genevieve's disciplinary time here at the puppy school was Scott's chance to prove himself capable of managing a station of his own—his next step up in the force. He'd been working hard to prove himself, and he wanted this chance at running a station so badly he could taste it. Call it how he was raised, but he had a lot to prove to his old man. Scott might not be military, but he'd have a position that his dad would be forced to respect. Afraid of a challenge? He'd make his father eat those words.

Even if Scott's promotion came with managing Genevieve Austin, which was no easy task. She resented her own father's intrusion into her career, but she benefited from it, too. The fact that she was here under Scott's supervision instead of in the unemployment line was proof enough of that. Scott had always liked Gen's spunk, but she'd gone too far this time. It wasn't spunk…it was spite. She was angry, and he wasn't a newbie's partner anymore. This was going to be a tightrope.

Scott was already thinking of that South Kingston station as his. It had been a long time since he'd stepped foot inside, but he could remember the place like it was yesterday. Except all of his memories came with the rosy glow of Genevieve as his partner. When he went back as commander, she'd be his subordinate, and he wouldn't be able to play favorites. No hanging out with her, or treating her more fondly than he would any other officer.

If he wouldn't say it to a six-foot, two-hundred-and-fifty-pound trooper, he shouldn't say it to Gen.

But that was easier said than done when they had the history they did. She *was* special…and it was hard to pretend otherwise.

Genevieve came up next to him and leaned against the fence. Her blonde hair was loose around her shoulders, ruffling in the warm wind, and her cheeks were pink from exertion.

"You're back," he said.

"I'm back." Her gaze was trained on Benjie, too, as he raced after a ball and caught it. "Do you know a young pregnant Amish woman named Alma who lives down the road about a couple of miles?"

"Uh—can't say that I do," he replied. "Why?"

Genevieve pulled her hand through her hair, untangling it with her fingers, and turned to him.

"I came across her on my walk today, and she'd lost a valuable watch—an antique that would definitely be unique and trackable."

"How unique?"

She held up her phone. "Something like this."

It was a Lange & Söhne watch—those were pricey sold new, let alone as an antique. He looked closer at the screen. "And you're wanting to—"

"Check the pawn shops and the like," she replied.

That was what he thought.

"You aren't here to work local cases, Gen."

"Maybe not, but it couldn't hurt."

She was already pushing back. It was subtle but there. She was finding other things to do out here—a little chore that wasn't part of the plan to get her back into a team-player attitude. This was Gen going solo. He chewed his lip, considering. If she couldn't handle working under him, it would be his job to let her go. Did she have to toe this line?

"Tell me again how you came upon this little case?" he said.

"I literally walked into it," she replied. "This wasn't intentional on my part. She was looking for a lost watch, and I asked a few details. Then I offered to help."

"We can hand that off to the local troopers," he said. "That's not really our jurisdiction."

"Can't do that," she replied. "She doesn't want police involvement."

"You are police," he replied.

"Yes, but I said I'd keep it unofficial and just take a look around for her. She preferred that. So we can't just hand it off. She won't talk to another cop about it. It's complicated."

"Complicated how?"

"There are only four suspects for who took the watch, and all four are very close friends. She's not looking to get anyone arrested, but she'd really like that watch back. It has great emotional value." She cast him a wry look. "And as you saw, it's worth a small fortune."

An Amish couple with a valuable antique. Where had they gotten it? They could probably pay off their farm with it.

"The Amish don't tend to have items that are

worth that much," he said. "If they're wealthy, it tends to be in livestock and land."

"I suppose these folks are an exception," she replied. "Anyway, she feels awful that it went missing, and she wants to get it back for her husband."

"Understandable," he said. "But we really can't—"

"Before you say no," she said, cutting him off. Her bright blue eyes locked onto his face and her fingers lingered on his forearm. "You're supposed to spend a week with me, figure me out, and report back to the commissioner, right?"

"Yeah…" Except all of his focus right now was on the gentle pressure of her fingertips against his arm.

"So, let's add this into our schedule. I promise to cooperate with all the K9-related activities you've got planned. I'll do my best to help you get Benjie ready for active duty. I'll be a model trooper. I'll make the most of the therapy sessions. You'll be able to write up a glowing review of my time here. You said we should help each other, and I'll make it my personal goal to make you look good. Okay?"

"I'm sure you were planning on that anyway," he said with a rueful smile.

"Of course." She smiled back. "All I'm asking is that we just take a little peek into this theft. It's unofficial, but who knows? We might be able to find that watch for her. And I have to tell you, I'm wildly curious about which of her friends took it."

Scott rubbed a hand over his jaw. It sounded like she already had quite a bit of information, and while this was definitely out of their jurisdiction, he was intrigued by what she'd said so far. Call it the cop in him.

"Okay," he conceded, "give me the rundown. How do we know it's one of her four friends?"

Genevieve spelled it out—the watch on the counter, the friends coming to quilt, the interest in the antique when the women saw it, and then its disappearance. No other visitors or family members, and her husband hadn't arrived home until after she'd noticed it was missing.

"So unless other information comes to light, it's definitely one of the four," he agreed. All of whom the victim had known for decades, most likely.

"That's what it looks like," Genevieve replied. "Living in a small community like theirs, it would be tough to trust any of these women going forward. She's going to need to know who did it, even if only for her own sanity."

Scott pressed his lips together and looked out over the obstacle course. If he got the station commander job and ended up her boss, he couldn't keep giving her preferential treatment. But he also would need her to work with him—for the good of both of them—and this was a great way to rebuild some of her trust in the system that had been letting her down. At least, that was what he'd tell the commissioner if it came up.

"You've got to be following me around anyway,"

Genevieve said. "At least this way we'd have something to investigate. Like old times."

Like those early days when he'd been partnered up with the gorgeous rookie and they'd spent their days patrolling the rural communities in their jurisdiction. Back when they used to laugh until their sides ached while they'd eaten greasy burgers or opened up about their personal lives while they'd been on traffic duty, watching for speeders. Those were the good old days…and she'd hit the right button, all right.

"Okay," he said. "We'll look into it."

"Thank you." She held his gaze for one glittering second then turned her attention to Benjie and Jan who'd come back to the beginning of the obstacle course again. "This might be a situation where she'll just be better off knowing who did it, but I hate it when good, decent people are taken advantage of."

"Me, too," he agreed.

"And I'm thinking, if we aren't going to be adding this missing watch to the National Crime Information Center or the FBI stolen articles file, then we'll have to move pretty quickly to make sure we catch the watch when it hits any local intermediary. It's worth a lot, and it might move fast."

Genevieve was smart, and she was a talented detective.

"There are two pawn shops around here," Scott said. "We can visit them both, give them a description and put the fear of God in them for moving a stolen article worth that much."

"Do you know them?" she asked.

"I'm acquainted. We'll go together and I'll introduce you. We should probably go this afternoon—before that watch disappears for good."

"What about puppy duty?" she asked.

"Let's take Benjie with us—give him some low-pressure practice being out there in the community."

"Deal." She nudged his shoulder with his. "This'll be fun, partner."

He couldn't help but smile back. She was going to be a tough one to manage because to her he'd always be her old partner and to him…she'd always be special. Maybe they both needed to shake this out of their systems, and a little local case might be just what they needed to find their new balance.

CHAPTER FOUR

THE TOWN OF STRAUSFELD was nestled next to Conestoga Creek, which was really a good-size river when it was in flood stage, swollen with winter melt and springtime rain. It was still wide, deep and muddy right now, and Genevieve could see it rushing past from the spot where they'd parked the cruiser along the waterfront drive.

The waterfront had a collection of old shops that had been there for decades. Most of the buildings were made from durable brick, while others were wooden with peeling paint and dilapidated clapboard. There were some old brick shops on the northeast end that had been spruced up and now sold specialty coffee and overpriced chocolate. Cafés sported colorful umbrellas in their outdoor dining areas, and a strip of grassy park afforded walking paths and picnic space next to the river.

On the shabbier end of the river walk were gift shops, a bakery and a second-hand clothing store with some vintage outfits on mannequins and antique china arranged in the window. The last building, a single-story wooden building, bore a sign with yellow lettering on a black background: Strausfeld Pawn—Cash for Gold and Guns. It was a rather gaudy sign that stood out from an otherwise picturesque strip of shops.

Scott had parallel parked on the street and they'd watched a middle-aged man in a baseball cap coming out of the pawn shop carrying some wrenches.

"The shop's owner is named Paul Miller," Scott said. "He's been cooperative in the past, but he can be a bit of a character."

"Gotcha."

"If you need me to step in with him—" Scott met her gaze then a smile crinkled around his eyes. Step in? She was a fully trained trooper. She'd be fine.

"You still hate that, don't you?" he said.

"I really do. I can handle him."

"No question. Just wanted to offer."

"Because you're a man?" she asked with a rueful smile.

"Nah, because I'm your boss for a week." He caught her eye and chuckled. "Come on. Let's get in there and see what we can find out."

Genevieve got out of the car and waited while Scott leashed Benjie. The dog's ears were up and his tail was high—he was excited.

"Benjie." Scott looked down at the dog meaningfully. "Stay calm."

Benjie panted, his glistening eyes on Scott. That dog loved him—she could see that plainly.

"Heel," Scott said, and he started toward the

door. Benjie trotted along next to Scott in a perfect heel position. Scott opened the door and nodded Genevieve through first.

A bell tinkled overhead and Genevieve did a quick scan of the store. There were glass display cases over by the register and cluttered shop shelves that held all sorts of tools from belt sanders to Weedwackers. She headed for the area by the register while Scott nodded to the man behind the counter.

"Hey, Paul," Scott said. "Busy lately?"

"Oh, about the same as always," the man replied. "How are you doing, Sarge?"

Genevieve looked over the display cases. By far the biggest selection of jewelry was a case of silver items. Rings, necklaces, earrings, pendants. The gold section was next and, for the most part, consisted of wedding bands and diamond solitaire rings that more closely resembled diamond chips, not stones. Who had pawned their wedding ring? she wondered. That was a heartbreaking thought.

Next to the jewelry, there were some watches. But none that matched the description of the piece she was looking for. One was a "Rollex"—misspelled and obviously fake. There was a woman's gold watch—slim, pretty—and an obvious old watch with a cracked leather band.

She looked over at Scott. Benjie sat obediently by his side, ears perked, waiting for a command. The man behind the counter was looking at her with an oily little smile on his face.

"Meet my partner," Scott said then compressed his lips at his mistake.

So this was all a little familiar for him, too, was it?

"This is Paul." Scott nodded to the slim man behind the counter.

"The pleasure is mine." Paul held out a hand to Genevieve. She ignored it, and after a beat, he smiled bashfully and wiped his hand down his shirt. "You new here? Will I be seeing more of you, Officer...?"

"Trooper Austin," she said. "And we're here, looking for a particular item. It's a gold Lange & Söhne watch. Brown leather band."

"I've got a watch with a leather band on display—" Paul started.

"That's a Timex," she said, cutting him off. "I saw it already. This watch is something special. It's an antique that could fetch quite a lot of money for the right buyer."

Paul pursed his lips then shrugged. "I'll keep an eye out. Maybe you could give me your number. I could give you a call and we could...talk about it."

He wasn't even smooth as he hit on her.

Genevieve didn't answer, pinning him a no-nonsense look instead. Scott crossed his arms over his chest and lifted his chin. He used to do that all the time when they were partners. She'd go question a perp and he'd just stand behind her that way— glaring down his nose at the guy while she peppered him with questions.

"Do you have many Amish locals who come through here?" Genevieve asked.

"A few."

"Amish women?" she asked.

"Yeah, I mean…they come by and haggle pretty aggressively. Normally, they're picking up gardening tools or a big pot, or something like that. I'll take pretty much anything someone wants to pawn, because I'll sell it eventually."

"Do Amish people pawn their things very often?" Genevieve asked.

"Yeah. I mean if you need some quick money, it's a way to get your hands on it. Like that bicycle over there—" He gestured to a far wall that had some old paintings leaning up against it, some long-handled gardening equipment, and a blue adult-size bicycle with a generously large basket on the front. "An Amish man brought that in. That's a new bike, too. He needed money fast."

"What for?" Scott asked.

"Don't know. I didn't ask."

"And the women?" Genevieve prompted.

"They're more cautious." Paul lowered his voice, although there was no one else in the shop to hear him. "If they've got a particularly controlling husband, they don't want to be caught pawning anything. They'll bring in kitchen utensils, pots, bowls, sometimes a handmade quilt… One lady came in with four forks. It was all she could swipe without her husband noticing. I felt so bad for her I gave her twenty bucks for them. I mean—

I won't sell them for more than twenty-five cents, but she looked desperate, you know?" He looked appealingly toward Genevieve. Maybe he thought she'd be impressed.

"You won't make a profit that way," Scott said.

"I considered it my good deed for the day. What can I say?" Paul shrugged and he shot Genevieve a slow smile. "I'm a decent guy."

She fought the urge to roll her eyes. "Have any Amish customers come in with anything...pricier?" Genevieve asked.

"Not really. That bike is the priciest thing. But, I mean, a nice quality bike like that is worth almost a thousand dollars brand new. I could get an easy five hundred for it."

"No jewelry?" she asked.

"They're Amish." Paul gave her a patient smile.

"I know, but...you never know. Some people might break some rules." At the very least, Alma and her husband had an unlikely and very expensive watch.

"No jewelry. They're simple people," Paul leaned back and eyed her insolently. "And they don't stay part of the community long if they break the rules, I can tell you that."

"Why?" she asked. She knew the answer, but she wanted to see what Paul would say.

"Because they'll rat each other out," he said. "Do you know how fast gossip spreads in a tight community that size? And if they're not abiding by the *Ordnung*—that's their rule book—the elders and the bishop will make a visit. If they don't shape up, they could get themselves shunned. You know about that, right?"

She did. It was when the person was ousted from the community. No one would speak to them, spend time with them, or even acknowledge them unless it was a life-or-death situation.

"So there's some good reasons for them to toe the line," Paul went on. "If they don't, they stand to lose everything—friends, family, everything. No shiny bauble is worth that much."

Genevieve was inclined to agree.

"If you could just keep your eye out for a watch that matches that description, and give us a call right away if you come across it, we'd appreciate that," Genevieve said.

"What about the money I give out? Will I get that back?" Paul asked.

"Within reason, we'll see what we can do," Scott said.

"If you'd give me your number…" Paul's attention turned to Genevieve again and he smiled hopefully at her.

Scott pulled a business card out of his pocket and handed it over. "That's mine. Feel free to call me directly. Thanks, Paul. I appreciate it."

Paul took the card, deflating just a bit.

Genevieve smothered a smile.

Benjie stood up, perhaps sensing that the encounter was finished, and when Scott tugged the leash, he followed Scott obediently as they headed for the door.

The bell tinkled again as they left, and when the door swung shut, Scott looked over at her.

"What do you think?" he asked.

"That man's telling some truth, but I'm willing to bet he's holding back a lot," she replied.

"Yeah, they all do," Scott muttered. "But I think we kept him hopping fast enough that he was telling more truth than usual."

She grinned. "I missed this. We used to be good at this, remember?"

"What do you mean 'used to be'?" Scott headed back toward the cruiser. "There's another pawn shop in the next town over. Let's head over there next."

Scott's serious gaze softened. That look—so much like the way he used to look at her when they were partners as regular troopers—made her melt just a little. Suddenly, as they stood on this sidewalk, it could have been six years ago, when they'd known each other better than anyone. She'd known his coffee order, his birthday, his favorite snacks and the exact way to push his buttons. Other troopers had joked that he was her "work husband," and they hadn't been too far from the truth. They'd had something special, the two of them. And she'd missed it deeply when it was over.

She had a feeling she'd miss this all over again when her time here was done, too, and there wasn't anything she could do about that.

THAT MORNING, before Genevieve arrived, Scott had had a good long talk with Commissioner Taylor, and he'd discovered two things. One, Commissioner Taylor was more approachable than he'd expected; and two, he truly cared what was happening with Genevieve.

He'd known the man was friends with Constantine Austin and his family. But Commissioner Taylor had also been her mentor. He'd known her since she was a young teenager, and he'd watched her grow up.

Those were the kinds of connections that regular people just didn't have, and it seemed that the commissioner was both ready to let Gen go, and deeply concerned for her emotional welfare.

"She might open up to you, Scott," he'd said. "You used to be partners, and I know she really respected you. I'm hoping that will help smooth your path a bit. I need to know that she's okay... or if she's not okay. But she's angry and she's closed me out. She's closed her father out, too. As the commissioner, I should fire her. As her dad's friend... I need to find out what's going on under the surface."

That was the first time Scott had considered Genevieve might not be okay, and the worry lingered. The Genevieve he knew wasn't the kind of woman to thwart authority in such a manner. He didn't only need to prove to the commissioner that she could work with him, he needed to make sure she was okay for his own peace of mind, too.

The commissioner had definitely pushed the right button there.

Now, sitting next to her in the car, he couldn't help but steal a look at her while he drove down the familiar narrow highway toward Benton. She looked withdrawn and a little sad.

"So, what did I miss in your career?" he asked casually.

"Nothing yet. I'm angling for detective," she said. "I like putting all the pieces together. I like making things make sense."

That checked out. She always had been the type to pick at something until she was satisfied.

"Like this missing watch?" he asked.

She leaned her head back. "Yeah, just like this watch. I guess I sympathize with Alma's situation. When you have people close to you who you can't trust, that's hard to deal with. I know what that's like."

"Who can't you trust?" he asked.

"My father, for one," she replied. "He doesn't want me to succeed. And Commissioner Taylor is another. Did you know that he wrote me my recommendation letter for the force?"

Scott glanced at her in surprise. "I didn't know that."

"Yeah, well…he did. He argued with my dad and said that I should be able to pursue the career I wanted to. And then he proceeded to overprotect me on the job. Of anyone, I thought I could trust him to have my back. But he's got more than my back. He's got my career in a stranglehold."

"It's complicated," he said.

"Definitely." She sighed. "Honestly? When I told him what I thought of him, I was talking to Tom—the family friend, the man I used to be able to speak my mind to."

"He does care, you know," Scott said.

"Well, now I've wounded his pride."

"So you feel alone," Scott murmured.

She didn't answer, but her expression did soften when he looked over at her. Scott slowed to the reduced speed limit as they came to the outskirts of Benton and he realized that he wasn't so different. He didn't trust his father, either. It hurt, but at this point he was pretty sure his dad was waiting for him to mess up again. And Scott was determined to prove him wrong. While Sergeant Allan Simpson didn't have the money or the clout that Constantine Austin had, Scott's father could take him out emotionally.

Scott parked in the small parking lot to the side of the Benton Pawn Mart. He took Benjie out again and leashed him.

"In the interest of opening up a bit," Scott said slowly, "I really do need your help with Benjie. I meant it when I said I'd messed up with this dog, and my conscience isn't easy about him. I'm not making connections to your situation when I talk about him. I… I got too attached to him."

There. He'd said it. Partly. During a time when

he'd been wrestling with his own demons, maybe he'd let Benjie be too much of a comfort to him, too. That bond hadn't been Benjie's fault. Scott had needed someone…and he'd been doing his best to keep his mind off of Genevieve at the time.

Weak. That's what his dad had called him, right? Maybe he was.

"There's no shame in loving a dog, Scott," Genevieve said softly.

"Well, my love put a stranglehold on his career, too, so…"

She smiled, her warm eyes meeting his. It felt better to have opened up more honestly with her.

"What can I do to help?" she asked.

"Well… Benjie has been behaving perfectly with me," Scott said. "Why don't you take him and we'll see if he continues with this good behavior? That would help."

It would reassure Scott, at least. He bent down and ruffled the top of Benjie's head with the tips of his fingers. And in his heart, he silently begged the dog to just do that… There was more riding on this next week than Benjie could possibly understand.

Scott gave her a quick demonstration on how to hold the leash, how to give the K9 more slack or call him back in to heel. Genevieve wrapped the leash twice around her hand, keeping Benjie in close to her side. Yeah, she had it. She looked down at the dog and he looked up at her.

"Are we good, Benjie?" she asked and then a smile glittered in her eyes. "Heel."

Benjie stayed close to Gen's side, and Scott opened the door, letting them go in first.

The owners were a married couple. Scott had dealt with the two before and had always found them to be organized and incredibly honest. Melanie Trent's hair was long and curly, and she was wearing a long skirt and a peasant blouse the same shade of natural gray that highlighted her hair. The last time he'd been out this way, he'd had a cough and she'd given him some homemade throat lozenges that had worked phenomenally well. Her husband, Neil, wore khaki shorts, sandals and a T-shirt with a logo on the front that Scott didn't recognize.

Neil pulled out a thick ledger and plunked it on the counter in front of Scott.

"It's all here," he said. "You can see every item brought in, and what happened to it. No watches like the one you described, though. I'd remember that. Those are incredibly pricey. I'd never sell it here. If someone brought it in and didn't come back for it, I'd find a private buyer for a piece like that."

"Do you know Paul Miller in Strausfeld?" Genevieve asked.

"Sure, he owns the pawn shop out there," Melanie said.

"Yeah, that's right."

The Trents looked at each other then back at Scott and Genevieve.

Neil added, "In fact, we were looking for an authentic bumper for an old Volkswagen we've been restoring, and he happened to have one. The Bug's worth more than you think—one that's in good condition."

"Did you buy it from him?" Scott asked.

"He gave us the bumper," Melanie supplied. "He called it a professional courtesy. It was really kind of him. He's a decent man."

That did sound like a kind gesture. Paul had mentioned doing some good turns for the local Amish in his area, too.

Benjie started to sniff around the shop, and like Scott had showed her, Genevieve let out his lead to give him some freedom. She followed the dog closely as he followed his nose—along the edge of the display case and behind the counter.

"Do you have something back there we should know about?" Scott asked.

Benjie pawed at the ground and sat, and Scott came around beside Gen.

"Oh, that." Melanie bent down and pulled out a cardboard box of dog biscuits. "Sorry, I'd have offered but I know you don't like us distracting working dogs."

"Benjie!" Scott looked at the dog, exasperated. "Seriously?" After all of their work, he was alerting them to Milk-Bones?

Benjie looked up hopefully, cocking his head to one side.

"No!" Scott said. "No doggy treats while you're at work."

"You sure?" Melanie asked, giving the box a shake.

"Very." Scott nodded toward the cupboard. "Do you mind if my partner just takes a look in there?"

Melanie shrugged. "Be my guest."

Genevieve squatted down and looked around inside the cupboard. She pulled out some boxes—one contained mousetraps and the other had bug repellent. She put the boxes back and closed the door.

"Thanks for letting us take a peek," she said, casting Melanie a disarming smile. "We're training the dog, you see."

"Well, you're a very good boy," Melanie said to Benjie, and Benjie wagged in response.

"Benjie, on me," Scott said, taking the leash from Gen. The shepherd immediately focused on Scott and sat down, obedient and still.

"Thanks for your time," Genevieve said. "We appreciate it."

"Any time," Neil replied and draped an arm over his wife's shoulder.

Scott gave the leash a tug and Benjie trotted obediently by his side as they headed out of the shop.

"What was that?" Gen asked once the door was shut.

"That was a drug alert," he said. "Or blood. Those are the scents he's trained for. You didn't see anything else in that cupboard?"

"Nothing." Gen shook her head. "Unless they've

got something hidden under the counter floorboards, or... Do you want to go take the place apart?"

"Either that, or he really wanted a biscuit," Scott said. "And, Benjie, if that's the case, I'm going to be really disappointed in you." Benjie's ears drooped and Scott felt some compassion alongside his annoyance. "So how come you're good as gold for me, and not for Gen, huh?"

That was another problem.

"Has he always been like this?" Genevieve asked.

"What?"

"Bonded to you exclusively?"

Scott's conscience tugged painfully. That had been the problem exactly. "He was perfect for me in training when he was a puppy. But he wouldn't transfer well to another officer. I thought with time he'd figure it out and work with a new handler the same way he did with me. But...he didn't."

"It's too bad you couldn't just be his handler," she said.

Yeah, that would be simple enough if Scott were staying with K9, but he was finally moving up in his career—and he'd worked too hard to get this chance. Station commanders didn't have dogs at their sides, but, all the same, there was one rebellious corner of his heart that wished he could.

"Benjie is a really good dog. He's just chosen the wrong guy," he said. "I'm not an option for him. He's got to learn to trust and bond with another handler or..."

Or he'd end up in a kennel a lot of the time and really lonely. That thought gave Scott's heart a squeeze. Even if Scott took him home as a pet, he'd be working long hours, attending meetings, doing a lot of computer work…and Benjie would be home alone. Benjie needed a job, or a very specific home—someone else's. Not his. The K9 career for Benjie was easier to provide by far.

They got back into the cruiser and Scott started the engine but didn't put the car into gear. For a moment, he just sat there then he looked over at Genevieve. Sunlight slanted through the window, lighting up her features, glowing across her creamy skin and backlighting some wisps of hair around her face. This had been the line he'd balanced for the better part of three years while they'd been partners—teetering on the edge of falling for her based on a moment just like this one.

"Do you want ice cream?" he asked.

Her pale eyebrows rose and a smile touched her lips. "Wouldn't turn it down."

"Good." He faced forward and shifted into gear. He knew an Amish-run place that had the creamiest soft serve on earth. They had puppy cones there, too, and he'd never trained a dog that didn't love a taste of ice cream.

He pulled out of the parking space and started in the direction of Yoder Dairy. It was on the way back to Strausfeld, so there wouldn't be time wasted.

"So, what's your take on Paul Miller?" Genevieve asked.

"Uh—" He signaled a turn. "He's a bit shady, but he's cooperated in the past. You know how it is, Gen. Not everyone is pure as the driven snow, but that doesn't make them criminals, either."

"True," she said. "And the Trents had good things to say about him. He seems to do people good turns—you included. But I have to wonder what he gets out of it."

Scott smiled ruefully. "I'm not saying he doesn't benefit by being seen as a good guy... But most folks have an angle."

"True enough," she replied. "I'm just hoping these people tell us if that watch comes through their shops. Because even the Trent couple strikes me as... I don't know...not past fudging the books if it meant a big enough payday, you know?"

He knew exactly what she meant, which made a case like this—unofficial or not—that much harder to navigate. They were looking for a single missing item—snagged by an Amish lady at a quilting session.

The Yoder Dairy was located on a paved side road outside of Strausfeld. It was a medium-size place—larger than most Amish establishments—and had become popular by word of mouth alone. Everyone in these parts knew of the Yoder Dairy.

He steered into a spot next to the buggy parking. Several buggies sat there, the horses tied to a hitching post and enjoying the warm June sun.

An Amish family, each with an ice cream cone in hand, was just coming out—parents who looked about as old as Scott, six kids trailing after them.

They got out of the car. Scott leashed Benjie and the dog heeled perfectly as they headed past the rambunctious children toward the shop entrance. Scott opened the front door for Genevieve, and as she slipped into the store ahead of him, the scent of her perfume lingered near him. Yeah, he'd forgotten that unique torment of working with Genevieve. She was one hundred percent off limits, but also had a way of tugging him after her, too. Nothing had changed in that respect.

He followed her inside, Benjie next to him. There wasn't a lineup, so they went to the Amish girl at the cash register.

"Hi," Scott said. "I'd like a vanilla cone, a pup cup and... Gen?"

"Twist cone, please," Genevieve said.

Scott paid, and they waited in silence while the girl got their cones ready. She handed them over the counter carefully, and Scott squatted to give Benjie his treat, too. The ice cream was as good as it always was—creamy, just sweet enough, and perfect—but he watched for Gen's reaction as she took her first bite. She shot him a smile and nodded. Yeah, it was good.

They thanked the girl who'd served them, Benjie finished his small taste of ice cream, and they headed back outside into the warm sunlight. Everything out here smelled faintly of cattle—there was no getting around that near a dairy. The Amish family leaned against their buggy as they ate their cold treats. He watched Gen's eyes move over the cow-dotted pasture, past the white barns and over to the rolling hills.

Suddenly, she turned toward him.

"Scott, what would you do if your best friend stole from you?"

"Uh—be pretty upset, I guess."

"What would make you steal from a friend?"

"I'm not sure. Some pretty deep resentment?" he said.

He thought about that. "Toward Alma or her husband?"

"Good question. It could go either way. But they're her friends, not his."

Genevieve took a bite of ice cream, pursed her lips then licked them. He could almost see the gears clicking away.

"What I wouldn't give to sit down with those women and hear their side of this," Genevieve said thoughtfully. "I don't like it when people don't act the way they should. It doesn't make emotional sense."

"You used to say that a lot," he said. Right before she'd figured out that the little old man on the bench was a drug mule or that the smiling lady running the store was hosting gambling in the back rooms.

"Because that's the clue," she said. "If people aren't acting right, their actions aren't matching the emotions they put out there, or their emotions aren't matching the situation...then there's a reason. And I want to know why."

She also never stopped until she found it. His mouth went dry. Well, maybe Scott should be glad that she had a case to sink her teeth into, because if she turned that sharp curiosity onto him, she'd unravel his motivation for his actions pretty fast.

He'd had feelings for her. He'd been halfway in love with her. He'd known he wouldn't be able to hide it for much longer, and he'd known who her father was. It had been both as complicated and as simple as that.

He'd much prefer she just leave well enough alone and didn't go digging after making "emotional sense" of him. She'd be happier, by far, if she didn't look any deeper at all.

CHAPTER FIVE

THE NEXT MORNING, the district psychotherapist arrived while Genevieve was working on an online anxiety management course she'd been assigned to complete. Her therapy appointment was for ten and she finished the online module just in time. She closed her laptop and headed downstairs. Wendy was at the front desk and motioned her through to the kitchen where Genevieve found the therapist waiting. Her mug of tea smelled minty.

"Good morning, Trooper Austin. It's a pleasure. May I call you Genevieve?"

"Sure," Genevieve said. She shook the woman's hand.

Dr. Darlene Schaber was a short, plump woman with a tendency toward layered clothing. She wore a long, asymmetrical skirt of a dusty mauve color. There was a white tunic on top of that, some jangling, clattering, wooden jewelry and a bulky coral scarf pulling her graying hair away from her face. The look was finished off with ballet flats.

"Call me Darlene," Dr. Schaber told her. "We're about to get awfully personal, so we might as well keep it on a first-name basis. Let's move into my office, shall we?"

While Darlene beckoned welcomingly toward the office wing of the first floor, Genevieve couldn't help but feel this was punishment. Online book-work about anxiety, anger management and coping mechanisms was hard enough, but sitting with a therapist—one she'd been ordered to see—was a different kind of humiliation.

Genevieve followed Darlene down a hallway toward a sunny room with large, bright windows. They were partly covered with a linen blind, letting in soft light but blocking any view of the outside that might be distracting. The room itself was all different shades of white and tan. Two cream-colored armchairs flanked the window. There was a box of tissues sitting unobtrusively on the windowsill next to a flourishing spider plant. A pale-pink-and-oatmeal-flecked rag rug covered the polished wooden floor, and several nondescript pictures of muted nature scenes hung on the walls. It was a room meant to relax a person and not influence them in any way.

"Have a seat," Darlene said. "I always love coming out to Amish Country. This is just such a lovely area. So calm. Refreshing." Darlene nodded a few times. "That's what it is. Refreshing. I leave here feeling renewed."

Genevieve sank into an armchair—it was incredibly comfortable—and Darlene took a seat opposite her. She balanced a leather-bound folder on her knee and she made a couple of notes with a ballpoint pen.

"So…" Darlene looked up. "What brings you here?"

"Disciplinary action." Genevieve gave the woman a tight smile. Amish Country wasn't leaving Genevieve feeling refreshed in the least.

"Yes, but why?" Darlene fixed her with a meaningful look. "And I don't mean what exactly you said to the commissioner. I've had the rundown on that. It happened. It's in the past. It doesn't interest me. What interests me is the *why*."

Genevieve sighed. Yes, the why. She'd crossed a line. She'd vented on the commissioner in a way she never should have.

"I don't want to lose my job, Darlene," she said. "I'll tone down the attitude and there will be no more trouble from me."

"That's a Band-Aid," Darlene replied. "What made you so enraged that you blasted our commissioner with the honest truth? That's what I want to know."

Genevieve blinked at her. "You believe what I said?"

"I've done my homework." She smiled faintly. "You've been working for the state police for five years, and you haven't moved beyond your current position. You're obviously well-liked and smart, but…as for action? You haven't seen much of it."

"Well, that's what makes me mad," Genevieve

said. "Why hold me back? Why hire me, train me, and then wrap me in cotton?"

"Why do you think that is?"

"Because of my father."

"Hmm."

"You disagree."

"It's not my place to agree or disagree. I want to know what you think."

Genevieve could feel her old irritation rising. "You'd have to know my father to really understand. He's wealthy, powerful and used to getting his way. And he loves me. I'm not saying that my father is a terrible person. He's just…not used to being told no to anything."

"And you think he's the one who has held you back."

"I'm positive."

"What if he hadn't?" Darlene asked. "What if it wasn't him? What if it was something else?"

"Then what reason would there be to keep me out of harm's way?" she demanded. "There is none! My father wants to keep me from getting hurt out there. He and Tom Taylor are good friends and Tom—sorry, Commissioner Taylor—is doing my father a favor."

"That's one story we could tell," Darlene said. "Let's set it aside for a moment. Give me a different story that would explain it all."

Genevieve shook her head. "There isn't one! Unless I'm simply not that good at my job," she said with a bitter laugh.

Silence from Darlene.

Genevieve blinked at her. "Is that what you think? That I'm not a good cop?"

"It's not about what I think," Darlene murmured. "It's about what *you* think."

"I *am* good at my job. I can handle myself out there."

"Except, you haven't had a chance to prove it, so..." Darlene murmured.

Was she trying to poke a tender place? Was this on purpose? Looking at the mild-faced woman opposite her, Genevieve had to assume that it was. Was this some kind of test?

"I do incredibly well in training exercises. I've always been able to handle situations in my years on the force. I could do more. This is just like—" Genevieve stopped.

"Just like...?" Darlene asked. "Go on. We were getting somewhere."

"All right." Genevieve leaned her head back.

"When I was twelve, I decided I wanted to make my own fortune. My father was very supportive of this. My mother was alive then, and she said I'd be inheriting a fortune, so I should focus on charitable contributions. Anyway, I wanted to sell hand-embroidered tea towels. Actually, it was some cross-stitched flowers, but I was very proud of my work, and I cross-stitched until my fingers bled.

"Then I took my stack of towels to a craft fair and set up my little table. No one stopped to look. My presentation was terrible. Just a little girl with a glitter-encrusted poster board and a pile of towels. And then one of my father's friends stopped. He admired my workmanship and bought a towel. That was Tom Taylor. Then another lady I didn't know bought two. And I was elated. I sold out of my towels and there was a bidding war over the very last one. It ended upselling for a hundred dollars. I was so excited."

"Wow…" Darlene looked dubious.

"Yeah. Obviously, my father had set it all up for his friends to make me feel good." Genevieve smiled ruefully. "My cross-stitched flowers weren't worth much."

"Your father was being kind," Darlene said.

"Until he got tired of it," Genevieve replied. "He said he'd take some of my towels to his office to see if anyone wanted to buy them. I got the driver to take me there the next day because I wanted to check on the display. I was taking this very seriously. I saw my towels in a garbage can in the break room. And when my father saw me, he told me this big lie about how they'd sold out right away, and he pulled out his wallet and gave me some cash. I knew then that he'd just been patronizing me."

"Did he do this sort of thing often?"

"All the time. I was part of a beauty pageant, and one of the judges owned a car dealership. Dad bought a brand-new car the day before the pageant. I won."

"You don't think you won because of your beauty?"

"We'll never know, will we?"

"But you think this time he's holding you back rather than helping you win. This is different."

Genevieve couldn't help scowling. "He doesn't want me to be a cop. He wants me to do something safer. Anything safer. He never liked that I pursued this career."

"Do you think he'd try to get you fired?"

"No! He'd never do that. He just wants to keep me safe—make sure I don't see any danger. He thinks that's his way of supporting me."

"What happened to your mother?"

Tears misted her eyes then and she blinked them back. "You obviously know if you're asking that now."

"Humor me."

"She was shot. She was doing some charitable work in a rough area of town, and she was held up. She tried to be kind to the robber. Bystanders said she told him that she thought he could succeed in life. That she believed in him. He shot her."

Genevieve thought about the moment her father had told her. He'd been crying. His eyes were red and watery, and he'd said that her mother had died immediately. There was no suffering. The suffering would be theirs.

"Is that why you wanted to become a cop?" Darlene murmured.

The first night in the house after her mother's

death, she'd pulled out her mother's bathrobe and slept with it. It had smelled of her face cream and her skin... It had smelled safe. She'd sobbed all night.

"It factors in," Genevieve said. "I want to see justice served. I want to keep the streets safe so that a well-meaning lady can hand out sandwiches and still make it home for dinner." Her voice shook and she swallowed against that growing lump in her throat.

"Do you think your father is afraid of losing you the same way he lost his wife?"

"I'm not handing out free sandwiches. I'm a trained trooper. This is entirely different."

"To you it is."

"In reality it is! My mother was a well-intentioned volunteer. I'm a trained cop."

"Your father probably sees everything through the lens of that deep loss he experienced when your mother was killed."

"Probably." Genevieve shook her head. "I'm not calling him a monster. I'm saying he's interfering!"

Darlene wrote something down and nodded soberly.

"So, what are we doing here?" Genevieve asked. "Are we going to defend my father's interfering in my career? Has he gotten to you, too?"

"Do you really think that?" Darlene asked, looking up again.

"I don't know..." Genevieve rubbed her hands over her eyes. "Darlene, I'm being straight with you. I love my job. I want to be able to do my job without being held back because of my father's influence. That's it."

"Are you sure that's it?" Darlene asked quietly.

"Yes!"

For a couple of beats, Genevieve locked onto Darlene's gaze and anger surged up inside her. Why would no one listen? She knew exactly what the problem was!

"Well, we have another half hour together this morning. If you don't like the things we've been talking about so far, what would you like to talk about?" Darlene closed her folder and clicked her pen shut.

What did Darlene and the rest of the command need to see from her? If she knew, they could just skip ahead and she'd cooperate like they wouldn't believe. But this walking there, step by step, was painful.

It was going to be an exhausting week.

SCOTT LOOKED BACK toward the house. Barracks. That's what the state police called it because there were rooms for overnight stays. But this place was different and that big, rambling Amish farmhouse would never be regular barracks. There was something in Amish Country that was part of the place on a foundation-and-stud level and just couldn't be rinsed out with protocol.

Benjie and Konig lay side by side in the shade of an apple tree. The apples were small, green and hard this time of year, but they were plentiful. In the fall, officers would pick bags full of them and bring them home. They were sweeter and crisper than any apple you could buy in a grocery store. The dogs were relaxed, and it was nice to see them enjoying each other's company.

Konig came from Germany, and those dogs were like marines. Scott hoped he'd rub off on Benjie. If only the Dutch shepherd understood English.

"Konig," Scott said. The dog lifted his head, ears perked. *"Kommen."*

That was the one command Konig responded to. He got up and trotted obediently to Scott's side. Scott gave him a pet. Konig might be struggling with English, but he still needed affection and affirmation. These dogs were smart but they were also sensitive. It came with the territory.

"Abwarten." Wait. It was a command for the dog to hunker down and keep his eyes on his handler, waiting for further instructions. Scott started to walk away from him, and Konig trotted along next to him.

"Buddy, am I saying it wrong?" Scott scrubbed a hand through his hair. He looked over at Benjie, who was sitting up now in the shade, eyes pinned on Scott.

"Come on, Benjie," Scott called, and Benjie joyfully launched himself forward. He hated being left out, especially from anything Scott was doing.

When Benjie had returned two weeks ago and

seen Scott, it had been like a homecoming reunion. Benjie had wriggled, licked and whined so furiously that Scott had almost cried. Benjie had bonded to him as a pup, and something in that little canine heart had refused to let go...or to give another handler a proper chance.

The two dogs trotted along side by side, eyes bright and happy. Konig didn't need any retraining. He'd been in top shape from the moment he'd arrived on a transatlantic flight. He knew his commands perfectly—the German K9 unit he'd come from trained dogs on everything from search and rescue to military bomb sniffers. The problem wasn't Konig. It was their German—or lack thereof.

Scott had always had a soft spot for the dogs who struggled with something. They'd been drawn to him, too. Take Benjie. He was a good dog—talented, smart, good instincts. But there was something holding him back from doing his job perfectly. And while perfection seemed like a cruel expectation, they needed to get as close to it as possible for everyone's safety, including Benjie's. When he was on a job, it was literally life or death.

Scott had been drawn to people who struggled, too. Maybe it was because he identified with them. He and Gen had gotten along as well as they had because they'd both been a little scarred. At first meeting, she didn't look scarred, but under the perfect image she projected, she had her own issues. And he had his. Together, they were excellent cops. But they had also been friends with a strong bond. It was his problem that he couldn't make his emotions stop at that line with her.

And he wasn't normally a guy who struggled with boundaries! He'd been raised with boundaries as sharp as razors. His father had been tough and unyielding in absolutely everything. If anything, Scott was normally too reserved with most people.

He saw a flash of white from the corner of his eye and he looked to the Amish farm next door to see the woman who lived there coming across the mown grass toward him. She was petite, with a rounded pregnant belly draped with a white apron. That was what had caught his eye. This must be Alma. Both dogs turned and fixed their attention on her, too.

"Sit," Scott said. Benjie sank to his haunches. "Stay."

Konig looked between Benjie and Scott, then sat down, too. He was smart! Wouldn't it be ironic if they ended up teaching Konig English with Benjie as a K9 translator?

"Good morning!" Scott called.

"Good morning!" Alma had a covered basket in one hand. Her cheeks were pink and she was breathing a little faster by the time she reached him. She held out the basket. "I made some muffins and thought you and your officers might enjoy them."

He peeked under the white towel and saw plump

blueberry muffins with a sugar crumble on top. They'd be amazing.

"We really appreciate this," he said, accepting the basket. "We'll make sure to get the basket back to you."

"There's no rush…" She sobered. "There is a lady here. I met her yesterday. She's…about this tall—" she gestured with one hand above her head "—and she's slim. Blonde hair. Very nice-looking."

"Yes, Trooper Austin. Did you need to talk to her?"

Alma nodded. "*Yah.* I wanted to…to see her for a moment."

"She's busy right now. I can't interrupt her, but I could pass along a message."

"That's okay." Alma's glance moved to the basket. It was obviously her excuse to come over, and she'd have to invent another one.

"Alma, right?" he said.

"*Yah,* I'm Alma Hertz."

"Look, Gen let me know that she's looking into a situation for you," he said.

Alma's eyes widened and she took a step back.

"No, no," Scott said quickly. "It's unofficial. I know that. This isn't really police business, right?"

"*Yah,* that's right," she said quickly. "She was just going to give me advice. That's all. I don't mean to get her into trouble or…"

"She's not in trouble," Scott reassured her. "All I mean is, if you need to pass a message along to her about that situation, I can let her know about it."

"Could you?" Alma looked up at him hopefully, resting one hand on the top of her belly.

"You bet."

"Well, there is going to be a birthday party," Alma said. "My birthday party, actually. And it will be held at my home tomorrow. I thought that if she wanted to come to the party, she could meet all four of my friends there. It might give her better insight into them as…as women. As people."

It was actually a clever idea. Genevieve could get to know the women a little bit in a social setting—watch them, observe interactions, get a better idea of which woman had swiped the watch.

"That's a really good idea," Scott said. "What time does it start?"

"About four," she said. "There will be cake. Some ice cream. Some singing, and some visiting. You could come, too, if you wanted to."

"Thank you," he said.

"Danke." She smiled. "That's how we say thank you."

"Danke," he repeated.

Konig whined softly. The German was tugging at his heart, it seemed. The Amish spoke Pennsylvania Dutch, which was actually a German dialect, and it seemed to be Alma's proper accent that was affecting the dog so much. He looked down at the dogs—both sitting obediently.

Alma dropped her eyes to the dogs, too. *"Gute hunde."*

Konig's tail thumped the ground and he whimpered a little.

"Can I pet them?" Alma asked.

"Yeah, for sure," Scott said.

Alma reached a hand out to let Konig sniff her and then she stroked his head. Then she turned to Benjie and scratched him behind the ears. Konig nosed back in and she laughed, turning to pet the Dutch shepherd.

"He's a beautiful dog," she said, murmuring a few words in Pennsylvania Dutch as she stroked his head. The dog pressed closer to her and Scott tightened his hold on the leash. Alma didn't look scared, though.

"This dog is named Konig," Scott said. "And the other one here is Benjie. But Konig only understands German, which is why he's getting pretty excited when he hears German words from you."

"Really?" She proceeded to croon softly to Konig in Pennsylvania Dutch, and Konig just about melted on the spot.

Alma straightened with a smile.

"My name is Scott, by the way," Scott said. "And I'm sure Gen and I will be at your party. Thanks for thinking of us. Maybe we'll notice something that will help you out. We did go down to the local pawn shops, but they haven't seen the watch yet."

"That's good news!" Alma said. "So, it's still around. It isn't sold."

Or the pawn store owners were lying—another

very real possibility. But there was no reason to upset this poor lady over that possibility.

"That's what we're hoping," he said.

"If I can get that watch back to my husband, it would mean so very much to him," she said earnestly.

"We'll do our best," Scott assured her.

Alma looked over her shoulder toward the house and took a step back. "I'd best go, then," she said. "See you both tomorrow."

Alma turned and Scott watched as she walked back across the wide lawn toward her own property. Konig's eyes were locked on her retreating form, and his head dropped a little bit.

"I'm sorry, big guy," Scott said. "She speaks a language that you recognize, doesn't she?"

Amish women tended to stick pretty close to home, and they didn't fraternize with state police. He fully understood that…but perhaps there was someone local who could help him out with the German pronunciation for Konig's commands. That might be the solution to the problem with this German-speaking dog.

He ruffled Konig's head then reached over and pet Benjie, too, to keep things even.

What was the solution for Benjie, though? What was going to be the key to unlocking Benjie's potential with another handler?

When he turned around, he spotted Genevieve coming out the back door into the warm, June sunlight. There was something about the way she was standing with her hands in her jeans' pockets that made her look more vulnerable somehow. Therapy sessions could have that effect. He wondered if she'd want some space.

She might… He didn't want to overstep. Discussion about Alma's visit could wait. Genevieve wasn't there for him. And she wasn't even there by choice.

Benjie put his nose in Scott's palm, and he gave the dog an affectionate pat. Yeah, he'd always had a soft spot for the misfits.

When he looked up again, he saw Genevieve headed in his direction. He tried to tamp down the hopeful feelings that bubbled up inside him. That was quite enough of that. He was going to be her boss. This *couldn't* be personal between them.

"How'd it go?" he asked when she reached him.

"Oh…" She looked around, as if she might find an answer in front of her somewhere, then shrugged. "It was kind of intense."

"Yeah. It can be."

"Have you done one of these therapy sessions?" she asked, looking at him again.

"I got myself into some trouble with that relationship I mentioned. So, yeah. I had a few sessions."

"Oh. I didn't realize that. So you get it."

"Yeah. They can be really helpful. Just…get what you can out of it. I guess that's my best advice."

He'd had a few more voluntary therapy sessions after he'd transferred back to K9, too. He had admitted that he'd gotten too close to Genevieve as his partner. Not that he'd ever crossed the line with Genevieve, of course, but his emotions had slid past professional. They'd talked for three whole sessions, sorting out that firm and necessary line once more. It was in those therapy sessions that he'd made his choice to cut contact with Gen.

And he'd been right to do it, because look at him now. Genevieve was the crack in his armor.

"Is Darlene looking for a reason to fire me?" Gen asked.

"No." He met her stare. He wanted to reassure her there. "Everything said in those sessions is strictly confidential."

"Are you sure?"

"Absolutely. Don't worry," he said. "These sessions with Darlene are a chance to restart things and go in a better direction with more personal insight into what makes you tick. It's for you, not for us. Okay?"

She nodded and bent to give the dogs each a pet. "Yeah."

She was embarrassed, and seeing Genevieve humbled stung him, too.

Scott cleared his throat. "Alma came by. She invited you and I to a birthday party where all four of her friend suspects will be present."

A smile touched Genevieve's lips and she sent him a grateful look. "That's a nice distraction, Scott."

"I thought you'd like that."

"When is it?"

"Tomorrow at four."

"Solving crimes—even unofficially—is so much easier on me than delving deep into my personal issues." She straightened and fixed him with her eyes—those blue eyes filled with conflicting emotion.

"Me, too." Scott shot her a grin, hoping to reassure her.

She was off balance, and he wanted to be the one to give her a stabilizing hand. And who knew? Maybe they could both avoid the cracks in their armor by focusing on a theft instead.

CHAPTER SIX

THE NEXT MORNING, Genevieve and Scott stood in the back field and played fetch with Benjie and Konig. The morning was cool, although quickly warming up, and the air held a heavy, grassy scent. Genevieve already felt a little sweaty for the exertion and the warm sunshine slanting across the wind-rippled field. In the distance, Genevieve could hear a mower running—obviously not on an Amish property—and out here that out-of-place sound surfed the breeze like an interloper.

She'd slept deeply last night, despite her turmoil after that therapy session. Maybe it was the fresh air or the physical activity, but she hadn't slept that well in years. She looked over at Scott. He picked up the tennis ball that Konig had carried to him, pulled his elbow back and threw the ball out in a long arc. Konig zipped through the grass like a bullet, leaving a trail behind him. The dog looked happier than Genevieve had seen him yet.

Genevieve threw a second tennis ball for Benjie. While she couldn't quite get the distance that

Scott did, Benjie jumped and twisted to catch the ball in the air—a regular show-off.

Genevieve plucked her shirt away from her chest to get a bit of air movement. Benjie came back with the ball. She was still thinking about her conversation with Darlene, though. She was still sorting through it all.

"Drop it," she said.

Benjie obediently dropped the ball at her feet, and when she picked it up, he crouched down, eyes pinned to the bright green tennis ball. She threw again, this time getting some better distance.

"Nice," Scott said.

"Thanks." She watched as Benjie took off again.

"You seem quiet this morning," Scott said.

"I'm thinking...about my dad, actually," she said.

"Yeah?" Scott squinted in the morning sunlight.

"He thinks he's doing the right thing," she said. "He's convinced of it. He's being my dad, and that's the job as he sees it, you know?"

She loved her father, and as furious as she was with him, she was beginning to wonder if her unloading on the commissioner was misplaced. Maybe she and her father were due for a good heart-to-heart. If he'd open up...

"Every time I saw your father, he told me to take care of you," Scott said. "That's a normal thing for someone to say to a cop's partner, but he was more forceful about. It was the pause and the eye contact."

Genevieve laughed. "That's the same way he'd tell me to do well in school. I fully understand the pressure coming from him."

"Your dad came from a different generation," Scott said. Gen's father had been considerably older than her mother and he was in his early seventies now. "For them, the men protected their women. It was how things worked. There was an obligation there."

And Dad hadn't been able to protect Mom. Maybe there was something to it.

Scott threw the ball for Konig again and Genevieve did the same for Benjie. Both dogs were off at full speed once more, zipping out through the blowing grass.

"Times have changed, Scott," she said. "Dad needs to catch up."

"Times haven't changed that much." Scott cast her a wary look. "I mean yes. Times *have* changed, but there is something genetically coded inside of a man that makes him want to be the hero, the protector, when it comes to a woman he cares about. It can't be helped."

"Yes, I know. He's my father and he'll want to protect me. It's natural. But I'm an adult now. Back in my dad's day, the police force was a real guy's club, but I think we've all learned that women are just as tough as men."

"Tough? You bet!" he replied. "No one's questioning your toughness. It's not just about fathers and daughters, either. I'm talking about a man and a woman facing a threat together and…" Scott looked at her then shook his head. "Never mind."

Was he actually siding with her father on this? It felt like the entire force could see her father's point, and it was infuriating, because her father was wrong. Point blank.

"No," she said. Make him say it. "Facing a threat, *and*…?" Genevieve raised her eyebrows, waiting.

"And knowing that if you had to choose between her life and yours, you'd step in front of a bullet for her," Scott finished. His brown eyes flashed before he turned away and picked up the ball that Konig had dropped at his feet.

For a moment, she just stood there, her breath in her throat, watching as he flung the ball out further than he had done all morning.

Genevieve swallowed hard. "I had your back, too, Scott. I was equally armed and capable."

Scott turned back, and his emotions seemed more under control now.

"I know," he said, "but I had partners before you and after you, and I didn't feel that visceral need to protect…not in the same way."

The inequalities in their culture went very deep, and she'd spent whole evenings hashing out the subtleties with girlfriends. Had he just never thought this stuff through before?

"Just because I'm a woman?" she asked, incredulous. "I mean that's hardly fair for a male trooper, is it? He's got a family, too. He's got just as much reason to survive that shift. You take care of each other. Just because one trooper is female—"

"It wasn't because you're a woman." Scott's attention stayed fixed on that tennis ball as he hurled it out in the field again. "It was because it was you."

Konig took off and Scott watched the dog run instead of look at her again. Benjie sat motionless at her feet, the ball in front of him.

"Me?" she breathed.

Scott looked over at her, his eyes filled with agony, and her breath caught in her chest. "Gen, what we had back then…it wasn't just partners. You know that now, right?"

She blinked at him. They'd never crossed any lines. Ever. He'd always been so careful of boundaries, and now she understood why. Had he been carrying around some irrational worry all these years that he'd overstepped with her? Because he hadn't! Scott had been a perfect gentleman, and every atom of her being wanted to reassure him and soothe away that pain in his eyes.

"I think you might be a little hard on yourself because of the way things went south with that trooper you dated," she said, stepping closer. "You can be your own worst critic, Scott. You and I didn't date. I didn't once think that we were anything more than partners. You weren't crossing any lines, I promise you."

Scott chewed on his bottom lip then threw the

ball again. Konig went after it with the same exuberance as before.

She threw the ball for Benjie, too, but her throw was a pitiful one.

"I know I didn't cross lines," he said. "I knew what was appropriate and what wasn't, but what I'm saying is—that connection we had, that ability to finish each other's sentences, to understand each other's personal issues and to pull each other back when it was necessary...all of that? That wasn't just a professional rapport. Not to me."

Not to her, either. She'd never found it again—that amazing connection, but she'd truly believed it had been because they were troopers together. It had been special because of the shared sense of duty and the shared danger, right?

"No, that was being *partners*," she said. "Being partners means something."

He held her gaze for a moment then squatted down and picked up Benjie's ball. He stood and threw it, Benjie launching himself after it. Konig followed.

Scott said at last, "Who's your partner now?"

"Gibbons." Roy Gibbons was a twice-divorced trooper in his fifties. He was bossy, smart and perpetually trying to quit smoking.

"And?" Scott asked. "Tell me you have something similar with Gibbons, and I'll say I'm wrong."

Genevieve thought back to the long hours working together with her nicotine-patch-wearing partner who was still in love with his first ex-wife.

"I can wait." Scott's lips turned up into a rueful smile.

"It's different," she conceded.

"Okay. So…there."

"So what?" Genevieve demanded with a laugh. "We were friends, Scott. We were good friends, and good partners, and… I don't know the word for what we were. But, okay, you're right. It was special."

The dogs ran back up, Konig ready for another throw and Benjie trotting happily next to him.

"I don't know what I'm trying to prove," Scott said, and he picked up the dog-slobbered tennis balls between two fingers each. "Just that sometimes a guy feels like it's more than his duty to protect a certain woman…it's his fate. There's no actual choice."

He patted his leg and started back toward the house. The dogs followed him, heads and tails high. Was he bringing this back to her father now? Or was this about them?

"Scott!" she called.

He stopped and turned back. "What?"

"What does that mean?" she demanded, and she jogged to catch up. "Duty, fate, having no choice…"

"Nothing," he said.

"Just say it!"

He grimaced. He hated this—she knew that full well—but he owed her an explanation, too, and she wasn't letting him off the hook.

"I mean that sometimes a guy feels more than he should. Sometimes a guy wants to protect you more than is his right. Sometimes..." He blew out a pent-up breath. "I'm not saying it's your fault. It isn't! But there's something about you that makes a guy willing to walk through gunfire to keep you safe. What can I say?"

"Are we talking about my dad now?" she asked. "Or about you?" Because this was feeling like it had veered into a whole new territory that made her heart speed up just a bit.

Scott was silent for a moment, words seeming on the tip of his tongue, then he smiled faintly. "Your dad, of course."

But she heard the truth under his words. She'd always known their partnership had been something rare and beautiful, had never experienced a connection like it.

And because of that close connection, he'd cut her off. No discussion. No explanation. That had hurt, and it hadn't been fair. And now he was telling her that he'd felt that same duty to protect her and hold her back?

So, he was no different from the other men, was he? He was part of that boy's club, making decisions for her because he thought he knew better.

And right now, the realization that he was a willing part of that machine stung worst of all.

As FOUR O'CLOCK APPROACHED, Genevieve went up to her room to get changed for the party. She'd brought with her an all-purpose Chanel black dress. It fit perfectly and always shook out without a single wrinkle, and she was glad she'd thought to bring it along when she'd packed for the week. Her mother's voice still hovered in the back of her head: *You never know when you'll need to dress up. Better to be overdressed than underdressed.* What was the dress requirement for an Amish birthday party, anyway? Not jeans and not a police uniform. That much she could be sure of.

Genevieve pulled a brush through her long blonde hair and then twisted it up into a bun at the base of her neck. This was how the Amish women wore their hair—albeit they wore theirs under a white covering called a *kapp.* If she could mirror their look just a bit, maybe she could also gain their trust a little bit faster. There wasn't much time to glean information, and she'd need the women to open up if she was going to make the most of this event.

When she headed downstairs, Scott was already waiting for her. His khaki pants and blue polo shirt still shouted police. But that was Scott for you—he was a cop to the bone, and while she'd never seen his wardrobe at home, she was willing to bet that he had about four options he rotated through. He looked good, though—clean-cut, his graying hair making him look more like a silver fox. She watched his dark eyes flicker over her outfit and gave a nod.

"Conservative," he said. "They'll like that."

"That's what I was going for," she replied.

Wendy was just packing up her things for the afternoon, slinging a heavy purse over one shoulder.

"The Amish don't normally invite a lot of outsiders to their personal events," Wendy said. "I don't know how you managed it."

Genevieve glanced at Scott. She appreciated that he was keeping Alma's confidence and hadn't let on what they were up to.

"I'm just that likeable," Genevieve joked.

Wendy chuckled and shook her head. "You'll eat well tonight. That's for sure. They can put out a real spread."

"Have a good night, Wendy," Scott said.

"You, too." Wendy fluttered her fingers as she headed for the door. "See you all tomorrow!"

The door shut behind her, and for a moment, Genevieve and Scott were silent. They were alone in the house—for now, at least. They'd been alone in the car, alone with the dogs…but somehow alone in this old house felt different. She swallowed.

"You didn't tell Wendy what we're up to?"

"Uh—" Scott shrugged. "This little case is unofficial."

"Right." Their little secret. Somehow, she liked that.

"You look nice," Scott said.

"Thanks." She met his gaze. "So do you. You clean up well."

He shot her a boyish grin but didn't answer.

"So, what's our plan tonight?" she asked.

"We make nice, make conversation, let Alma introduce us to the right women, and we take it from there. But the Amish are unique in their gender roles—as you know. So those women aren't going to talk in front of me...and the men wouldn't take kindly to me chatting with their wives, either."

"Right." The Amish did have very conservative values, and the women socialized with women and the men hung out with men. It wasn't considered proper for married women to be standing around chatting with a man—especially an *Englisher* man.

"So, I'll interview the women, and maybe you can glean something from the men," she said. "Teamwork."

"Teamwork." He held out his elbow toward her. "Shall we?"

She slipped her hand into the crook of his arm and they headed for the door.

"This is wildly unprofessional," she said with a low laugh. "But office hours are over, and can I assume I get tonight off?"

"Yeah, you get tonight off," he said.

"Just checking."

They could go back to professional boundaries tomorrow morning. Tonight, she was going to enjoy sleuthing out a missing watch with her friend. Because of all things she'd missed from her partnership with Scott, their friendship topped the list.

Genevieve's hand rested on Scott's biceps, and he had to stop himself from acting like a fool and tensing the muscle for her benefit. He almost laughed at the thought. It was what young men did, a game for a guy chasing a woman, and he certainly wasn't doing that. But she felt nice so close to him, soft, warm and fragrant. And honestly, it just felt good having *her* there. No one else. Just Gen—the partner who'd slipped under his defenses and had ruined him for anyone else.

The Hertz farm had nine buggies parked neatly in two rows out front—he counted them as they made their way down the gravel drive. The horses were in a small pasture beyond, and he could hear the sound of children's laughter in the distance. The mouth-watering aroma of barbecuing meat mingled with the scent of a wood fire burning. When they got closer, he saw a big bonfire and a pot suspended above it. By the pile of corn husks being fed into the flames, he was pretty certain there would be corn on the cob soon enough.

Alma spotted them first. She was dressed in a pink cape dress—the cape dress being the garb of all Amish women—and she waved, heading in their direction.

Scott noticed a man watching her walk through the ankle-deep grass. He wasn't a big man, or even terribly intimidating, but there was a certain taking-care-of-business look about him. By the way the man's eyes were fixed on Alma—protective, gentle, alert—Scott was willing to bet that he was her husband.

"Hello!" Alma stopped a couple of yards short, and Scott and Gen closed the gap. "I'm glad you could come."

"Happy birthday," Genevieve said, warmth in her voice.

"Thank you." Alma's cheeks pinked. "All of our friends are here—and all four of my...particular friends."

Right. The suspects.

"That sounds good," Scott said. "How do you want to do this?"

"They're inside the house—the four of them." Alma licked her lips. "You two could... I don't know, get thirsty? I'll bring you inside and give you some iced tea or some lemonade, and I'll introduce you...as thirsty *Englishers*."

Scott smiled at the woman's humor. He glanced down at Gen, and she nodded. "That's a great idea. How are you holding up, Alma?"

"This morning, I put the coffee can with change and egg money in it upstairs under the bed," Alma said. "And I put my purse next to it. And I hate that. I hate worrying what our very dear friends will do when they come into our home. I need to trust people again."

Gen pulled her hand free of his arm and fell into step beside Alma. Scott stayed half a step behind on Gen's other side.

"You will," Genevieve assured the younger

woman. "When you find out who did it and why, it'll fill in those gaps for you. That's the hard part—not understanding what happened."

"It *is* the hard part," Alma agreed.

Scott stayed silent. Gen seemed to have a handle on this. But she was right—not knowing was the worst part of betrayal. He hoped that Alma would get the closure she needed. From Scott's experience, human vices all ran along the same lines, no matter what culture they hailed from.

They headed across the yard. In the front, some younger kids were playing a horseshoe-throwing game. The older kids—teenagers—were grouped together, talking, next to a volleyball net. Alma led the way through, waved at another woman who looked busy with toddler twins, and led them around to the side door. A screen door separated the kitchen from the outdoors, and Scott could make out the sound of women's voices in conversation in Pennsylvania Dutch. There was a bout of laughter just as Alma pulled open the door.

"Alma!" one woman called, and she started talking quickly in Pennsylvania Dutch. But when she spotted Scott and Genevieve, she stopped, and the room fell quiet.

"These are some friends of mine," Alma said, gesturing toward Scott and Genevieve. "They're thirsty. I thought I'd get them something to drink."

"Of course." The woman switched into English and smiled shyly in their direction. "Hello."

"This is Sarah Wiebe," Alma said. "Her husband and sons are outside with the men."

Scott gave Sarah a nod. She looked to be close to thirty, with a kind face and hands that had seen hard work. Scott noticed that her dress looked a little worn, too.

"And this is Constance Lapp," Alma said, gesturing to the next woman. Constance was short and plump, with a round face and pink cheeks. She looked happy—genuinely so. "Her husband is outside. She's newly married."

Scott gave her a nod, too. He knew from working in this area that a man had to be cautious with how friendly he was to Amish women. They had very firm boundaries.

"This is Miriam Smucker." Miriam was a more solemn-looking woman, but she appeared confident, too. She looked directly into Scott's eyes and gave him a nod in return. "She's my husband's cousin."

No mention of husband or kids, Scott noted.

"And this is Lily Huyard. Lily is getting married in a few weeks." The woman Alma gestured to had her back to them, and when she turned, she had two full glasses of lemonade in her hands. She handed one each to Scott and Genevieve.

"It's fresh," Lily said.

"Thank you," Scott said. *Danke.* That's how you say it, right?"

"Yah!" Lily smiled. *"Danke.* You were close." She said it with a slightly different accent.

The women looked over at Lily disapprovingly, and the younger woman's face reddened. She dropped her eyes and turned away. She'd crossed a line, apparently. This was probably because he was a man. Scott could already feel that he was going to be in the way here.

Genevieve shot the young woman a winning smile. "Congratulations on your engagement. Is your fiancé here?"

"Outside with the rest," Lily said, angling her head toward the window, but she didn't turn in that direction. Lily's eyes narrowed just a little as she regarded Genevieve. Yeah, he'd seen women react to her that way before. They only saw her flawless good looks. But Gen was a whole lot deeper than that. Scott took a sip of lemonade—just the right amount of tartness to it.

"And this is Scott and Genevieve," Alma said. "We met a few days ago, and I invited them to come to my party."

The women exchanged some looks. Obviously, having two unknown *Englishers* at her birthday party was a strange thing for Alma to do, but Alma plunged on.

"Is this your husband?" Sarah asked Genevieve. She seemed careful not to even make eye contact with Scott.

"No, we're friends."

All eyes flickered to him, followed by some knowing expressions on their faces. Friendship with a man meant something different to them, he could tell. They were assuming a romantic connection.

"Maybe I'll head outside and check out that bonfire," Scott said.

Genevieve looked up at him. He could see the sparkle there—she was having fun. She'd also get more information out of these women if he made himself scarce.

"All right," Genevieve said. "I'll find you in a bit?"

There was something sweet about the way she said it—almost like there was more than the friendship she'd claimed, but he wasn't going to get himself caught up in that. She was playing a part for the sake of some information.

Well, he could play the part, too. He ran a hand down her arm, gave her a warm smile. Surprise flickered in her eyes and then her cheeks pinked. This would have been torture for him five years ago, but now… Now, he had a better handle on his feelings.

"See you," he said, and he turned for the door.

Maybe he could get one of the men to open up a little. Who knew? Because the women in this kitchen had men out there connected to them. Maybe there was a man with a very expensive antique watch—in lockstep with a woman in this kitchen. That was a thought.

The Amish were very conservative when it came to their gender roles, but that conservatism was maintained in order to keep married couples close and united. There wasn't room for flirtation with the opposite sex. Not for married people, at least. And if a man wanted female attention, he could get it from his wife. Period. The same went for a married woman. The system, while very different from mainstream American society, had been preserved this way for a reason. The Amish were practical people.

But Scott had one question: Exactly how united were these couples? Because one of these women had robbed a friend.

GENEVIEVE STOLE A look as Scott left the house. Goose bumps ran up her arm where his fingers had lingered. She exhaled a soft sigh. Scott didn't know how a gesture like that could make a woman feel, obviously. And she knew they were playing a part to get the most from their investigation, but that had felt just a little too real. The reality was, if these women felt like Scott was attached, then he was safer. Their presence together at this party could be explained. Otherwise, they'd seem a little too…police-like.

The women in the kitchen seemed to visibly relax once Scott left, their conversation starting up again, but politely it was in English. A window was cranked open to let a finger of air inside. The women seemed used to the heat, though. They leaned back against the cupboards and their smiles relaxed.

"Did you all grow up in this community?" Genevieve took a sip of the lemonade.

"Yah," Lily said. "Born and raised."

"So you've known each other all your lives," Gen surmised.

A child started to cry and Sarah Wiebe glanced out the window—that maternal look on her face. The child's cries stopped and she relaxed.

"His *daet* has him," she said. Then, to answer Genevieve, she added, *"Yah,* all our lives. That's what makes living an Amish life so special. Our mothers were friends before us, and we used to play together outside when our own mothers stood in the kitchen chatting."

"That's really nice," Genevieve said with a smile.

It also made the theft that much more personal. But sometimes old friendships that began without any choice for the children could grow toxic over time. Pressed close together, unable to disentangle themselves, unable to get some space or to even rethink the friendship if it was no longer one that brought support and happiness...

"Sarah was the first of us to get married," Alma added.

"But her husband isn't from around here," the plump woman said. Constance—that was her name. "He came from Ohio looking for a wife."

"And took one look at her and he was smitten," Alma said with a laugh.

Miriam stayed sober, and so did Lily. Neither

woman so much as cracked a smile for their friend's happiness. Jealousy, perhaps?

"How did you know he was a good man?" Genevieve asked.

Miriam arched her eyebrows at Sarah meaningfully.

"He came well recommended," Sarah replied, but her tone had sharpened slightly. "And he is a good man. Every man has a little bit of history. Every man is human. We grow and learn, Miriam."

"I didn't say anything," Miriam replied.

"Everyone has history," Genevieve said with a shrug. "And everyone deserves a second chance."

"I agree," Sarah replied, and she looked out the window again. "I'm going to go find my husband."

She walked briskly to the door and the screen bounced shut behind her. The other women were silent for beat.

Finally, Lily said, "Miriam, you're going to have to apologize to her."

"I didn't say anything!" Miriam countered.

"But we know what you were thinking," Constance said. "The truth of the matter is, Zachariah Wiebe is a kind and loving husband and father. He adores Sarah, and his whole focus is on her and the boys. Whatever he did as a teenager is no reflection on him now."

"What did he do, exactly?" Genevieve asked.

"He got involved with some bad *Englisher* boys and stole some farm equipment," Alma said. "He was charged for it, and had to do community service. He couldn't find a girl to marry him in Ohio. They all knew his reputation."

"But he changed," Constance added. "I admit, I wasn't sure of him, either, when they first got married, but Sarah was certain, and he's proven himself to be a good man."

But it was something to note. A theft wouldn't be new ground for Sarah's husband if he saw a plum opportunity. Genevieve didn't dare ask any more about that now, though. She wasn't about to tip her hand about why she was there.

"Did you marry someone from here, Constance?" Genevieve asked instead.

"*Yah.* I've known him all my life. He was my neighbor when I was growing up. Our families did haying together every year. And Elijah and I walked to school together. Well, we all did—all us kids from both farms. We'd walk to school together, and Elijah always walked next to me."

"Did he get that job?" Alma asked.

"No." Constance's face fell. "He didn't. It would have been better pay, but at least he still has somewhere to work. For now."

"What job was he trying to get?" Genevieve asked.

"At the canning factory," Constance replied. "They pay pretty well—more than he makes as a farm hand at the moment. It would help us move out of his parents' *dawdie* house. But it's hard to get in there."

"*Dawdie* house?" Genevieve asked.

"It's a little addition to the main house where a *dawdie*—a grandfather—might live. An in-law suite, you *Englishers* call it," Lily said.

"Right." Genevieve nodded sympathetically. "I guess money would get tight."

"Always," Constance replied. "But I wanted just a little more space with my husband. His parents are wonderful—they are—but..." She shook her head. "Never mind. It's wrong to tell tales. It's fine."

"They mean well, of course," Miriam said. "They are good people."

"They are the best people!" Constance agreed quickly.

"They pressure her about having children," Lily said, glancing in Genevieve's direction. "As if she can control that! So it's hard for her to have that pressure from her mother-in-law every single day."

"I can only imagine." Genevieve winced. "I'm sorry, Constance. That sounds difficult."

"All the more reason for us to get our own place," Constance said.

"Soon—Elijah will get something better," Alma interjected. "He's a good man and a hard worker. Something will open up. It always does."

"I know." Constance forced a smile. She looked out the window and she fluttered her fingers.

"You flirt with your husband shamelessly," Miriam said with a low laugh.

"Who else can I flirt with?" Constance asked,

casting a grin over her shoulder, earlier worries forgotten, apparently. "I'm going to head outside."

"I'll go with you," Lily said.

"I'll bring some lemonade out to the men," Alma said. "Lily, grab those cups?"

The two women headed for the door with a jug of lemonade and a stack of plastic cups, leaving Miriam and Genevieve in the kitchen. Gen gave the sober woman a smile.

"How about you?" Genevieve asked. "Do you have a special guy out there?"

"No." Miriam looked down.

"Oh, don't worry about that," Genevieve said. "I'm single, too."

"What about Scott?" Miriam asked. "I thought he was your boyfriend."

"Oh…it's complicated." Shoot. She'd momentarily forgotten that she'd led them to believe that.

"Hmm." Miriam nodded. "I can understand things getting complicated. If I can give you some advice, though…don't drag your feet if you really like him."

"Why's that?" Genevieve asked.

"He might up and marry your friend instead. The one he said was like a sister to him."

Genevieve looked over at the woman in surprise. Miriam braved her gaze almost regally.

"Who did you love?" Genevieve asked softly.

"Elijah and I were courting for three years. I wanted to get married, and he was dragging his feet. So, I broke up with him. I thought I was just jostling him a bit—getting his attention. The next thing I knew, he was taking Constance out driving in the buggy, and in less than a year, they were married."

"Oh, that's…hard," Genevieve said.

"*Yah.* Very."

"But you stayed friends with her," Genevieve murmured. "If that were me, it would be too hard. I might understand, but I wouldn't be able to hang out with her."

"They're married. I'd best get used to it," Miriam replied. "Besides, I haven't told anyone yet, but… I'm leaving here."

"Going where?" Genevieve asked.

"Anywhere! I've saved up enough for a bus ticket, and I'm going to go to the farthest Amish community I can find. There are some Amish in Oregon now."

"That far?" Genevieve asked.

"I need a fresh start." Miriam's eyes misted. "I don't know why I'm telling you this!"

"Sometimes it's easier to talk to someone you don't know," Genevieve said, and unwittingly she thought of Darlene.

Miriam nodded. "When you live in a community this small, everyone knows you so well, but it can be stifling, too. People have expectations of you. I just want my turn at love and marriage."

Genevieve said, "I get it… I don't blame you."

"And I need to get away from Constance and Elijah. Even Alma and Joseph! It's just so much marital happiness, and I'm tired of watching other people have what I long for. I need to do something about it."

The screen door opened and Miriam stopped talking as Alma came inside. Alma crossed the kitchen, and Miriam straightened and then headed wordlessly for the door. She looked back once, meeting Genevieve's gaze, and then disappeared outside.

So now they had a woman with a husband who had a criminal history, a woman who needed money to get out from under her mother-in-law's thumb, and a woman who had grown resentful of her friends' happiness and had plans to skip town as quickly as possible.

Alma gave Genevieve a questioning look. "Well?"

"Three of the four have possible motives," Genevieve said. "The only one who doesn't seem to have any reason is Lily."

Alma nodded. "That's what I think, too."

"Give me more time," Genevieve said. "I've only just met them. Being a detective is all about listening for details. I'll pick up something, I'm sure."

Alma brushed a wisp of hair off her forehead and her eyes welled with tears.

"Hey…" Genevieve put a reassuring hand on the younger woman's arm. "It'll be okay."

"Some birthday celebration, huh?" Alma said, sniffling. "Happy birthday, Alma. I'm suspicious of my very best friends, and don't know who I can trust anymore."

"Don't worry, Alma. I'll do my best to get you answers."

Here was hoping that the answers Genevieve managed to dig up weren't going to tear Alma's life apart even further. Because that could happen sometimes. When you grabbed onto a thread, a whole life could unravel...

CHAPTER SEVEN

MOST OF THE men stood around the bonfire, chatting and poking sticks into the flames. It just seemed like the natural thing to stoke a fire. There was something elemental that made a man want to tend to a blaze. Some boys were off playing in the yard, but a few stayed close to their fathers, imitating the older men's stances and poking at the fire, too. That was just as elemental—a boy wanting his father's approval. Scott had been the kind of kid who'd tried to walk like his dad, talk like his dad, act like him in every way. Except he hadn't liked cadets, and his father's disappointment in him had started early. It would have been better if Scott had been one of the kids who'd cared less. Here was hoping these boys got more affirmation from their dads than he had.

Scott had cordially introduced himself to the group of men. Zachariah had caught Scott's attention, though. Sarah stood next to him now, one of the few women by the fire. Zachariah was a tall, solidly built man with a bushy beard and a shaved upper lip in the Amish style. And he was tender with his wife. Sarah looked upset, and he ducked his head to talk to her, one hand gently on her shoulder. Then his expression darkened and he guided her farther away from the group. The couple spoke with their backs to everyone else.

Alma's husband, Joseph, came up next to Scott.

"My wife explained why you're here," Joseph said quietly.

That was a relief. At least Alma and her husband were united in this.

"Just offering some help...if we can," Scott said.

"I didn't like this idea, but my wife was so certain that your...friend...could help us," Joseph said. "Personally, I'd rather let it go. It was only a watch. *Gott* knows what happened."

"Do you want us to stop?" Scott asked.

Joseph was silent for a moment. "My wife won't let it go at this point. Some men think they can tell their wives what to do. I'm not one of those."

"You're smarter then," Scott said with a smile.

"*Yah*, well..." Joseph sighed. "Look, between you and me, do you have an idea who might have taken it? With respect, I don't want to involve police. We can take care of this on our own. If I know who took it, I can talk to them privately. That's how we handle things—with discretion and a little grace."

"I don't know yet," Scott said.

The young man nodded, but he looked grim.

"That watch means a lot to you," Scott said.

"*Yah.* It was my grandfather's. It was also worth quite a lot."

"Do you know the exact worth?" Scott asked.

"A few years ago, I had someone appraise it and it was worth upwards of sixty thousand. But that depends on finding a buyer, and all that. It's... complicated, I've been told."

So he did know. Why wasn't this man angrier? Or was he just good at hiding his feelings?

"Would you have sold it?" Scott asked.

"No. We're having a baby. The first of many *kinner,* I hope," Joseph said. "And one of these babies will be a boy, and I'll leave that watch to my son. It'll be the watch that belonged to his great-grandfather. That's...meaningful. A connection to the past."

"So this is a big personal loss," Scott said. Although for such a personal item that Joseph never intended to sell, he had had it appraised.

Anger flashed in Joseph's eyes for the first time and he pressed his lips together into a thin line. "It's a very big loss. And someone here—eating my food, enjoying my hospitality—stole it."

The bonfire crackled, and Joseph moved closer to the blaze. He used a metal rod to lift the lid off the hanging pot. It was steaming but not boiling. He put the lid back.

"How did your grandfather get that watch?" Scott asked quietly. "I mean...like you said, it's worth a lot."

"He converted to the Amish faith," Joseph replied. "He was an *Englisher*."

"Oh! Why?" Scott heard it as soon as it came out of his mouth. "I mean… I'm sorry, that sounded crass. But what led him to this way of life?"

"My grandmother," he replied. "My grandfather already spoke German, so learning Pennsylvania Dutch wasn't too much of a stretch for him. And he fell in love with her. I've been told my grandmother was uncommonly beautiful in her day, and my grandfather was willing to do just about anything to marry her."

"That's rather sweet," Scott said, and he looked toward the house. He knew a thing or two about a woman who could make a man's heart stop in his chest. It wasn't just a woman's beauty, either. It went deeper. Scott also knew that the clock was ticking on Gen staying single. One of these days a guy worthy of her would capture her heart. He could see making a leap across cultures for someone like her.

"*Yah*, like your friend there," Joseph said, clearly following his line of thought. "That kind of beauty. She could turn heads."

"And the watch?" Scott asked, focusing back on the present.

"It was a gift from his own father. His family was well off—they ran a cloth factory."

"Do you have anything to do with your *Englisher* side of the family?" Scott asked.

Joseph shook his head. "No. They live a much

different life than we do, and my grandfather chose this. Some choices cut off other roads."

He could understand that all too well. And as if on cue, the screen door opened again and this time Genevieve came outside with Alma. They couldn't have been more opposite. Genevieve looked more like a socialite than an average woman at a birthday party, even though she'd gone for a more traditional ensemble. Her hair, pulled into a bun at the back of her head, shone like gold in the sunlight, and her black dress was cut in a way that modestly whispered *money*. Even her muted makeup made her look otherworldly next to the truly natural young Amish woman next to her.

The other women were across the yard at a table where the desserts were laid out. Scott had gotten a look at the pies—none cut yet—and some squares and brownies. There was a cake box there, too, and the women seemed to have opened that now and set it up.

There were three barbecues going, and the scent of roasted meat made his stomach rumble.

"I think it's time for cake!" one of the women called, and the kids and teenagers all whooped at the announcement.

A rendition of happy birthday sung in Pennsylvania Dutch started up, and Scott watched the happy faces of the Amish people as they sang. Alma's cheeks grew pink and when she looked toward her husband, he could see the instant connection they shared.

When the song finished, Joseph stepped up to speak. His wife beamed shyly at him.

"I can translate for you," an older man said, moving to stand next to Scott.

"I just want to thank you all for coming to celebrate Alma's birthday with us," Joseph said in Pennsylvania Dutch, but the old man next to him murmured the words in English. "It's been an exciting year for us with the wedding, and now our baby on the way. I'm just thankful for Alma as my wife, and for all the blessings we're enjoying together. We're thankful for all of you, too. So thank you for coming!"

Alma nodded her agreement and she headed down the stairs to stand next to her husband. Genevieve slipped past the couple and came up beside Scott. The old man smiled and hooked a thumb in the direction of the dessert table, discretely heading off. Scott leaned toward Gen and his arm pressed up against hers.

"They're nice people, aren't they?" Scott murmured.

"Very." But there was something in her voice. Scott looked down at her.

"We've got three solid suspects now," she said. "Motives galore. I was hoping for one clear suspect out of the bunch, but it's more complicated."

"Three…" Scott scanned the group of laughing, happy Amish folk. The women were rosy-cheeked, and the kids were all active and excited. The men looked proud, and healthy, and strong… Nothing was ever so simple or idyllic as it looked, was it?

The meal was delicious—barbecued ribs that fell off the bone, corn on the cob, and all sorts of desserts, including that big sheet birthday cake. The sun sank low and then dipped below the horizon. The families with smaller kids hitched up their buggies and left, and Scott figured it was a good time for them to make their exit, too.

The air was cool, and as he and Genevieve walked up the drive, Gen rubbed her arms.

"Walk closer to me," Scott said.

"You don't mind?" she asked, looking up at him. Her eyes shone in the low light.

Mind? As if that were possible. He caught her hand and pulled it through his arm so that her arm pressed to his side. She came up close against him, and he felt her give a little shiver. The warmth between them was spreading, though, and he found himself feeling warmer, too.

"Thanks," she said. "That's better."

Yeah, it did feel better. Maybe tonight didn't have to count. They could ease themselves into the professional distance they'd need later. Besides, she was cold in her dress, and he couldn't just let her shiver, could he?

"So, I found out where the watch came from originally," Scott said, and he told her about Joseph's grandfather.

"Wow…" she murmured. "He was willing to make some really big changes just to be with her."

"Yeah, I guess he was," Scott agreed. Something had shifted in her mood, though, and he looked down at her. "I thought it was a beautiful story."

"It is," she agreed. "I haven't come across a man yet who'd change anything in his life to be with me. I mean…a couple would have gladly spent my father's money."

"Not the same thing," Scott said.

"No."

Not that Gen didn't deserve a hundred times more than she got romantically, but he was glad that there wasn't a man who'd lived up to her expectations yet. He knew he was being petty and jealous, but if he'd had an actual chance with her, he'd move heaven and earth to make her happy. Any man who wouldn't didn't deserve her. She didn't want Scott like that, and he could accept it, though. If some other guy could make her happy, put her first, meet her hopes and fill her heart, he could accept that, too. He might not like it, but he could accept it.

A buggy with electric headlights shining came clopping up behind them and they stood back to let it go by. Scott couldn't see the adults inside, but he did see two pale round children's faces in the back of the buggy as it passed.

"The right guy would change whatever he had to in order to be with you," he said.

"You'd be surprised," she said. "They aren't so keen on changing, or giving, or… I don't know, accepting me as I am."

"Then they're not good enough! Some guys try to make a beautiful woman feel less than worthy so they aren't so scared of losing her," he said.

"Negging. Yeah, I've heard of it."

"Sounds like you've come across it, too," he said. "Gen, you're stunning. You're like a walking goddess. I mean…women pay all sorts of money trying to look the way you do."

"Oh, hush." But she chuckled. "Do you really think that, Scott?"

"Uh—yeah. I do."

"I never thought you did," she said.

He blinked at her and slowed to a stop. "Are you serious? Why wouldn't I?"

"Because I was a friend. A partner. I wasn't a romantic interest."

It was oddly naïve of her to think he'd be ignorant of all the things that made her special just because he'd always been careful to maintain the boundaries of their friendship.

"It wasn't like I was blind," he said, softening his tone. "I'm still a man, you know. Women like you come around once in a lifetime. You should know your worth—and it's got nothing at all to do with your father's money, or your good looks. You're the whole package. You're a catch, Gen."

She didn't answer, and maybe he'd said too much. His stomach sank. Actually, he'd definitely said too much. What was wrong with him?

Her cheeks colored and she looked down.

Genevieve was just as beautiful on the inside as

she was on the outside. And any man who missed that was obviously an idiot. Any man who tried to drag her down so he didn't feel so insecure didn't deserve a second of her time. That was a cold, hard fact.

GENEVIEVE SNUCK A look over at Scott. His attention was focused on the road ahead of them, and as they crested the hill, she could see the K9 training grounds rolling out beneath them. Had he really meant that? He'd never said anything so directly before. He'd rolled his eyes when she'd told stories about dates gone wrong, or he'd suggest she "throw that one back" when he figured she'd had a boyfriend who was beneath her, but he'd never said what he thought of her before. He'd always been a solid friend—never once even approaching that line between them. And there was some safety in that—Scott had been the only man she hadn't worried about encouraging too much or leading on. Had she been naïve?

"I thought you were the one guy who would never see me like that," Genevieve admitted.

"Seriously?"

"Yeah." It was the truth.

"What about me gave you that impression?" he asked.

"You were respectful. You never hit on me. You—"

"I was decent," he said.

"I guess."

He huffed out a short laugh but he didn't say anything else.

Had she offended him? She went to pull her hand away, but the pressure from his arm to hold her there intensified just enough. She leaned back into his side.

"I'm still decent," he said. "You don't have to worry. For the record, though, I'm enjoying walking with you like this."

"You monster," she joked.

"No, I mean—" He looked over at her, his eyes wary, but his grip on her arm still firm. "Look, Gen. I've liked all of this. I'm enjoying working a case with you again—unofficially, I know. But I'm also enjoying just being Scott and Gen again. More than I should, maybe."

"I'm liking it, too," she said. "What do you mean 'more than you should'?"

"I can't be the one to hold you back."

"You think that by being yourself with me again, *you'll* hold me back?" she asked. "Ironically, at the moment, you seem to be the only one who isn't trying to." Where was this coming from?

"The commissioner is serious, Gen."

"Yeah, I know him pretty well."

"He needs to see a respect for the ladder, no matter who your superior officer is. Right now, that's me. While it doesn't change the way I feel about you, it does change how we can act together. We're on a clock here. And I don't think that I'm helping matters by being too…friendly."

Scott let go of her arm then and she felt the rush of cool air between them. Why did that feel like rejection? Electric lights lit up the obstacle course and the drive that led to the farmhouse. In an Amish area where the only light this time of night came from kerosene lamps or bonfires, the lights at the K9 training facility stood out like flares on the countryside. They were almost back.

"We were friends once, Scott. I thought we were getting there again," she said.

"We are. But this is work, and we've got to play the game." He sounded more reserved now, and she wanted to reach out and smack him. He thought he was doing her a favor by helping her to see him as the senior officer here?

"You were always ahead of me in this job," she said. "That hasn't changed. We always managed to deal with it."

"It's different now, and you know it," he said.

Because she was being disciplined, had two strikes against her already, and was there to mend her ways. And Scott was her boss for the next week as she navigated this humiliation. Very nice of him to rub that in.

"Look, Gen, if you end up getting into more trouble because of me—"

"Oh, give it a rest!" she snapped. "Yes, I'm in trouble. Yes, I'm here to do my time and prove I'll still be a team player. That doesn't make our friendship problematic!"

He didn't answer her.

"Maybe I could just go elsewhere. Sometimes you need to move to a new place to get a proper clean slate."

They turned down the drive. There were a few lights illuminating the paved drive, and a whisper of tree-cooled breeze wound around her legs and arms. She felt goose bumps rise, but she stayed a solid twelve inches away from Scott.

"You don't have to leave," he said at last.

She shook her head. "I've already created problems for myself with the commissioner. It's complicated."

"He told me that he wants you to work out," Scott said.

"If he did, he wouldn't have left this job to you, Scott."

She hadn't meant to snap that out, but the realization had been growing all day. Tom Taylor had sent in her old friend and partner to be her SO during her punishment. That wasn't out of kindness. He'd chosen Scott exactly because Gen wouldn't see him as her SO and wouldn't toe the line with him. Tom was giving her enough rope to hang herself with rather than outright firing his friend's daughter.

"I think he asked me to do it because he thought I could," Scott retorted into the ringing silence. "Maybe he figured our friendship would help."

"Scott, you want to fix everything." Her voice shook. "But you can't. Okay? You can't fix me, or my father, or the commissioner's response to me.

That's a very old dynamic that started long before you even entered the force. Right now, I don't need you to be a guiding influence or my boss. I need my friend."

"That's going to tank you," he whispered.

Genevieve clenched her jaw. Couldn't he see it? Couldn't he see how impossible this was already?

"You really want me to talk to you like a friend?" Scott asked, and for the first time, his eyes glittered with anger, too.

"Please!"

"Fine. You're talking about walking away from your career. I know you think you'll find something better out there, but the state police is the best of the best. You made the cut, and now you're walking away because it's hard. You'll regret it."

"How do you know what I'll regret?" she countered, her tone sharp. "You ignored me for five years!"

"I was—" He scraped a hand through his hair. "I was trying not to miss you, okay?"

She blinked at him.

"You were my partner, not my girlfriend! And I missed you like we'd broken up, like I was walking away from a romance." He clenched his jaw. "That's the truth I didn't want to tell you. Maybe you can see why—I look like an unprofessional idiot. I made you feel like you'd done something wrong, but you never had. It was me. My messed-up emotions around moving to a new position weren't your problem, okay? I'd already made mistakes romantically on the job, and I couldn't be seen doing that again. Besides, I was sparing you the awkwardness of telling me that I was only a friend, and myself the embarrassment of having to hear it."

He'd missed her that much... The realization slipped under all her defenses and she felt tears well up her eyes.

"You did?" she whispered. "Because I missed you, too, Scott. I really missed you. It did feel like a breakup—but for me, it was the kind where the guy just ghosts you one day and quits taking your calls. And I'd thought you cared."

His agonized gaze met hers and her heart flipped in her chest.

"Oh, I cared..." he breathed.

"I needed to hear that." With every fiber of her being, she'd needed to hear that he'd cared, that their friendship had mattered to him, too!

Scott's brown eyes embraced hers, and he looked so deeply forlorn that she thought her heart would break. What she wanted was to wrap her arms around him, breathe in the smell of him, and make this aching in her own chest stop! She took a step toward him, but Scott seemed to understand her intent because he nodded in the direction of the house.

"We're on camera, Gen."

Right. The video surveillance all the state police buildings had. She nodded and dropped her gaze. The last thing they needed was video of them crossing professional boundaries. Even if she left, he had a future here and a professional image to maintain.

"So maybe that distance was necessary," he said gruffly.

She rubbed her hands over her chilly arms.

"You're cold." Scott's voice softened. "Let's get inside."

A light in one of the bedrooms upstairs flicked on and Genevieve saw the outline of one of the dog trainers moving past a curtained window. They wouldn't be alone tonight—which was for the best.

Scott had always been special to her, too, and maybe he'd been right about taking that distance, after all. He was just a little too easy to fall for. And just because two people could start something didn't mean they had what it took to maintain it.

CHAPTER EIGHT

THAT NIGHT GENEVIEVE lay in her narrow cot, watching the moonlight shine like silver on the wall through the open curtains in her room. Leaving the state police had been only an option before tonight, but saying it out loud today had changed that inside her. She didn't have a future here.

Why did that make tears rise up? This was a job she loved, yet it was more that. She'd spent a long time being angry with Scott. And tonight she'd found out that he'd had his own worries, but he'd cared. If she walked away from the state police, she'd be walking away from him, too.

She could see that their close friendship might have looked bad to the powers that be. They might have misinterpreted things, and a friendship they didn't understand could have ended a good cop's career. She didn't want that for him.

But she'd cared very deeply for Scott, and tonight she'd had to wonder…had she been expecting too much from a friendship? Had she been accidentally going over the line? Maybe she'd also been way closer to Scott than she should have been. Because tonight had been a wild relief. Being close to him, being relaxed with him… it had been healing.

"Oh, I am over the line…" she moaned, rubbing her hands over her face. Scott had always been more than just a partner to her, but he was right. Their feelings had crossed professional boundaries. She had to rein this in and focus on the case in front of her or she'd really overstep, and the last thing she wanted was to make Scott look like he was crossing lines when he wasn't. He was a good cop, and he was trying to protect her career. If she really cared about him, it was time for her to protect his.

DR. DARLENE SCHABER sat in her chair in her office that next morning, her fingers steepled in front of her lips as she watched Genevieve pace the room.

"Here's the thing," Genevieve said. "We've got four women, three of whom have motive. All four have opportunity. But this is a much different culture, and I'm lucky to have gotten as much information out of them as I already have."

"Hmm…" Darlene nodded.

"I'm looking at money as a motivator right now because of the value of the missing watch. Sarah's husband was in trouble with the law as a teen, so he might have some financial woes no one else knew about. Constance needs money so she and her husband can get their own place away from her intrusive in-laws…"

"Is this really what you want to talk about this morning?" Darlene asked.

Genevieve stopped her pacing. "What?"

"You have me for two hours." Darlene's ivory bracelet slid down her arm as she lowered her hands. "I understand you're preoccupied with this missing watch, but do you think it's possible that you're using the case to distract yourself from deeper problems?"

Genevieve sighed. "I told you last time. My problems are pretty surface-level. I have an over-protective father who is great friends with the commissioner. That's it."

"We talked about your mother last time. Are you avoiding that?" she asked.

"No. My mother died when I was a teenager. I've dealt with her passing."

"Hmm."

"I have."

Darlene made a note in her notebook.

"Have you given any more thought to why your dad is so protective of you?" Darlene raised her eyebrows.

"Because I'm his only daughter," she said. "And he's always seen me as his little girl. Not a grown woman. Not a competent cop. His little girl."

"Do you feel like his little girl still?"

"Nope." Genevieve shot her a roguish smile. "That's my problem."

"Therapy isn't about winning," Darlene said quietly.

Genevieve sighed. "I'm sorry. I'm not trying to be difficult here. It's just no one believes me when I say very plainly what my problem is."

"I do believe you," Darlene said. "I'm a woman who has worked her way up for the last thirty-seven years in this industry—hitting glass ceiling after glass ceiling. Trust me, I get it. But I also know that problems are never surface level. They have roots that dig down deep."

Right—and while men played games with her career, she was the one being forced to find the roots of problems. Not them.

"Is it fair to blame me for something someone else has done?" Genevieve asked.

"This isn't about blame. It's about feelings."

"I don't like digging down deep into feelings," Genevieve said.

"Why not?"

Genevieve laughed softly. "Because it's uncomfortable!"

"Why don't you come sit down? Pacing around like that, you seem to be on the attack. This time isn't about winning or losing. It's about facing your own emotions. You've faced a lot. You've showed an incredible amount of courage in standing up for yourself. I've never known any other trooper to tell the commissioner exactly what they thought of him."

"It's either bravery or stupidity," Genevieve said, but she did slide into the cozy chair opposite the older woman.

"Tell me something about yourself that has nothing to do with your job," Darlene said.

"That'll be tough," Genevieve replied. "My job is a huge part of my life. I've been aiming for this since I was a teenager, and I had to fight my dad every step of the way. It's become an integral part of who I am."

"Have you ever been in love?"

That question took Genevieve by surprise. "I've had boyfriends, of course."

"Ah, but boyfriends and being truly in love don't always go together," Darlene replied. "Have you ever experienced the real thing?"

She thought back over the men she'd dated. She had experienced a very close relationship that had turned out to be quite foundational... She wouldn't name names, though. "The closest relationship I've ever had was with a former partner. I know you don't want to hear that, but he and I were closer than I was to any boyfriend."

"So you were in love..." Darlene said softly.

"I didn't say that!" Genevieve cast about inside herself, looking for what she'd felt when it came to Scott. It had been complicated, and powerful. "He was my partner, and yes, I think our friendship went beyond the job, but there was no crossing of lines. Ever."

"Lines don't have to be crossed physically for emotions to develop," Darlene replied.

She was right. Emotions had developed between them, and now they were blossoming again, but what she said here in this session could get Scott into trouble. He'd been through this before—held back because of a workplace indiscretion. She couldn't put him in that position again, especially when he hadn't done anything wrong.

"I was trying to say that no, I haven't been in love," Genevieve said. "I've dated, but I've never felt truly passionately in love with any of them. And my closest friend was my partner. I think if I get romantically involved again, I need to find someone I can have that kind of depth of relationship with."

"And what parts of the partnership felt particularly fulfilling?" Darlene asked.

"Our ability to open up, to talk about anything," she said. "We were very comfortable together. We knew each other incredibly well, and we looked forward to our shifts together. I think that comfort and truly liking each other is important. Too many people end up in romantic relationships with people they don't truly like on a very deep level."

"That's insightful."

"But that isn't limited to romantic relationships. I mean how many times do we make a good friend just to have her talk badly about us behind our backs?" Genevieve asked.

"Does that happen to you often?"

"Doesn't it happen to you?" Genevieve asked.

"Not often. But it sounds like you have some experience with this."

Again, she was alone on an island—the odd one

out, the woman with the wildly different experience in life.

"Never mind," Genevieve said.

"No, I think this is important. What happens when you make friends with women?"

"Well, if it's a woman from my father's social circle, there's a lot of comments about my looks—how they wish they had my bone structure, or how they starve themselves to get as thin as I am... That sort of thing. Then I hear from others that they thought I was snooty, or they didn't like something I said. Heaven help me if I share something personal! That'll be picked apart."

"And women you'd meet who are less affluent?" Darlene prompted. "Are they different?"

"No, they judge me based on how snooty I seem to be because of my father's money. They think I'm out of touch and I can't understand their problems. It's difficult."

"It's jealousy, on both fronts," Darlene said. "Jealousy because of your natural beauty, and jealousy of your family's wealth. It's simple."

"I suppose you're right."

"Someone else's jealousy is outside of your control. That's a them problem, not a you problem."

"I know." Oh, how she knew. She'd had to make her peace with this a long time ago, but it was isolating, too. An idea sparked at the mention of jealousy, though. Jealousy was a powerful motivator for a lot of ugly behavior...possibly even the theft of an expensive watch. It brought out the worst in anyone who fell prey to it.

She'd been thinking about financial need, but maybe the person who had stolen the watch had done so out of jealousy and spite. Maybe someone who'd felt that Alma had more than she did emotionally.

"Genevieve?" Darlene said.

"Sorry, I just thought of something to do with the stolen watch." Genevieve felt her cheeks warm. "I know that's going to drive you nuts."

Darlene laughed. "It's all linked to criminal investigation for you, isn't it?"

"Seems to be," Genevieve agreed.

"You seem to have a very good understanding of human nature, which is why you make a good investigator," Darlene said. "And I think you can use that critical curiosity on yourself."

She already had, and what she'd come up with was that she'd been overly attached to her first partner, possibly even feeling something akin to love. That was not useful for career growth—at least, not talking about it to Darlene.

"Maybe we troopers are better off being a little less self-aware so we can focus all of that curiosity onto our cases," she said with a joking grin.

"What happens when you retire?" Darlene asked.

"We fall apart and turn to drink." Genevieve was still joking, but Darlene's expression remained serious.

"You need to know who you are apart from the

job, Genevieve," Darlene said. "Jobs come and go. If your entire identity is tied up in what gives you a paycheck, you're on very shaky ground. Trust me."

Darlene's gaze was a little more direct and flinty than usual, and for a moment, they just looked at each other. Was that a warning about the longevity of her job around here?

"I appreciate it," Genevieve said meekly. "And I'll give it some thought."

She'd also walk down to the Hertz farm and have a chat with Alma. She needed to ask a few more questions about the women she'd met yesterday. Like, who might have reason to be jealous of Alma's simple but happy life?

SCOTT HELD THE rubber gun in one hand, Benjie sitting at attention twenty yards off. He adjusted the padding over his arm. The sun was bright and the sound of cattle from the neighboring farm melted into the surroundings.

Scott had been out of sorts all morning. He'd said far too much last night—confessing that his feelings had crossed the line back then. He'd avoided her for years for some very good reasons. Then, one moment in the moonlight with her hand in the crook of his arm, apparently, he couldn't keep his mouth shut. And that frustrated him. Gen was still his kryptonite, but the least he could do was maintain a bit of dignity. That hadn't happened last night.

"Benjie, gun!" Scott barked.

Benjie leaped into motion. He sped across the grass, bounding over an overturned wheelbarrow that Scott had hidden dog treats beneath as a distraction, and lunged at Scott's protected arm. He felt himself stumbling backward with the force of the dog's weight and bite, and he landed hard. But he had a grin on his face.

"Release," Scott said, and Benjie let go, panting happily.

"Good boy, buddy," Scott said. "That's five for five. You're doing great."

Benjie had turned a corner in his training, but it had only happened when Scott had started spending more one-on-one time with him—letting Benjie come inside the house and trail after him as if Scott was his handler. It wasn't the best idea, but Benjie had looked so desperately sad that Scott had relented. If Benjie wasn't going to make the cut, that was no reason to emotionally deny the dog some comfort.

These dogs were not tools to be passed around. They were more like a policing partner—they were part of absolutely every element of the handler's life, and in return the dog's loyalty was unswerving. And it seemed that Scott also had a few issues around boundaries with a partner in the field. So who was he to judge poor Benjie? He was hoping that Benjie could be reunited with his partner, but if that wasn't possible, it wasn't right to make the poor guy suffer, either.

But today, Benjie was doing great.

"So why won't you do this for another cop?" Scott asked the dog, but he felt a rush of protectiveness for Benjie, too. He was a good dog—a really good dog—and he was trying hard. If only Scott could simply keep him. He'd miss this furry face when Benjie was sent back to his handler again, but Vince was off for a couple of weeks with his wife, who'd just had a baby. So, for now, it was just the two of them.

"You're supposed to be good like this for Vincent," Scott said, pushing himself up to his feet. "Come on, let's go find your treat."

Benjie bounded back toward the overturned wheelbarrow, then pushed his snout under it and came out with a dog biscuit held between his front teeth. He eyed Scott, waiting for permission.

"Eat it," Scott said.

Benjie crunched down on it happily.

"Hiya," a male voice said, and Scott turned to see Joseph standing a few yards off at the fence, his arms crossed over his chest. "Well-trained dog, there."

"Thanks. He's a good dog, but he's better for me than for anyone else," Scott said. "How are you, Joseph? Come on over. It's fine."

"Good, good." Joseph nodded and he squeezed through the rails of the fence. "Just thought I'd come by and see what you were doing over here. Alma says there's a dog that speaks only German."

"Well, he understands only German," Scott

said, chuckling at the Amish man's humor. Joseph laughed, too.

"Would you like to meet him?" Scott asked. "He really cheers up around German speakers. I'm doing my best with some commands, but he doesn't like my accent."

"Maybe I can be of help," Joseph said. "My family used to raise dogs years ago. Terriers. But we stopped when we started worrying about the homes the pups would go to. You have limited time where you can sell them and they're still young enough for a new family to easily train. And sometimes you have a choice—be left with two or three pups or send them to homes you aren't certain of. It was too heart-wrenching. We stopped."

Scott led the way to the kennel. Konig lay comfortably in his kennel.

"Time for a rest, Benjie," Scott said, and he opened Benjie's kennel door. The shepherd looked up at Scott plaintively then hung his head and went in.

"Sorry, buddy," Scott said softly. "Konig needs his turn, too."

"That dog is yours?" Joseph asked.

"Benjie? No, he's not mine. But I trained him and he was sent back to try and undo a few bad habits. The problem is, he's bonding to me."

"*Yah*, I can see that," Joseph agreed. "He wants to be where you are. He's chosen you."

"But that wasn't part of the plan," Scott said,

shaking his head. "I'm just supposed to be a pit stop, not his destination."

"Ah…" Joseph nodded then turned to Konig. He said something in German, and the K9's tail started to wag.

"See?" Scott said. "He loves his mother tongue, this dog."

"Don't we all," Joseph said. "There are lullabies that can only be sung in Pennsylvania Dutch, and at the age of twenty-five, I still tear up when I hear my wife humming them in preparation for our own baby. There is something about a mother tongue that wraps around a man's heart. I think it's the same for dogs."

Scott looked at the man thoughtfully. He was an observant man—perhaps more so than Scott had given him credit for.

"Could you help me with a few of these commands?" Scott asked. He picked up a clipboard that was hanging outside Konig's enclosure.

"For sure and certain."

For the next few minutes, they went over the German pronunciations. Then they took Konig outside and gave him some commands, watching him retrieve toys, sit, wait, lie low and go for a gun arm. Konig was powerful, fast, and obeyed instantly, so long as the command was said with the right accent.

Scott spotted Genevieve coming across the yard toward them. She had on a pair of jeans, running shoes, and a pink cotton top with ruffles along the neckline that looked pretty on her. He shouldn't be noticing that about her—but he always did. When they'd been partners, he'd trained himself not to notice that kind of detail, but Gen always made an impression. Always.

He tossed a ball for Konig one last time.

Gen strode across the grass in her purposeful gate. There was something about her that tugged at his heart in spite of all of his best attempts to keep it under control. Not just her beauty—something about her spirit that tugged at his in return. Cutting himself off five years ago really had been his only option. That, or tell her how he'd felt—and that could have been career ending.

Genevieve reached them and she cast Scott a smile then turned to Joseph.

"How are you, Joseph?" Her tone was bright, cheerful—focused. He knew that tone. She'd thought of something.

"I'm *gut. Danke*." Joseph's face pinked just a little bit. Yeah, she had that effect on a lot of guys.

"I was going to go have a chat with your wife—" she began.

"That might be best," Joseph said quickly, dropping his gaze.

"But since you're here, it might be better to talk to you. There are things that a man will notice that a woman won't," she said frankly. "For example, your wife is very loyal to her friends, and she might not see things about those women that you will."

Joseph stilled. He looked up at her after a moment—she had his attention now.

"Now, this is for you—right?" Genevieve asked. "We need to find out who took that watch so that you can have some peace and know who you really can trust in your own home…right?"

"Yah." Joseph fiddled with one of his suspenders.

"We've considered who might have taken the watch because of financial need. If that were the case, Constance springs to mind because she is stuck living with her in-laws and she needs space with her husband. But that costs money."

"Yah, that's true," he agreed.

"And if we just look at red flags, Sarah's husband was in trouble with the law in his youth…he could have gotten back into some trouble."

"It's possible, but I would be very surprised," Joseph said. "He's a good man. He works very hard, and he loves his family. He's careful, too. He won't touch a drop of liquor, and he's personally reported some young men who'd started gambling to the bishop."

"Hmm…" Genevieve was thoughtful. "That's good to know. But another motive occurred to me today." Her eyes flickered in Scott's direction. In her therapy session, maybe? "Jealousy."

"Jealousy…of us?" Joseph squinted at her.

"That's my thought," she replied.

"It makes sense," Scott agreed. "People can get

really tied up in jealous thoughts. It can make them act uncharacteristically. I've seen it a lot."

"But jealous of what, exactly?" Joseph asked.

"That's what I'm asking you." Genevieve softened her tone. "It was one of those four women, Joseph. One of them did it. What might they have been jealous about?"

Joseph considered for a few moments then said, "Constance's husband, Elijah, has been having a hard time keeping a job. He means well, but he can get distracted easily and he gets bored. She's asked me to talk to him before and give him some advice on how to keep things together. So, if she were jealous—and I'm not saying she is!—then it might be because I'm steadily employed."

"That's a good start," Genevieve said. Her gaze flickered to Scott again and she pulled a pad of paper and a nub of pencil out of her pocket. She jotted something down. "What about Sarah? Her husband has a criminal history?"

"*Yah*, but he's an ideal husband. That man's life begins and ends with her and their *kinner*. He works hard, he focuses on the job in front of him, and he goes home to his wife with a full heart. Sure, he has a history, but he's a good husband. She's got nothing to envy here."

"And your cousin Miriam?" Genevieve asked. "Is she related to you on your father's side or your mother's?"

"My father's," he said.

"So that watch…could have gone to her?"

"It was a man's watch," Joseph said, sounding surprised.

"It could have been something she saved for her future husband," Genevieve said.

"I don't know. My grandfather gave it to me. There wasn't much else he had from those days when he was English. I suppose he wanted me to have it."

"Did Miriam ever mention the watch?"

"Once or twice. Mostly out of curiosity. She wanted to see it. It did belong to our grandfather, so…it makes sense."

"She could have felt that the watch should have come to her," Scott said. "Is she older than you?"

"*Yah*, by a few months." Joseph's face fell. "She might have thought that… But would she have robbed us?"

It was a possibility, Scott had to admit.

"What about Lily?" Scott asked. Genevieve had been quick to dismiss her because of her upcoming wedding, but she was one of the suspects, and he wasn't so quick to discount her.

"Lily Huyard is quite young," Joseph said.

"True, but she's old enough to be getting married," Genevieve said. "How is her family? Do they struggle financially?"

"No, they do well," Joseph replied, and he shifted his weight from foot to foot. "They're well-respected people, too. Her father is the bishop in our community."

Joseph crossed his arms over his chest again and

looked down at his feet. He was holding something back, Scott was certain.

"Did you know her before you married Alma?" Genevieve asked.

"Not well." His words were curt.

"Did you…court her…at some point?" Genevieve guessed.

"I did not!" Joseph retorted. "I knew who I wanted to marry, but…" He huffed out a breath. "Before I married Alma, when Lily was all of seventeen, Lily had her eyes set on me. She… I don't know. She had a crush."

"How did you find out about it?" Genevieve asked.

"Lily told me herself. She said she thought she could make me happy, and she asked me to consider her."

"Were you courting Alma at the time?" Genevieve asked.

"*Yah.* It's shameful of her, I know. But she was young and it was just a crush. I just saw her like a little sister. I told her that I was flattered but that I was in love with Alma, and that I was going to marry her."

"Did you tell Alma about this?" Scott asked.

"*Yah.* I did. Lily was embarrassed and begged me not to tell Alma, but I don't like holding things back from her. I told Lily so. Anyhow, my wife was the one who introduced Lily to her fiancé, Vern. And now Lily is over the moon with happiness. Sometimes young people do silly things. That's all it was."

"All the same, there might be some resentment there," Genevieve said quietly. "Speaking as a woman, of course. She might have truly believed she was in love with you."

"That's all over and in the past now," Joseph said. "She's getting married in a matter of weeks. She'll have a husband and *kinner* of her own soon enough. I think she should be able to just start her life—put anything ugly behind her. She deserves a second chance."

"I agree. You're happily married, and soon she will be, too." Genevieve smiled.

Joseph glanced between Scott and Genevieve, but his gaze came back to Scott.

"*Danke* for looking into it for us. I understand if you can't find anything—"

"Give us a few more days," Scott said. "You never know what we'll dig up."

Joseph licked his lips then nodded. "Well, good. I'd best get back home. Chores are waiting."

"Of course." Genevieve smiled brightly. "Say hi to Alma for me."

Joseph nodded and turned to leave. For a moment, they watched him as he slid back through the fence and headed off in the direction of his own farm cross country.

"He's still hiding something," Scott said.

"A hundred percent," Genevieve replied and shot

Scott a grin. "You want to crack this case as much as I do, don't you?"

That smile could still pull him in. He shrugged. "What can I say?"

He did want to solve the case with her…and he wanted to talk to her, and drive with her, and listen to her talk, and just be near her. He'd forgotten that smile she got when she felt like she was getting closer to an answer. And when they made an arrest? He used to feel like he'd handed her the world, and he wanted to feel that way just once more.

He was a glutton for punishment, wasn't he?

"Do you feel like taking a walk?" Scott stroked a hand over Konig's head. "We could take Konig and Benjie out. I've got a few German commands that I can say properly now."

"Actually, I would," she said, and he saw his own relief mirrored on her face.

It was a terrible idea going off alone with her, but he couldn't help it. How on earth was he supposed to be Genevieve's boss when he felt like this?

CHAPTER NINE

GENEVIEVE PULLED HER hair away from her face as a breeze whispered past, letting the cool air reach her neck. Scott had the dogs on leashes, and they trotted ahead, tails and heads up, as they headed across the wind-rippled field of lush grass toward the tree line ahead.

"I think you might be on to something with the jealousy angle," Scott said.

"It brings out the worst in people," she said. "Maybe even sweet little Lily."

Lily was obviously less innocent than Genevieve had originally thought when meeting her… but then, youth didn't always equal innocence. Besides, there had been a certain knowing air about the girl. Alma obviously wasn't threatened by her, but that didn't mean Lily's feelings didn't run deep.

"Except, she's got her own fiancé now," Scott said. "I doubt she still harbors feelings for Joseph now."

"She does have her own wedding coming up. But if she'd really thought she loved Joseph, or felt embarrassed by his rejection, or perhaps felt he'd led her to believe that he was interested in her, too..." Genevieve was just thinking out loud. "I mean we agree that Joseph is definitely hiding something, right?"

"Definitely," Scott said.

"It could be that Joseph was flirting with Lily, leading her on a bit. Maybe he liked the attention and things got out of hand." She looked over at Scott. "Guys do that, right?"

"Not good guys," Scott said.

"But it's in the realm of possibility," she said. "He would have been pretty young. Maybe he was flattered by the attention. Maybe he didn't get a lot of girls flirting with him, and a pretty girl batting her lashes in his direction might have stroked his ego a bit."

"That's possible," he agreed.

"And if she held on to some resentment around his treatment of her—brushing her off as too young after having led her on..." Gen tucked a hand into her back jeans' pocket. "Joseph seems to think she was just a girl being silly. Well, maybe she saw the watch and did something else silly— took something that belonged to him."

"Maybe it wasn't for the money," Scott agreed. "Maybe it was for the memories."

"Or out of spite," Genevieve said. "She was sitting in his home, quilting with his wife, knowing that he loved Alma, and Alma has him. That might have stung. She might have wanted to do something to hurt them—make them suffer just a little."

"But what about this fiancé of hers?" Scott asked. "You don't think she loves him?"

"I think all of this can be a whole lot more complicated than Alma wants to believe." Genevieve sighed. "I just hope the truth doesn't make her more miserable than the theft."

"I agree," Scott said.

A path became clearer through the grass and Scott's hand touched her back, nudging her closer to him so that they could walk on the trail side by side. His fingertips lingered on her back just for a moment and then disappeared, and she felt a trail of goose bumps run up her spine.

Stop it, Genevieve, she mentally told herself.

"Speaking of men behaving poorly, I never did like the guys you got involved with…" Scott said. "I mean the two that I met."

"I know." She smiled ruefully. "My taste has improved."

"I'm glad to hear it." He nudged her arm with his. "You deserve the best, you know."

"The best these days are already married or simply not interested."

"I don't believe that." He shot her a joking grin. "I'm a catch, and I'm still single."

He was a catch. There was no doubt about that.

"You're stubbornly single," she laughed. "I could have had you set up and married five times by now."

"Maybe I'm holding out for the best, too."

No. From when she and Scott had been close,

she knew it wasn't that. Scott was sweet, honest, interesting, good at his job…and he was also scared of commitment. His experience with the coworker who'd accused him of unprofessional conduct likely hadn't helped his ability to trust in love.

"You've always been skittish when it came to commitment," she said.

"That's not true."

"No? I watched several women—nice, attractive, available women—show you attention. And a few you liked, but you never did anything about it," she countered. "I was paying attention, you know! I was watching."

"Were you?" He chuckled uncomfortably. "So you think I can't commit?"

"Oh, you can. You're just scared of getting it wrong," she said. "Because your parents broke up—you mentioned that a few times. It was hard on you. You thought they were the perfect couple, and then things went sour." She knew he'd watched his parents' divorce when he was a young teen and it had left him wary. And that he had an incredibly complicated relationship with his father, which had only gotten worse when his parents had split.

"I probably talked too much back then," he said.

"Maybe so, but I understand you better than you think," she said. "No one will be perfect, Scott. That's the scary truth. But two imperfect people could make each other really happy."

Scott's eyes lingered on her and he looked ready

to say something, but instead he just gave her a small smile.

"I'm serious," she said. "Maybe I can help you, too."

"By quickly meddling in my love life before we part ways again?" he asked with a low laugh.

"Maybe." She nudged his arm back. "Once upon a time, I knew you very well. And your history hasn't changed. I'm just not up to date on your newest issues."

"You did know me well." His eyes softened. "I won't argue that."

"So, if you think I'm wrong about your parents' divorce and all that, then tell me…what's kept you single? Is it because of that bad experience with the colleague you dated?" she asked.

"You really want to dig into this?" he asked. His voice was warm, though, and he passed her Konig's leash. She accepted it and wrapped the loop around her wrist. The dog pulled her forward in his exuberance.

"I really do," she said. "Catch me up."

Would he tell her? The truth was, she did want to know. She still cared.

"I'm single because I know what I'm looking for. It's just…hard to find."

He wanted the perfect match—the woman incapable of hurting him. That was her guess, at least. He was more vulnerable than he liked people to know.

"Maybe you're looking for something unrealistic," she suggested.

"Nope. I know it's out there. I've seen it before."

That was a new twist. Maybe he'd met a couple he aspired to be like.

"So, describe this ideal woman for me," she said. "What's she like?"

"She's smart, capable, intuitive, kind…"

"I could give you five women right now who match that," she retorted.

"She gets me," he went on, his tone softening. "She understands what makes me tick, and I'm safe with her. When I have a hard day, she's gentle with me. And she trusts me in the same way—she's willing to lean on me, too."

They were getting closer to the tree line now, welcoming shade stretching toward them to beckon them into the trees.

"You want her to be your best friend," Genevieve said.

"Yeah."

"A best friend and the love of your life—that's a little harder to find," she said ruefully.

He shrugged. "You asked."

As they reached the tree line where the path through the grass opened onto a path that led into the forest, Scott pulled Benjie in and undid the leash. Genevieve did the same for Konig, and the dogs trotted on ahead into the shady undergrowth. The tree cover made the air cooler and wind rustled through leaves overhead. The skit-

ter of small animals—ground squirrels, probably—rustled through some dry undergrowth, and
overhead birds called to each other. It was like a
whole new world.

"Benjie! Konig! Wait! *Abwarten!*" Scott called.
The dogs both obeyed.

"Nice," she said with a grin.

"Thanks. Joseph helped me with some pronunciation."

They caught up to the dogs and Scott gave them
the command to go on ahead. The dogs ran off,
noses to the ground.

"It wasn't the divorce, exactly," Scott said, picking up the thread of their conversation.

"No?" She eyed him curiously.

"I had a career objective," he said. "I needed to
achieve it."

"That's a weak excuse," she replied. "The right
woman can make that easier."

"Maybe," he said. "But it's not my parents' marriage that's held me back from finding the right
woman."

He looked like he was about to say more, and
she held her breath, waiting… One of the dogs
barked, sharp and clear, and Scott straightened,
the moment broken.

"That's a signal," he said. "Benjie's found something."

SCOTT LED THE way through the brush toward the
sound of Benjie's bark. He'd stay by whatever he

found until Scott told him he could stand down. But he glanced around at Genevieve as she followed.

Gen was trying to figure him out, and he wasn't sure he liked that. She was curious about what made him tick...what held him back... But the truth of the matter was, back then, it was Genevieve who'd made him tick! She was the baseline, the one who influenced absolutely everything. Why hadn't he dated other women? Because none had measured up to her!

Twigs snapped under his shoes, and an angry squirrel chattered at them from high in the trees. Benjie stood next to a fallen log, some sort of tubular carrying case held by its handle in his mouth. Konig came trotting over, leaping across a gully that passed between them, his tail low and his glittery eyes alert. He seemed to sense that they were working now—playtime over.

"Come here, Benjie," Scott called. "Let's see it."

Benjie came and dropped the object at Scott's feet. He picked it up and turned it over. The case was leather and, by the looks of it, hadn't been out there too long. But it was dirty and one end was soaked through. He opened the clasp and pulled out a piece of cloth. On one side, it was covered in strings and tatters, but when he turned it over, he realized it was a beautiful piece of embroidery. It was about as big as a place mat, and it depicted a storm coming in over rolling farmland—the colors of the threads showing impeccable detail.

Tiny fence posts delineated one farm from another, small red barns and tiny dots that looked like cattle... The artist hadn't signed it, though, and one small corner of work looked to be incomplete.

"Is this something you use for training?" Genevieve asked.

"No, we use rags soaked in scent, not pieces of embroidery," he replied. "And not in leather satchels like this one, either."

"Who would leave something like this in the woods?" Genevieve said.

"It couldn't just be dropped," Scott said. "It was buried."

"Unless a dog buried it."

"A possibility, but it wouldn't be one of ours. It goes against their training..." His mind was spinning forward. A puppy maybe? The younger dogs were more inclined to follow their instincts that way. But where would a puppy have gotten it?

"I guess it could have been dropped and then buried by a dog," he conceded. "But who would be out here carrying around a satchel of embroidery?"

"Unless this is stolen property, too, like the watch," she said. "Maybe someone stashed it away until people forgot about it."

"Do we have a thief at work in this community?" Scott murmured.

"That missing watch might be less isolated than we thought," she replied. "But we still have only four suspects."

"Unless one of our suspects is working with someone else—a bigger network."

"Maybe," she agreed. "But a watch worth tens of thousands of dollars is in a different league than a piece of embroidery…"

He looked down at her and a smile flickered at the corners of her lips. "Let's check out that hiding spot."

That would take crossing the gully, at the bottom of which a small stream trickled. He backed up, took a running start and jumped it. It was wide enough that it wasn't an easy leap. He turned around and waited while Genevieve did the same. She backed up, took a running start and leaped. He caught her arm as she landed, and she leaned into him, getting her balance. His heart stuttered and he tried to push away those old rising feelings.

Catching her was something he'd done a hundred times before—often while they'd been searching for something, like they were now—but this time, he found his hand around her waist, and she was so close that he could smell the faint aroma of perfume. She fit perfectly in his arms—a detail he wished had changed over the years! But it hadn't. She was still the perfect fit against his side and the perfect height so that when he looked down at her and she blinked up at him, kissing her would take just the smallest dip of his head. Her lips were parted and her breath was coming in soft puffs from the exertion of the jump. And suddenly, the only thing he could think of was her lips and how close they were…and she wasn't moving away from him…

Whoa. He needed to step back or he'd find himself following through. He swallowed and let go of her.

He could see the faint scatter of freckles over her cheekbones, and one eyelash lay next to her nose. He reached out and brushed it away.

"Oh…" she breathed.

"You okay?" he murmured.

She looked up, blue gaze meeting his, and if his heart could have stopped, it would have. This was torture.

"Yeah." Genevieve stepped back, but some color bloomed in her cheeks. People thought she was gorgeous when she was confident and taking over a room, but very few got to see this side of Gen. She was prettier still—completely herself with no mask in place. This was the version of her that left him helpless.

"It was by that log," Scott said. Maybe he could pretend that hadn't happened.

Genevieve's eyes flickered toward him before she turned her attention to the fallen log. She squatted down and reached underneath it.

"Nothing…" she murmured and then heaved against the rotting wood. It rolled slightly. There was a little dugout hole, but it was empty.

He looked down at the embroidery again.

"Is this worth anything?" he asked.

"I have no idea, but it looks pretty intricate."

Genevieve stood up and came over to look at the piece. She frowned. "Someone wouldn't bother taking it if it weren't worth something, would they?"

"We can check if there were any robbery reports filed," he said. "Unless the motive for taking it was less financially driven and more personal."

"Spite?" She raised her eyebrows.

"It's a possibility. I'd be curious to know why, though."

"Me, too." A smile touched her lips. "People are interesting, aren't they?"

The dogs sniffed around the log, but there didn't seem to be much else to find. Scott scanned the area. They were in a patch of woodland that butted up against two other fields.

"I wonder who owns the land around us," Scott said, gesturing.

"I'm willing to bet it's all Amish," Gen replied.

"Me, too." And somehow, that didn't help, because the Amish stuck together. But Alma might be able to give them some insight.

They headed back toward the main path the way they'd come.

"Can I ask you something?" he asked.

"Sure." She was composing herself again, that mask coming back up.

"Do you think you could work with me again?" he asked.

"Are you looking for a new partner?" She flashed him a teasing smile.

"No, I meant…could we work together like this—me as your sergeant?"

That smile faded and Genevieve turned away. He could see her profile, her tensed jaw. "You mean could I call you 'boss' and fall into line?"

Not so much fun to think about, he had to admit, but yes, that's what it amounted to.

"Nope, I don't think I could." She turned to face him again, the playful smile gone. "But that doesn't mean everyone else won't. Don't get me wrong. It isn't that you lack leadership skills, or that you're not boss material. You asked if *I* could, not if you had what it took." She waggled a finger at him. "Watch how you phrase things."

He wasn't looking for reassurance that he had managerial skills. He was looking for the key that would make their working together possible.

"What would it take?" Scott asked.

"I'm not your target trooper," she said. "Other troopers will have no problem accepting your authority and respecting your leadership. Don't even worry about that."

"What if you were my target trooper?" he queried.

Genevieve smiled faintly. "A cop like me, with an attitude problem and a tendency to tell off her superiors? I doubt you have to worry about many more troopers like me. Scott, I wasn't just being nice. I'm serious. You'll make a good leader. You already are here in the K9, aren't you? People respect you. You do the job well. What's making you question your abilities?"

He shook his head. It wasn't his abilities he was questioning—it was the flexibility of his relationship with *her*. Could he and Genevieve work together and still remain civil if he was her boss and she was his subordinate? That was what he needed to know. Because he wasn't sure it was possible…

"Thanks," he said. "It'll be fine, I'm sure."

He wasn't questioning his own ability to lead. He was worried about his ability to work with Gen and keep things fair and professionally distant. Could they do that? Maybe when she found out he'd be her boss, personally, she'd see what they needed to do and it would be a nonissue.

For her, at least. How was he supposed to pretend that Gen was just another trooper under his command?

CHAPTER TEN

As THEY HEADED down the path, stepping over tree roots and arms brushing against each other, Genevieve wondered what he meant about wanting to know if they could work together. She knew that working with her was his test, but she could give the powers that be what they wanted there. Why was he worried about that? Was she considered *that* difficult?

Scott caught his boot in the undergrowth, and she slipped her arm through his to steady him. He shot her a smile and gave her arm a gentle squeeze.

"Do you remember when you were a brand-new rookie and I was assigned to you?" Scott asked.

"Of course."

"Well, you were supposed to be a trial by fire."

"What?" She barked out a laugh.

"They wanted me to mess up. They wanted to make sure I wasn't going to be hitting on just any pretty young officer who came along."

Genevieve let out a slow breath. "That sounds unnecessary."

"They disagreed."

"But you obviously passed the test."

"I suppose I did."

Genevieve nudged his side. "It's been long enough now that I don't mind admitting that I had a crush on you back then."

Scott's steps slowed and she looked up at him to find his dark gaze locked on her.

"Really?"

"Come on, Scott, you were more mature, more experienced, good-looking…"

A smile quirked the side of his lips. "Good-looking, huh?"

"Oh, stop, you know you're good-looking," she said with a short laugh. "And when you're new to the job, and everything comes at you at once, and you've got this stable, strong—"

"Good-looking guy—" he added with a rueful smile.

She nudged his arm with her shoulder and laughed. "Shut up, Scott! Yes, fine. A good-looking guy whose job it is to show you how things work, and how to do the job, and how to keep your cool and act stronger than you are… I'm just saying, it's easy to start idolizing that guy a bit."

"Then you got to know me, of course," he chuckled.

"I did." She grinned. "But you're still pretty loveable, even once you topple off the pedestal."

Loveable. That was a strong word, and she hadn't meant for it to come out quite that honestly. She'd meant to say something that would brush it all off, but she was just blathering out everything, and getting more and more awkward. Scott was the only one who could throw her off balance like this. With everyone else, she had some poise.

"I'm loveable?" He stopped short on the trail and the dogs carried on ahead, noses to the ground. Again—that very strong word. It wasn't fair to call her on it.

"You're— Oh, stop it, Scott!" She didn't want to admit to any of this. "The thing is, when two people spend as much time together as we did, they'll either bond or…hate each other."

"And we didn't hate each other," he said, his voice low.

Not at all. In fact, having thought about their relationship in a new light, she was starting to wonder how deep her own feelings for him had gone. And she was realizing that he was right—the connection they'd shared was not just an ordinary partner relationship. Their feelings had been unique, and incredibly special. But it wasn't their fault, either—she was sure of that.

"So, what I'm trying to say, I think," she said, going back over the bumbling trail of her thoughts, "is that we're cops, not robots. We have emotions, and of course we can handle that like adults. But you aren't alone in that. And I don't think having feelings in our job is a weakness."

Did that cover it? Standing on the trail, birds twittering overhead and a cool breeze whispering over her skin, Scott's dark eyes met hers. What

was it about him that could root her to the spot like
that? He reached up and touched her chin. Then
his finger moved down her jaw.

"I *really* missed you, Gen," he said softly, and
his tone sounded beaten.

She could ramble on for twenty minutes and
make herself look like a girl with a stupid crush,
and Scott managed to pull it all together with one
heart-stopping line. Her breath was lodged in her
throat. She should move. She should back up...
But his touch seemed to immobilize her. All she
could think was that Scott was feeling like he'd
failed, but he had never failed her. If anything, she
felt like he was hers again—her partner, her best
friend, and very much her business. And standing this close to him, with his breath touching her
lips, in her mind, all she could see was an image
of herself rising up onto her tiptoes to kiss him.

But then she felt a canine nose butting in between them, and a flush of heat hit her face. Benjie looked up at them.

Saved by the dog.

"Sorry," she said.

Scott smiled ruefully. "If I'd met you any other
way and you hadn't been my partner and my colleague, I'd have asked you out."

Her heart hovered in her chest but she didn't
answer.

"And you'd have wisely turned me down." Scott
started along the path again, and glanced back.
"But I would have tried. For the record."

Her muscles seemed to unlock then.

"And if I'd said yes?" she called after him.

Scott stopped and turned, the leather satchel over his shoulder and a private smile on his lips. "If you'd been foolish enough to take on some emotionally wounded cop, you mean?"

"Yeah." She lifted her chin. If she'd met him and somehow glimpsed the treasure he was under all his layers of armor... If she'd sensed he was better than the rest...

"Under all this, I'm a hopeless romantic. And not so scared of commitment as you think. I'd have married you, Gen." Then he laughed. "See? You dodged a bullet."

Scott turned and continued on the path, and her heart hammered in her throat. All that time together, their connection weaving into something more powerful than they'd had any right to...

"Come on!" he called. "Don't worry. I know the lines, and I don't cross them."

He'd proven that all too well. Well, maybe she wished he would have crossed them—said how he'd felt, maybe showed her what was bubbling away inside him. But Scott's iron-strong integrity was what made him such a good cop.

And such a disappointing bullet to have dodged.

WHEN THEY GOT to the farmhouse, Wendy stood outside with a K9 officer, pointing out the different sections of the training grounds with the end of a ballpoint pen. They couldn't hear Wendy, but she aimed the pen toward the kennels then toward the obstacle course. She paused and waved when she spotted Genevieve and Scott, and the trooper shaded his eyes to get a better look. A horse-drawn wagon had parked in front of the house, too, and Genevieve could just make out some teenage boys unloading something from the back of it.

"Who are the Amish people?" Genevieve asked.

"They take care of the lawn," Scott replied. "Looks like duty calls."

"Let me take the embroidery," Gen said. "I want to show it to Alma. She might know something about it. And it's only really of use to us if it's connected to the theft, right?"

Scott looked down at her with a certain gentleness in his eyes and handed the satchel over. What she wanted was an escape—they'd both said too much, and she needed a little cushion between them, some time to let their words settle.

"Sure," he said.

"Thanks." Her voice sounded breathy in her own ears. His words had sunk deep down inside her, where she'd covered them over for safekeeping. He'd have married her? She warmed at the very thought.

Of course, they were colleagues at the time, and they *weren't* dating. She'd never unlocked that hopeless romantic in him. They'd been connected professionally, so there was no romantic connection possible. But he'd felt that much for her! She'd never made a man feel that deeply for her in her life.

She'd attracted men, sure. She'd made their eyes light up with hope. They'd seen dollar signs. They'd seen a climb up a social ladder. They'd seen a beautiful woman, and they'd seen a threat, believing she wouldn't stay interested. But they'd never seen what Scott had seen in her.

Not once.

A work partner wasn't supposed to be the bar she measured all other men by, and she reminded herself of that a few times as she headed on past Wendy and the K9 officer and up the paved drive. She didn't look back, either. The last thing she needed was video proof of the expression on her face when she glanced back at her old partner.

Alma was outside hanging laundry on the line when Genevieve walked up. Her pregnant belly seemed to have grown even in the few days since Genevieve had first met her, and she leaned against the railing, straining to reach as she pinned a towel to the line. She looked up when she heard Genevieve approach.

"Hello!" Alma called.

Genevieve waved and watched as Alma pinned another two towels to the line before Gen reached the porch.

"You look busy," Genevieve said.

"A wife is always busy," Alma said, but her eyes sparkled with a smile. "We believe if you find the joy in the work, you'll always be happy, and your home will always be sorted."

"We believe something similar," Genevieve said. "We say if you love your job, you're never really working."

Or, more realistically, Genevieve realized, if you loved your job too much, you were always working. That's how a workaholic was born. She and Scott had spent long hours taking overtime together. Always working. Always professional... And maybe she was a little disappointed in that now.

"What do you have?" Alma asked, nodding toward the satchel.

Right, this was a woman who had work to do.

"We came across this in the woods," Genevieve said. "One of the dogs dug it out of a hiding spot."

She watched Alma's face, but there was nothing in her expression that said she'd seen the satchel before. Genevieve opened it and pulled out the embroidery. Alma's mouth opened wordlessly, and she held the piece draped over the palm of one hand. She ran her fingers across the stitches.

"Do you recognize this?" Genevieve asked.

"It's beautiful work," Alma murmured.

"But have you seen it before?" she pressed.

Alma looked up, seeming to shake herself free. "No, not this piece in particular. But I know who made it."

"Who?" Genevieve asked.

"Linda Yoder. She's the best. The absolute best.

None of us could ever match her skill—even when her eyesight was getting worse! Toward the end, she was working with magnifying glasses and her granddaughter would hold a light close by. She passed away last year."

"She was a member of your community then?" Genevieve asked.

"*Yah*. She was very sweet. Everyone loved her. She was ninety-two when she died."

"Was there ever any talk about her work going missing?" Genevieve asked.

Alma shook her head. "No. I mean she was always working on something, though, no matter how slowly."

"You're sure this is her work?" Genevieve asked.

"Of course. You see this?" She held up the embroidery again. "The way these gardens are arranged like that—Linda was the only one who did that. And you see the birds? How their wings look almost like they're in motion? That's Linda's work. I guarantee it."

"What did she do with her pieces?" Genevieve asked.

"She sold them."

"Did they sell for a lot?"

"I'm not sure."

"Did she give them as gifts ever?"

"Sometimes. Smaller things—nothing this big. Unless she made something for her daughter."

"Does her daughter live close by?" Genevieve asked.

"In Kentucky."

"Oh." Genevieve smiled. "Has she been home recently?"

"Not since the funeral two years ago."

"Can you think of any reason why someone would hide this?" Genevieve asked.

Alma shook her head. "That just seems crazy to me. It doesn't do anyone any good hidden away."

"Do you think someone might have stolen this?" Genevieve asked. "Is there any reason why they might?"

Alma shook her head again. "I don't think so. It's a strange thing to steal when you could just apply yourself to learning embroidery yourself. If someone stole this, that just seems…mean."

"Yeah, it does," Genevieve agreed. It seemed spiteful.

"Would you like to come inside for a cup of iced tea?" Alma asked. "I made some earlier."

Genevieve smiled. "I'd like that. Thanks. Let me help you get those clothes on the line first, though."

"Would you?" Alma brightened. "That's so nice of you. I won't turn you down."

Alma's entire face lit up in the most radiant smile. She was beautiful, this petite little Amish woman, and Genevieve could see exactly why Joseph had fallen in love with her.

Yes, if anyone had taken that piece of embroidery, it did seem like a rather mean thing to do, didn't it? If it was connected to the missing watch, the picture was starting to darken.

Scott sat in his swivel chair, his feet up on his desk. Behind him, out the open window, he could hear the soft shushing sound of the push mower outside his window. They'd hired an Amish family to take care of the grounds, and those boys came out like clockwork once a week to keep the grass trimmed with their push power mowers. Three brothers were doing the front lawn—all teenagers, and all focused hard on the work in front of them.

One of the boys called something to his brother in Pennsylvania Dutch. The brother answered and they carried on. These kids were good workers, and Scott was always impressed by the work ethic of their Amish neighbors out here. Kids worked hard—no whining or complaining—and they were worth the wage they earned, that was for sure.

Scott's office was only his for two weeks, so he hadn't put any of his own personal effects out. The office belonged to Sergeant Ellen McKale, and she had a wedding photo on the corner of the desk. When Ellen married, she'd been in her fifties, and her hair was prematurely white. She'd made a beautiful bride, and her husband looked positively smitten.

That photo had been giving Scott some hope these days—but he'd never admit it to anyone. He hadn't taken the matrimonial plunge, and it seemed like every time he knew someone getting married, it was a niece or nephew, or someone younger than he was. But this picture of Sergeant McKale and her husband made him feel happy. That was what a mature marriage looked like, and one of these days, he hoped he'd be able to find the right woman to settle down with, too. Because he'd told Gen the truth—he was a hopeless romantic under it all.

The problem was, he was looking for someone who might not exist—a woman who took his breath away, who he could trust with his life, and who wasn't a colleague. That was a harder combination to come by than he'd appreciated in his youth.

He pushed back the regrets. He had a job to do, and it was time for Scott to reach out to Benjie's handler, Vince Haas. They needed to run a few routine training exercises with Vince and Benjie together. And maybe it showed how tired he was this week, but he was feeling a bit depressed at the thought of linking Benjie up with his K9 partner. It was a reminder that Scott would have to say goodbye to Benjie again, and he'd been avoiding thinking about that, too.

"What has happened to me?" he muttered as he opened up his computer and tapped out an email to Vince.

Hi, Vince. This is Scott at the K9. Just checking in to see what day will work with your schedule to come run some exercises with Benjie. I don't want to take up any of your paternity leave, but as soon as you're back at work, I want to bring you over to the K9 to work with Benjie in person. He's doing well, but we need to put the two of you together...

He was trying to distract himself from thoughts of Genevieve, honestly. What was it about her that made him say exactly what he was thinking? Because that was a problem here! He could face every other professional relationship with a backbone of steel, but when it came to Gen, he'd opened his mouth and blurted out that if he'd dated her, he'd have married her!

It was true. She was the kind of woman he'd have held on to. He'd have done whatever he could to make her happy, and he would have committed. Hard. Even if she broke his heart. Even if he cared more than she did. He would have been in it for keeps.

But that wasn't the kind of thing he was supposed to tell his old partner! If only he could stop seeing her as his partner and start seeing her as a trooper who was going to be under his command. And that was very solidly his problem, not Genevieve's.

Maybe she was right—maybe she was treated differently because of her looks, because of how other people felt around her, instead of based upon her abilities. Because look at him! Was he any better, telling her how he felt about her as if it had any bearing upon their relationship today? He had to stop this. She deserved professionalism, and he could not be part of the problem.

His cell phone rang and he grabbed his ear buds and picked up the call. It was the commissioner.

"Commissioner Taylor, how are you?" Scott said as he answered the call.

Scott leaned over and closed the window for quiet and privacy.

"I'm not too bad," the commissioner replied. "I'm calling to check in with you about Genevieve."

Right to the point. "Uh…what did you want to know?"

"How it's going?" the commissioner said.

"Good, actually," Scott replied.

"Have you gotten her to tell you what's going on with her?"

"Like, what she's upset about?" Scott asked.

"Exactly."

"Well, sir…" Scott sucked in a deep breath. "It seems to be exactly as straightforward as she said when she arrived. She's upset because she's been held back. She's a trained cop who knows the job and who hasn't been able to prove her abilities because she feels that every time there is an assignment that would be more physically difficult or might expose her to danger, it's handed to someone else. She believes that it's because her father has asked that she be protected. This makes her feel disrespected and like she isn't trusted with the job."

Scott could hear the commissioner's sigh. "She blames me personally," Commissioner Taylor said. "And that's because I'm friends with her father. But I haven't targeted her maliciously."

"I didn't mean with malice, sir."

"That's good," Commissioner Taylor said. "I'm sitting in an office far from her department. When her commander assigns her duties, it's based on the department's needs and on the strengths of the officers available. This is about getting the job done to the best of our abilities. As a team."

"Right. Of course," Scott said. That was what he needed to hear.

"I'm going to level with you here," he said. "Constantine Austin gives a great deal of money to various state police charities. He's donated money to renovate the original headquarters, and he funds a couple of charities that help troopers recovering from on-the-job trauma. He also has some politicians in his pocket. When Constantine asks for a favor, we sit up and listen. I will admit that, in Trooper Austin's training, we went a little easier on her."

"You went easier on her?" Scott asked, still processing what the commissioner had said.

"What did your commander say to you when you were assigned to her when she was a rookie?" the other man asked.

"He said…" Scott sighed, his mind going back.

"He said to look out for her and to make sure she didn't get hurt. But we do that for every rookie!"

"Some more than others," Commissioner Taylor replied. "Some need a little more backup than others do, and that's no fault of their own. She came from privilege. She'd never even been to a rougher part of town, but she was smart and dedicated. So...we worked around a few things and made sure that she was protected. There was no way I was making any call to her father saying that she'd been hurt, or worse, killed, in the line of duty. Her father might fund charities for traumatized troopers, but I wasn't letting his daughter become one of them. That's called teamwork. But if she's upset that we're not sending her in to assignments as if she were a 250-pound marine, then she'll just have to stay upset."

"So she has been treated differently."

"She's an Austin. The world treats that kind of wealth differently. I don't think she actually wants to be tossed into general population, if you know what I mean."

"She's been held back," Scott said.

"She's been kept safe. And when you climb in leadership, you start having to deal with complicated situations. Genevieve Austin is a good trooper, but if anything happens to her, her father will unleash lawsuits on us that will never end. He's got the money to do it, and I know him—when he's focused on retribution, he gets it."

No, Constantine Austin was not a man to mess

with. Scott had known that all along. Then something occurred to him.

"What happened to his wife's killer?" Scott asked.

"He was jailed, and Constantine has a whole team of lawyers dedicated to making sure the man never sees the light of day. Any time he comes up for parole, they're ready for him. Like I said—when he's focused on retribution…"

Not that Scott blamed the man in this case. He'd do the same thing if he had that kind of money behind him and he'd lost the love of his life.

"And if all goes ideally, in a few weeks, you're going to be her commander," the commissioner went on. "You'll be assigning cases. Let me ask you—will you be taking Trooper Austin's father into account when you do that?"

It would be Scott's job to look at the bigger picture, and he exhaled a slow breath.

"I'll have to, I guess."

"And do you think that Genevieve will work with you while you do that?" The commissioner's tone had firmed.

Did he? Would Genevieve accept his call when he said that she wasn't getting an assignment? Would she be able to see him as her commander with all the respect and authority that came with it? Or would she call him out?

When he hadn't answered, the commissioner went on. "Scott, I understand this is going to be tough. But you have to look at Trooper Austin and decide if she can be a part of your team or not. She's got two strikes, and the fact that she's still employed is *because* I am her father's friend. If I wasn't, she'd have been fired on the spot. So you need to decide two things. One, do you want this job with all the responsibility and complication that comes with it? And two, if you get this job, is Genevieve going to be a productive part of your team? Is she going to take the assignments you give her or not? And you've got until the end of her time at the puppy school to figure that out."

"I really want to work with her successfully, sir," Scott said.

"We all do, Scott! We all do. But will she be part of that team, and will she respect authority? Will she obey orders? We can't have a station where the commander doesn't have his troopers' respect and cooperation—whoever that commander happens to be."

"I do see your point, sir."

"Good."

And while Scott understood the threat her father posed to the state police, and the help he provided, that wasn't Genevieve's fault, either. She just wanted to serve and protect, and he'd do everything he could to help her.

Her father was looming, and the commissioner was capitulating to the wealthy man's demands. Like it or not, Genevieve wasn't getting a fair shake. She'd been right all along.

"And I think I can get her respect and cooperation." Scott sounded more sure than he felt, but this was Gen's career on the line!

"I'm glad to hear it," the commissioner said. "You're a good leader, and if you say you can do it, then I believe you. Genevieve Austin is a good trooper. She's good at her job, and she's a truly decent human being. I want her success here—I really do."

"Me, too, sir." Scott swallowed. "Sir, is there any way we can transfer her to a different station? That might change the dynamic."

"No," he replied. "I care about Genevieve as a person, and as a trooper. But this is her last chance. I'm not transferring her around, making her anyone else's problem. I should have fired her on the spot for her insubordination. I'm still incredibly angry about that. So, this is her last chance. She either can work with you, or she finds a different career path. I'm not bending anymore."

"All right, sir. I understand."

"You take care," the commissioner said. "And keep me posted. If you need any support, let me know."

"Will do, sir."

As Scott hung up the call, his stomach felt like lead. The commissioner *had* been holding her back, but Scott could understand why. Constantine Austin was a powerful friend, but an even more powerful enemy. And when Scott became Gen's boss, it would be his job to make sure she stayed safe, and keep that balance. She was going to hate that a lot! And the only chance he had of making sure she'd respect his orders and protect her job was in getting their professional boundaries back. Because the commissioner was tired of this precarious balance, too, and he was ready to let her go. With cause.

Scott was going to be part of the problem, wasn't he? Or was this just a situation where the added responsibilities of leadership meant he couldn't be Genevieve's friend after all?

As if on cue, there was a tap on his door and he dropped his feet to the ground and straightened.

"Come in," he said.

The door opened and Genevieve poked her head into the office. "Busy?"

"What can I do for you?" he asked. She blinked at him. Yeah, he could hear the difference in his voice, too. "Come in, Gen. Sit down."

Genevieve entered, the leather satchel tucked under one arm. She shut the door behind her and slid into a visitor's chair in front of the desk. She looked wary now, her blue eyes locked on him.

She wasn't the one who was messing this up—it was him. Whatever he felt for her shouldn't matter. She was his junior officer, and he needed to get things back on track immediately.

"What brought you by?" he asked.

"Our case, actually." She placed the satchel on his desk. "I showed Alma that piece of embroidery, and she recognized the work. She's confident that it was done by a local master embroiderer named Linda Yoder. She's passed on now, but she used to sell her work—so how much it was worth, I don't know. But this was definitely made by a local artist."

"Any idea if it's stolen?" he asked.

"It seems that way," she replied, and she leaned forward. "I helped her out with some chores, and it got her to open up a bit more. It seems that her husband's cousin, Miriam Smucker, who was there when the watch went missing, was incredibly upset about being left out of her grandfather's will. She had been close to him, but he only left items to the men. He had some archaic view of things, I suppose, and Miriam is a bit of an Amish feminist. She thinks that a woman shouldn't have to get married to be considered equal in the community, and she's even been working with a group of other single Amish women to create a sort of sisterhood where they support each other and even pool some resources to help each other start up businesses."

Scott raised his eyebrows. This unofficial case was tugging him back in.

"She sounds impressive," he said.

"And apparently, she told Alma in confidence a few weeks ago that she was incredibly hurt to have been left out of the will. She saw it as her grandfather's way of telling her that he disapproved."

"So…she might have had some good reasons to take the watch herself," Scott said.

"That's my thought."

"Hmm."

"And guess who she's been meeting with quite often to get business advice?" Genevieve's lips quirked up in a sly smile.

"You're just going to have to tell me."

"Our friendly local pawnshop owner, Paul," she replied. "I'm thinking we owe him another visit, don't you?"

This was starting to feel like regular police work. "Gen, you're looking into this unofficially."

"I know." She shrugged.

"Alma wants to know which of her four friends took the watch. That's it. Even if you catch Paul with the watch, you'd have to get Alma or Joseph, or both, to press charges. What are your chances of getting that to happen?"

Genevieve sighed and for a beat she looked at him. "I don't know. But I want to get the lay of the land. That's it. Something fishy is happening here, and I think some good people are being taken advantage of."

Scott hesitated. He trusted her gut, and there was enough evidence here to at least get his hackles up, even if he couldn't hand out charges.

"We might not be able to see this one through, Gen," he said.

"I know. But I want to try."

Genevieve always did have a way of tugging him right along with her plans. But this time she was right. There was something up in this sleepy

Amish community. The question was, could they do anything about it if the Amish people in question didn't want police involvement?

CHAPTER ELEVEN

THE NEXT DAY, after therapy and dog training, Genevieve got into Scott's cruiser and did up her seat belt. The vehicle was hot and stuffy from sitting in the sun. She'd changed into jeans and a blouse—it just seemed like a more casual approach would be most effective at the pawn shop today. The back door opened and Benjie hopped up onto the seat, tags jingling, his tongue lolling out in a happy pant.

"Are you happy to be coming along?" she asked the dog, and Benjie turned in a circle, getting comfortable. Scott slipped into the driver's seat a moment later and did up his seat belt, too.

Benjie panted from the back seat, his nose lifted toward the partially opened back window. The drive into town was a pleasant one, and when they entered Strausfeld, they found a parking spot along the waterfront, a short walk from the pawn shop.

It was a busy shopping day and tourists ambled down the scenic walkway, taking pictures next to the muddy fast-flowing river as it rushed on beneath the stone-arched viaduct that carried trains across the river and onward to their destinations.

Scott took Benjie out of the back and leashed him. Benjie immediately went into a close heel and stayed alert.

"He's doing well," Genevieve said.

"Yeah. I'm pleased with his progress," Scott agreed. "I'm bringing his handler in in a couple of days to see if Benjie will behave this well with him. He's been on paternity leave, or I would have had him here sooner. I think Benjie's ready to go back to work." The shepherd regarded Scott with a look that could only be described as adoring, and together they headed down the brick walkway in the direction of the pawn shop.

A few Amish families strolled along—one woman pulling a wagon behind her with three little kids inside. Another Amish couple walked, a proper eighteen inches between them, but the way they glanced at each other spoke volumes about their feelings for each other. That was definitely a date. A family, with everyone from grandparents down to a babe in arms, had laid out a picnic on the stretch of grass next to the water, and Genevieve watched them for a couple of beats, feeling a rising wistfulness inside her.

Ahead of them on the walkway, Genevieve saw a plump Amish woman she recognized heading in the direction of a pawn shop, a bag under her arm. She disappeared inside.

"That was Constance Lapp," Genevieve murmured.

"Yeah, I saw her. I wonder what she's doing at

a pawn shop. Not quite the place for a reputable Amish wife, I'm thinking."

They picked up their pace and closed the distance. When they opened the front door, a bell tinkling overhead, Constance was at the counter with the owner, Paul. She looked over her shoulder at Genevieve and Scott, and her face bloomed red.

Paul leaned closer, said something quietly, and slipped some money into her hand. Constance wadded it up in her fist and bee-lined for the door.

"Let's divide and conquer," Scott murmured, and Genevieve headed for the door to intercept Constance.

"Hi!" Genevieve said with a smile. "How are you? I'm Alma's friend. We met at her birthday party."

"Right. Hello," Constance mumbled, eyeing the door.

"What brings you here?" Genevieve asked.

"I, uh…" She pulled her hand with the money in it behind her back. "It's private."

"Your husband doesn't know you're here, does he?" Genevieve asked, lowering her voice.

Constance shook her head. "No. He doesn't. But we need some extra money and… I'm not doing anything wrong. It's things I own, anyway. Things I brought when we got married."

"Oh?" Genevieve asked, pitching her voice to sound friendly and interested.

Constance relaxed a bit. "Just a washboard. They can fetch quite a good price in some places. They're common here, but in the city, people pay good money for an Amish washboard."

Genevieve had gotten a glance at the bills in Constance's hand. She couldn't tell how much money was there, but it was over fifty.

"Do you come often?" Genevieve asked.

Constance shrugged, her cheeks still red. "I come when I have to. I know what you're thinking—I should get a job. But we're trying to start a family, and once we do, I'd be at home with my little one. So..." She looked at Genevieve imploringly. "Please don't tell Alma about this. It's private, and very embarrassing. They'd all think my husband doesn't provide properly, and he's trying so hard!"

"It's okay," Genevieve said. "I won't mention it."

"Thank you..." Constance almost wilted with relief. "I have to get home, though. I have baking to do, and some sewing for the craft sale."

"It was nice to see you," Genevieve said.

"*Yah.* You, too." But by the way Constance rushed out the door, it was clear that Constance couldn't wait to get away.

Genevieve headed over to the counter where Scott stood. Scott glanced at her.

"Paul was just telling me that he often overpays Constance for items she brings in," he said.

"Why would you do that?" Genevieve asked.

"Look, it isn't easy for Amish women," Paul said. "They have to rely on their husbands financially, and their husbands can't always provide enough. That is Constance's situation. So when she comes in with some little item, I overpay her. Call it my act of charity." Paul shrugged sheepishly.

"How do you know about her situation?" Genevieve asked.

"Everyone in her community knows," Paul said with a short laugh.

"But you aren't part of that community, are you?" Scott said.

"I'm ex-Amish," Paul replied.

Scott's eyebrows rose. "Are you?"

"Yeah. I'm Paul Miller. That's a pretty Amish name, isn't it? I'm number nine of our fourteen siblings. Six of my siblings are still Amish—including my little sister, who is good friends with Constance."

"And your sister is…" Genevieve said.

"Vivian Miller. Well, Hofsteder. She's married now."

So, none of the suspects. Genevieve mentally struck that off her list.

"Look, Constance doesn't know that I know about her situation," Paul said. "And I'd appreciate it if you could keep it that way. It would only embarrass her. As it is, she thinks she's bringing me stuff that I really want, and that I'll be able to sell somewhere for a big profit. So I can help her out, and she doesn't need to be the wiser."

"That's really kind," Genevieve admitted.

Paul shrugged uncomfortably, and Genevieve pulled out the satchel and opened it.

"Speaking of items that might be worth some-thing, we came across this piece of embroidery," Genevieve said, and she handed the cloth across the counter.

Paul picked it up and turned it over in his hands. His eyes lit up and then he immediately squashed the reaction.

"Yeah, yeah…if you wanted to leave this with me, I could give you… I don't know…thirty dol-lars."

"What's it worth?" Genevieve asked.

"Oh, it depends on the buyer."

"Who would buy it?" she pressed.

"There are collectors of Amish art. This is a Linda Yoder piece, right?"

"So you recognize the artist, but it's only worth thirty bucks?" Genevieve asked.

"Hey, I've got to make my profit, too, right?" Paul said, spreading his hands.

Clearly, Paul was capable of lying and play-ing the game when he needed to. This bit of em-broidery was obviously worth quite a lot. They'd have to try to return it to whoever was the right-ful owner.

"We aren't selling it," Scott said. "We were just wondering what it was worth."

"Oh." Paul's expression dropped. "Well, like I said, it would depend on who was buying it. Where did you get that?"

Genevieve didn't answer and she peeked over at Scott. His expression remained granite.

"Okay, well, we're going to head out," Scott said, reaching across the counter to shake Paul's hand. "Good to see you, Paul."

"You bet." But Paul's gaze followed the embroidery as Genevieve tucked it back into the satchel.

As Genevieve, Scott and Benjie headed out the front door into the sunlight, Genevieve looked at up Scott curiously.

"I've got a few questions for Paul," she said. "What's his interest in this piece of embroidery, for example?"

"It's probably worth a small fortune," Scott replied.

"And he lied about it."

"Sure did."

"If he's lying about that, what else is he lying about?" she pressed.

Scott stopped on the walkway and caught Genevieve's attention. "Gen, we need to drop this investigation. Now."

Scott knew she'd fight it. He understood it, even. He hated walking away from an obviously shady situation just as much as she did, but they couldn't pursue this investigation. He pulled Benjie into a tight heel and they headed down the sidewalk. Genevieve strode next to him and cast him a frosty look.

"Why?" she demanded.

"Because we'll never make any of it stick, and he's the pawn shop owner. He's our first contact between stolen goods and the crooks who took them for this entire area. We cannot antagonize the man, especially when we can't press charges."

"We could press charges," she countered.

"We will have no witnesses!" he retorted. "Didn't you hear him? Not only does Alma have zero desire to see one of her very good friends charged with a crime, no one in that community is going to stand up before court and identify any stolen goods. He's one of them!"

"If he left after his baptism, he's shunned," she replied.

"He's obviously not if Constance is in semiregular contact with him. If he were shunned, there'd be no Amish in that shop, and she wouldn't have risked being seen going in. No, there's no way he's shunned, which means even though people would be offended that he didn't stay with the faith, he's still someone's son, someone's brother, someone's uncle, someone's nephew."

"True…"

Scott paused and looked at her. "Good. So you see why we can't do this—not now."

"What if I convince Alma to press charges—if we find that watch?" she asked. "She might do it!"

"Not if the bishop tells her not to, she won't. And she'd have to get his permission first or she could be in bad standing. We aren't dealing with an individual here. We're dealing with a community. It's completely different. You know this."

"That man is lying to us," Genevieve said, meeting his glance. "How much can you trust him anyway?"

"He's all we've got right now! So if all we're going to do is antagonize him, then we're not ahead."

Genevieve sighed. "You're being overly cautious. He's banking on that!"

"I'm being pragmatic, and I'm pulling rank, Gen. Walk away."

Her glare breathed fire and they carried on back to the cruiser. When they got to the vehicle, she snapped, "This is not the Scott I remember."

"No, I'm not," he said, hauling the rear door open and staring at her over the roof of the car. She was doing the exact thing that would make managing her so difficult when he became her commander. Could she accept his position of authority? "I'm your senior officer, and I'm giving you a direct order, Trooper."

Then he pointed, and Benjie jumped into the back seat. He closed the door and got into the driver's seat. For a moment, he wasn't sure what Genevieve was going to do, but she finally got in and slammed her door shut.

"I can't believe you're pulling rank on me." She turned on him. "There is a thief at work here. There's a pawn store owner who's dealing in stolen goods—and you used to trust my gut on this stuff. Someone is flagrantly breaking the law!"

Scott's stomach sank. She wasn't going to accept the order. But this was his fault, too. He hadn't kept that line firmly drawn since she'd arrived.

He'd been pulled back into their friendship, too, and it wasn't possible to be friends with the troopers under his command. Command was lonely, but that line had to be absolute, and he could see why.

"You care deeply," he said slowly. "I see that. But as your senior officer—"

"As my *friend*," she interjected hotly. "We're doing this together, I thought."

"As your boss!" he shot back as he flung the car into gear and pulled out.

Genevieve didn't answer and when he looked at her, her face flushed pink and she averted her gaze. Was that embarrassment? Somehow having embarrassed her was worse than infuriating her. He'd rather face her rage than this.

"Gen, I'm going to lay it out for you," he said, putting the car into Drive and pulling out onto the road. "I've been offered the command position of your station. And if you and I can't work together effectively—and that means you taking orders from me and not questioning me—then the commissioner has said that will be your third strike and your career here will be over."

"You're going to be the commander at my station?" she repeated.

"Yes."

She was silent for a few beats, her lips pressed together in a tight line. She was angry—he could feel it emanating off of her.

"And you tell me that now?" She turned her fiery scrutiny onto him. "How long have you known?"

"I'm not even supposed to be telling you now," he said. "But I thought you needed to understand."

"So all this time, you've been telling me this is about my career, my future, and really it's about yours."

"It's about both of ours!" he stormed. "My career and yours. I have a future to think about, too, you know!"

"You lied."

"I…omitted a few details."

"For me, that's a lie."

"I know. And I'm sorry. But you understand why I had to, right?"

"Is this what you want?"

"The job? Yes! Of course. It's everything I've been working for. But to be your boss? No!"

She was silent again.

"If I end up being your commander, Gen, I can't tell you everything. You'll have to just take my orders and trust them."

"I don't obey *anyone* without question," she said.

"You know what I mean."

"Let me get this straight. If you end up my boss, I'm not allowed to disagree? I can't speak my mind? I can't point out a danger that hasn't been noticed yet, or a clue that's been overlooked? I have to snap my heels together and salute? That's how this is going to be? Every commander I've had has had an open-door policy for their troopers."

No. No, he didn't want that distance with Genevieve, and that was the problem! He wanted equality with her…he wanted her in his arms! Blast it all.

"If I'm going to be your commander, Gen, then we can't be—" He looked over at her miserably. "We can't be *this*!"

"Friends," she said, her voice thick with emotion.

"Yeah." And he hated that as much as she did. "Look, this is my career, too. I've worked long and hard to make up for my own mistakes. You've got a father who holds you back, and I've got a father who's never believed I'd succeed. This chance at command is a huge step up for me, and I have a few things to prove to myself, to my father, and even to my superiors. This is my opportunity!"

"I understand," she said quietly.

"I've worked my tail off."

"I know. I said I understand." But her voice was still clogged with emotion, and he hated that. Because this felt like a breakup, or the ending of a friendship. And in a way, it was. But it wasn't because he was a bad guy, either.

"I don't have a rich father behind me," he said, merging onto the highway. He knew this drive like the back of his hand, and the car seemed to almost navigate to the K9 Center of its own accord.

"So you think I can't possibly understand how hard you've worked?" she asked with a bitter laugh. "I've worked just as hard to prove myself because of him! You and I both have issues with our fathers."

"Yeah, but you've got a safety net that I don't have," he replied. "So maybe you get more credit for your hard work considering that you've had that safety net all along. But if I lose this opportunity, or I get myself fired? I mess up my future. I underfund my retirement. I don't pay off my house. I sink into debt. There are very big consequences waiting if I mess things up. My old man isn't giving me a thing."

Not a compliment, not an ounce of respect, and sure as hell no money to catch him in his retirement years.

"And I've got an inheritance coming," she murmured bitterly.

"I don't mean that as an accusation," he said. "But our situations are different."

"I don't want to mess up your future," she said quietly. "I know how hard you've worked. I know you deserve this. And yes, it'll be hard for me because when I look at you, I see the Scott I knew so well. But I'll deal with that."

"Thank you…" he breathed. "I want this to work. I want us to be able to show the commissioner that we can work effectively together, and I want your job to be safe, too. Clean slate. Fresh start. I won't be holding you back."

She was silent and he glanced over at her to see her biting her bottom lip, her eyes trained on the window.

"Gen?" he said.

"So we really can't be friends," she said.

"No, I don't think we can. Not like before. Maybe we can work you up to a commander position of another station, and then we can pal around again." He shot her a grin. "There's no saying we can't both climb, right?"

Just not as buddies. Not yet. Not when he was going to be her commander.

"Okay," she said. "I understand how things stand now. I'm sorry I overstepped. If I'd known from the start, I would have handled things differently. So…that's on me."

"Gen, I don't regret these last couple of days," he said. "I've had fun with you."

He shot her a hopeful smile.

"Me, too." She blinked quickly and cleared her throat.

Being faced with her again, this was hard, because he didn't want to be Genevieve's boss. Did he want to command? Yes! But he didn't want to be over *her* head. He didn't want to be so far removed.

Heavy the head that wears the crown, or something like that.

Scott reached across and squeezed her hand. She squeezed back, and for a moment, he just held her hand, because it was such a wild relief to touch her.

"Can we do this?" he asked. "Can we work together at the station?"

"Yes." She sounded more sure than he felt, and

she gave his hand a final squeeze and pulled her fingers free. "We can do this. Starting now."

He put his hands back on the steering wheel. Maybe he should have told her where things stood sooner, because she seemed to be phenomenally more capable of handling this than he was, after all.

"You'll be a good commander, Scott," she said. "You'll be great. You'll also need an ally in the station to start, and I'll be yours. Just stand by your word and don't hold me back from doing my job."

"It's a deal." It was more than a deal. This was his promise. And it might put him in some hot water with the commissioner, but she deserved a fair chance to prove herself and climb.

And if he were permitted to be friends with her, he couldn't ask for a finer friend than Genevieve.

CHAPTER TWELVE

WHEN THEY GOT back to the K9 Center, Scott headed out to do more work with Benjie and Genevieve went inside, intending to go upstairs and change. That was her excuse, at least. She just needed a few minutes of silence to process everything. Her mind was spinning and her heart hadn't caught up.

They couldn't be friends. At all. This was a test run for Scott, managerial practice with her because he was going to be her boss. And Tom thought this was a good idea?

She'd suspected before that Tom had chosen Scott specifically to make this week harder on her. Was he trying to get rid of her without out-and-out firing her? One moment of angry honesty and she might have completely ruined her own career.

"Are you okay?" Wendy asked as Genevieve numbly headed for the stairs.

"Hmm?" She looked back over her shoulder. Wendy sat at the reception desk, her silver-gray hair sprayed into perfect shape on her head. But her countenance had softened, and Genevieve saw more compassion there than she'd seen before.

"Yeah, I'm okay," Genevieve said. "Thanks."

"You know, this is tough for everyone," Wendy said. "Every trooper who comes through here for disciplinary reasons—it's hard."

"Right." She dropped her eyes.

"Look—" Wendy got up from her seat and came around the desk. "I've seen a lot of troopers come through. Some stay obstinate and rude. Others work hard because they want to keep their jobs. But you're different. You're… I don't know. I don't mind telling you that I was impressed to hear that you fought for your job like you did. Not many would go toe-to-toe with the commissioner. All you'd really have to do is accept the easier cases and coast. You'd be set."

"I don't coast gracefully," Genevieve replied with a faint smile.

"I can tell." Wendy nodded. "And it's to your credit."

"Thanks."

"I admit, I thought I'd see something different out of you," Wendy said. "I saw a beautiful woman with men falling over themselves to make life easier on her, and I thought I'd be watching you take advantage of that. But you don't. And I'm sorry I jumped to conclusions."

"Oh!" Genevieve looked at the older woman in surprise. "It's okay. I get that a lot. I really appreciate you saying so, though. It makes me feel less crazy."

"I just thought you could use a little encouragement around here," Wendy said. "We women have to stick together, right?"

Genevieve felt a smile tug at her lips. "We do."

"I left a pack of cookies up in your room," Wendy said with a wink. "Sometimes a little shot of sugar improves things."

"You're an angel," Genevieve replied. "Thank you."

Wendy went back behind her desk and Genevieve headed up the stairs. Was it possible to have a future in the Pennsylvania State Police, after all? But it would involve working under Scott and letting their friendship go. That stung more than anything else.

"And it shouldn't!" she told herself as she closed her bedroom door behind her. As promised, there was a package of chocolate-chip cookies lying on the center of her neatly made bed. She picked up the package, opened it and took a cookie.

Wendy's sympathy was remarkably comforting. Funny how women even a decade or so older had the power to build her up or tear her down. Maybe it was because she'd lost her mom, but she'd seen the phenomenon with other women, too. There was power in a comforting word coming from someone who'd lived a little longer.

Her cell phone rang and she pulled it out of her pocket to see her father's number there. She sighed.

"Not now, Dad," she muttered, and she let it go to voice mail. It started ringing again. It looked like he wasn't going to give up that easily. She picked up the call.

"Hi, Dad," she said. "I'm kind of busy right now."

"Then tell them your father has called you and you need a moment," her dad barked. "Because I know where you are, and whatever you're doing can wait."

So news had gotten to him now, had it? Had Tom told him?

"Fine," she sighed. "If you know where I am, then you know I have other things to focus on."

"What happened?" he asked, his tone softening. "Tom Taylor told me that you displayed gross insubordination."

"I did."

"Why?" Her father sounded truly baffled. "That isn't like you, Genevieve. I know you better than anyone, and you are not the type to flout authority. You're a state trooper today because of your firm belief in keeping the law."

"I believe in justice," she retorted.

She could hear him sigh. "And what miscarriage of justice brought this on? Because Tom tells me that I'm at fault. And I don't believe it for a second!"

Genevieve let out a slow breath. "Dad, did you tell Commissioner Taylor to make sure I stayed safer than other troopers on the job?"

"What?"

"That's not an answer," she countered. "Did you?"

"I might have." He was silent for a moment.

"You're my daughter. What's the use of having a dad like me if I don't throw my weight around on your behalf once in a while?"

No one else got their paths paved. Not the other troopers. Not Scott. It wasn't fair for her or anyone else.

"They've put me in bubble wrap," she said. "I'm not able to get out on tough cases, because they might be dangerous. I can't prove myself. I certainly will never earn a commendation this way. If this continues much longer, I'll be behind a desk for the rest of my career!"

"I'm sure that's an exaggeration…"

"It's not. I'm not just another trooper, I'm Constantine Austin's daughter. And you've got them knotted up because you're holding money over their heads. You'll donate large sums, so long as your daughter is kept out of any kind of danger. And if anything happens to me, I imagine there's a big stick waiting. Am I wrong?"

Silence. She'd take that for agreement.

"So, at this point, Dad, I haven't had the same work experience as my colleagues. I've never faced down the dangers other cops have faced because I've been *protected*. Guess what that makes me?"

"Genevieve…"

"Inexperienced!" She answered her own question. "It means that at first they held me back because they wanted to please you, and then maybe to make sure you didn't sue them for any injury I might have gotten. But now…" The realization dawned on her with sudden horrible clarity. "But now, I have a feeling they're holding me back because they have to. I *don't* have the same experience as other officers. I'm not ready."

She sank onto the side of her bed, her head feeling light.

"Who told you that?" her father barked. "I'll make a few calls—"

"No, you won't," she said, her voice quiet and heavy. "That's what's been scaring me all this time—that nameless dread in my stomach. That, at this point, I'm actually not good enough for those tough cases, am I?"

"Genevieve, you are just as good—"

"I'm not as experienced, Dad." She cut him off. "And that's because of a lot of things. But the fact remains—smooth seas don't make sailors. And safe cases don't make a trooper, either."

"Genny, I asked them to make sure you didn't get hurt—not to keep you from getting experience," her father said.

"It's the same thing, Dad. How do you think any of us learn?"

"I was protecting you—"

"You have actually put me in more danger!" she retorted. "Training and experience mean I can handle myself. It's a dangerous job, period. And I don't have the same experience the other troopers have. That means I'm at risk!"

Her father was silent for a couple of beats then she heard him sigh.

"I'm sorry. I thought I was helping. You know I'd do anything for you."

She was silent, processing.

He added, "I thought I'd give you an edge, keep you safe, let you climb without risking life and limb." His voice softened again. "I'm really sorry."

She felt herself softening, too. "It's okay, Dad."

"Should I tell Tom it's definitely my fault and get him to let you off the hook?" he asked.

She groaned. "And how is that different from all the other ways you've protected me? Dad, there's no getting me off this hook. I looked the commissioner in the face and told him exactly what I thought of him. The fact that I wasn't fired on the spot is credit to you, as it is. If I was anyone else's daughter, I'd be in the unemployment line."

"All right… So what do they have you doing as punishment? I'm assuming it's not too tough. I heard it's stuff like playing with dogs?"

"Not exactly. There's therapy, dog training, and it's definitely not a game… I'm looking into a little local theft. It's nothing too strenuous, though. Don't worry, there's no abuse happening here."

"Okay," her father said gruffly.

She thought of her conversation with Darlene and tried to see where he was coming from. "Dad, I know you worry," she said. "And I will be careful. I promise you that."

After saying their goodbyes, she felt drained. Maybe it was the dose of truth that Scott had given her, or maybe it was the realization that potential didn't matter a bit. She'd fallen behind in acquiring the experience she needed to be an effective cop.

Maybe Scott would keep his word and let her get that invaluable experience on the streets. Or maybe she'd be better off starting anew with a city police force in another state. She could start fresh, climb the ladder, and do it all without her father's protective shadow.

Maybe at this point she shouldn't blame the commissioner, or her commanders. At this point, they had probably been holding her back because they'd had to.

She rubbed her hands over her face. Maybe she'd have to stop fighting this with attitude and simply buckle down and do the work. Other people might have been at fault for meddling in her career, but she was the only one who could fix it now.

Genevieve looked out the window. Another K9 officer was working with Konig, using what looked like hand signals. And Scott stood off to the side, watching Benjie run through the obstacle course. Benjie had sped up over the last few days—he could launch himself through that course at a full run.

Progress took hard work, and she had work to do, too.

SCOTT SQUATTED DOWN and gave Benjie a good rub behind the ears. Benjie darted forward and licked his mouth. Scott grimaced.

"Dude, I know where that mouth has been!" Scott said, but he laughed all the same.

Some dogs would work their hearts out for food rewards. Some would do just about anything for a game of tug. Benjie was different, though. His motivation was entirely emotional. It was about his bond with his handler, and he'd do anything for a partner he loved.

That thought hit rather heavy and Scott's regard tore up toward the house. Yeah, he'd had a partner he'd do pretty much anything for, too.

"Good boy," Scott said, and he stood again. "Good job! Let's run it again, okay?"

Dogs enjoyed doing something well. They were like people that way. Once they caught on to how they were supposed to do a job, there was enjoyment in simply excelling at it. Dogs also asked for less from their human partners: affection, a sense of duty, a balanced diet and good training. It wasn't the emotional labyrinth that he'd gone through with Genevieve. Maybe Scott was just a man who needed simpler commitments.

And yet Benjie wasn't simple at all, was he?

Scott leaned his elbows on the rail and watched as Benjie sped through the course once more—up the ramp, over the rope bridge, over three successive hurdles, then down through the pipe...

"He's doing well, huh?"

He turned to see Genevieve come up beside him. She kept her distance, though, and leaned on the rail a couple of feet from him.

"Hi," he said. "Yeah, I'm really pleased. Vince is coming tomorrow, so we should be able to send him back to work again."

"Good for Benjie." She smiled. "How can I help today?"

"With Benjie?" he asked.

"Yeah. What can I do?"

Something had changed in her—he could feel it. She'd lost some of the steel in her spine. Was it because he'd told her that he'd be the commander of her station? It had to be.

"Well, we can go through a few more weapons drills with him," Scott said.

"Let's do it."

She wanted to be allowed to face the tough stuff, and maybe today could be practice for him, too, in letting her flex her abilities a bit.

"All right," he said. "You wear the padding this time. I'll be the victim."

"Do you think I'm ready?" she asked. "This is your call, Scott."

This was certainly a meeker version of the woman who'd tossed him to the ground a couple of days ago. He wasn't sure how he felt about that. But his feelings shouldn't factor in. She was obviously trying to cooperate and defer to him as her senior officer, and for that, he'd choose to be thankful.

"I know it's my call." He gave her a rueful smile. "Of course, you're ready. But more importantly, Benjie is ready."

She rolled her eyes. Yeah, that was better—

closer to the spunky Gen he knew. He shot her a grin. "Come on."

They walked together past the obstacle course and toward the kennel building. Benjie loped along behind them.

"So, yesterday you ordered me to lay off this case with the stolen watch," Gen said.

"Sure did." He gave her a sidelong look.

"You don't want me to mess with the pawn broker and ruin any good intel we might get from him in the future," she said.

"Bingo."

"Are you ordering me to stop looking into the four suspects?" she asked. "What if I just…observed them? And I left the pawn broker out of it?"

Scott rolled it over in his head. She was asking permission, at least. And keeping it to the farm and away from the pawn shop would certainly relieve his current worries.

He looked over at her.

"If I said no?" he asked.

Her jaw tightened but she shrugged. "I'd cooperate, boss."

"I hate that a lot," he muttered.

"I thought this is what you wanted!"

It was what he needed, not what he wanted. Those were two different things.

"It'll take me a bit to get used to," he admitted.

Genevieve's eyes crinkled into a smile. "Good, because it'll take me a bit to get used to, too, but it doesn't mean we can't do it, right?"

Fighting her, he could at least put his back up and get irritated. But cooperative, mature Gen was almost tougher to deal with because his heart relaxed then and went tramping over in her direction. None of that was her fault, though.

"Of course, we can," he said. "And thanks. We're two mature adults."

"Very mature." She laughed, her eyes sparkling. "At least we can play the part, right?"

Dang. She knew how to soften him up.

"Look, if you want to ask a few questions of the women who were there, and as long as Alma is on board with it, I'm okay. It's unofficial."

"Thank you, Scott."

"But it has to stay clear of the pawn shop."

"Yes, sir."

Nope, he wasn't going to like being called "sir" by her, but he couldn't exactly fight it. He opened the door to the kennel building and gestured her in first. She passed by him, that floral scent of her perfume lingering near him. The dogs inside yipped happily. They were being fed by one of the workers there.

Scott led the way through to the cupboard where the padding and rubber weapons were kept.

Benjie sat at Scott's feet and looked up expectantly. He knew the drill now, and this was an exercise he seemed to enjoy. Scott sorted through the pads and tossed her one that looked like it would fit. She tried it on and nodded.

"Here," he said, handing her a rubber handgun.

She accepted the toy and tucked it into the back of her jeans. Gen was tougher than she looked. She had a lithe, elegant look to her, like she'd be almost fragile, but that was far from the truth.

"How fast can you run the mile?" he asked.

She told him her time, and Scott pressed his lips together. She could stand to improve. "Well, here's the thing. When I take over the station, everyone is going to be giving me the time it takes them to run a mile three times a week. It's what my commander does here. She posts the times, too, for everyone to see where they rank."

"Okay…" She smiled faintly. "A little public shaming?"

"A little public incentive." He shot her a grin. "I know how competitive you are."

"So it's just the honor system?" she asked.

"Of course. If you can't trust a trooper to tell the truth, they don't belong on the force."

She nodded. "Where do you rank?"

"I'm number two."

"Who's number one?"

"A guy who's ten years younger and determined to keep ahead of me," he replied with a grin. "If I had the time, I'd beat him. Or die trying."

She snorted. "Yeah, that's the Scott I remember."

"So, let's start tonight," he said. "We'll finish Benjie's training for the day, and then we take him for a mile run."

Benjie loved going on runs.

Genevieve nodded. "Sure. Let's do it."

She wanted to be treated like everyone else, so he'd do just that. But he had some high expectations from his team, and cardiovascular endurance was important.

They headed back outside again to the green space.

"Stay. Wait," Scott said casually over his shoulder and continued walking, expecting obedience. He got it. When he turned again, Benjie was sitting, eyes trained on him, without even the twitch of a muscle.

"Okay, Gen. Manhandle me."

Genevieve chuckled, tugged on her protective sleeve and pulled the imitation gun out of the back of her jeans.

"Ready?" she asked.

"You bet."

She slid an arm around his shoulders and yanked him back, off balance against her. She held the gun up and waved it around.

"Benjie!" Scott called. "Gun!"

Benjie was off like a shot, body stretching out as he settled into a full run. He was an impressive dog from this vantage point. Suddenly, he veered off course, circling around.

"Oh, no…" Scott muttered.

Benjie was angling for a hamstring instead of the gun. But as the dog came around, he lunged and caught Genevieve's padded wrist from behind. They both staggered forward, and Gen fell hard on her stomach, the breath whooshing out of her in a huff.

"Release, Benjie," Scott barked, and Benjie released his grip and looked up expectantly.

Every instinct in Scott's body wanted to scoop her up, but he held himself back.

"Good boy, Benjie," he said, putting a hand on the dog's head, and Gen pushed herself onto her knees, her rib cage straining as she tried to pull in a breath.

"You okay?" He couldn't keep all the worry out of his voice. He squatted next to her.

Gen finally gasped in a ragged breath and she nodded, panting.

"Knocked the wind out of me," she wheezed.

Gen would never be just another trooper. Not to him, and for whatever illogical reason, he'd always see her as a woman first. That was a problem working in the field. She couldn't be a woman first. She had to be a trooper—a hundred percent. But the man in him wanted to protect her, spare her moments of pain like this one, and be the strong one for her.

And that was even more dangerous territory. He held out a hand to her and she clasped it, and he tugged her to her feet.

"You good?" he asked.

Her face was red from the exertion and she nodded. "I'm good."

Anything more would be unprofessional. He bent over and gave Benjie a good head rub.

"Good boy, Benjie," he said. "You went for the gun hand, after all, didn't you, buddy?"

"He took me down," Genevieve said. "Very efficiently. Good boy, Benjie!"

But Benjie's gaze stayed locked loyally on Scott, tongue lolling and eyes bright with the happiness that came with praise. Not just anyone's praise—it was Scott's approval that Benjie wanted.

"Oh, Benjie," he sighed, bending to give the dog another good pet.

He would miss this dog. Really miss him. But his job right now was to return a properly trained K9 officer to his handler.

CHAPTER THIRTEEN

LATER THAT AFTERNOON, Genevieve jogged next to Scott along the paved road, their running shoes pounding the asphalt. If Scott pushed his troopers on the track, then she'd give him some times to compete with! Benjie ran next to Scott at an easy pace.

The shade on either side of the road was welcome, a dappled stretch of cool relief. Sweat sprang out of her as she ran, the warm day feeling hotter for the exertion. Scott's shoes slapped the pavement, barely a glisten on his forehead. He sped up, passed her, and then turned around, running backward and grinning at her. He was lean and relaxed—looking far too handsome for his own good.

"Pick up the pace, Austin," he said. "We've got a hill coming up."

They were headed down the road toward the Hertz farm, but first there was that big hill between them. She would have groaned, but that would waste energy, so she shot him a scathing look instead.

He laughed and turned forward again. She caught up to him and they started up the hill, her lungs already heaving.

As they set off, they slowed a little bit. The shade melted away into farmland on either side, and a cow looked up, slowly chewing her cud, and watched them pass. If Scott wanted to be a show-off, Gen would give him some competition. She sped up, lengthening her stride and pulled ahead of him as she powered up the hill.

He hustled, as well, matching her pace, but his breath was coming a bit faster now. Good! Let him work for it. She cast him a grin.

"I'm not *that* out of shape," she huffed.

Scott chuckled, but he was puffing now, too. Benjie was the only one who seemed to be unfazed. Genevieve couldn't keep this up forever, but she could make her point now! As they crested the hill, she suppressed a grunt of relief, and they headed downhill on the other side. She could see the Hertz farmhouse from there, and the clothesline, now empty. Alma seemed to be working in a flower garden in the front yard, kneeling among the plants with a bucket beside her.

"The Hertz farm makes a mile," Scott said. "We'll stop there for a breather then run back."

"Deal…"

Her legs were getting heavy. The downhill stretch was much easier, and she picked up her pace to match him. Well, almost match him. He stayed half a step ahead of her, and she had a feeling that he could maintain his lead no matter how fast she ran.

Today, at least.

As they came up to the Hertz mailbox, she slowed to a stop, breathing hard. Benjie was panting, his tail high and eyes bright.

"Hello!" Alma called, coming up the drive. Her dress had dirt streaks down it, but a smile wreathed her face. "Who won? That looked like a race!"

"He did," Genevieve said, straightening. "But that's not going to last."

Scott just grinned at her, not looking daunted in the least.

"Do you want some water from the pump?" Alma asked.

Genevieve looked over at Scott and he nodded.

"Yeah, thanks, that would be great," he replied.

They followed Alma down the drive and she led the way to the pump beside the stable. She gave the handle four or five good heaves and water rushed out. Genevieve put her hands under the icy flow and took a deep drink. She rubbed her wet hands over her face and stepped back to let Scott drink, too. He gave Benjie a slurp out of his hands first then scrubbed his hands under the water before taking his own drink.

"I don't mean to pester you," Alma said, looking up at Genevieve bashfully. "I know you're very busy, but I was wondering if you had figured out anything about the watch?"

Scott straightened and wiped his mouth. "Alma,

would you be willing to press charges against the person, or the group, who stole it?"

"Group?" Alma said weakly.

"If the one who stole it was working with others," Genevieve explained gently.

"No! No, no, no. I don't want to press charges," Alma said, shaking her head. "I just… I wanted to know which of my friends… You see…" Alma turned toward Genevieve again, her face flushing slightly when she glanced toward Scott. "A woman's friends are the ones she goes to for advice. They're the ones who know if I'm hurting, or if I need to be told I'm wrong. They're the ones who know everything about me! If one of my friends is not really my friend, I need to know which one. I can't have someone who would hurt me in so close to me. Do you understand?"

"Completely," Genevieve said. "But I'm going to need to see your friends again—ask a few more questions. With the information I have, I can't tell for sure, and I can't just make a guess. That would be wrong."

"*Yah*, that would be very wrong. They're coming tonight to work on a different quilt," she said. "Just the four of them."

Genevieve felt a little rush of energy. "Do you think I could come by?"

"*Yah*. Please do. Come and chat with us. Maybe, *Gott* willing, you'll notice something. I need to know!"

"I get it," Genevieve said. "You do need to know. But can I give you one little piece of advice?"

"Okay?" Alma looked up at her.

"In general, you're going to want to keep your personal things with your husband private. You don't know when someone is happy for you, or a little jealous. Or even if they talk behind your back. I'm not married, but in this job, I've seen a lot."

Alma nodded. "It's wise advice, all the same. Will you come tonight? My friends will arrive after dinner. About seven."

"Yes, I'll come," she replied.

"Danke!"

Scott angled his head at the road. "You ready to run back?"

"I'll have to be!" she said. "I'll see you later, Alma!"

Genevieve fell into pace next to Scott as they jogged back up the drive. The momentary shade of those overhanging branches was decadent, and then they emerged into afternoon sunlight again as they hit the pavement.

"I see why this matters so much to you," Scott said, his voice bouncing with his footfalls.

"So you're okay with it? This isn't crossing the line?" she asked.

"It's fine," he replied.

She puffed along next to him. "Even if she doesn't press charges, she needs to know."

Then they hit that hill and their focus went into

running. But Genevieve was going to do her best to give Alma the closure that she needed. One of those four women was no friend of Alma's, and the sweet Amish woman deserved to know which one.

THAT EVENING, Genevieve put on her sensible black dress again, slipped on her black flats, and took her cruiser down the road to the Hertz farm. She wasn't sure how late she'd be staying, and she didn't want to be walking alone down dark country roads.

When she parked in front of the house at about seven thirty, there were buggies already parked beside the stable and horses in the corral. Alma's friends had arrived, it would seem. Joseph came out of the stable when she pulled up and gave her a somber nod.

"Good evening," she said, slamming the door. "How are you?"

"Good...good," Joseph said. He eyed her uncomfortably.

"Are you going to avoid the house for the next few hours?" she asked jokingly.

"*Yah*, probably," he replied. "There's work enough to be done outside."

"I can only imagine," she replied with a friendly smile. "It's nice to see you."

He nodded and she turned toward the house. Joseph didn't seem as keen about her help as his wife was, and she wondered if there was a deeper reason for that. It could just be that she was an *Englisher*. That would be enough. All the same, he hadn't seemed surprised to see her, so Genevieve figured his wife had told him about the invitation. The couple communicated—that was a positive.

She headed up the steps and before she could knock, the door flung open and a rosy-cheeked Alma greeted her with a smile. She rubbed the side of her pregnant belly and stepped back.

"Come in," Alma said. "It's so nice of you to come. You *can* sew, can't you?"

That hadn't been mentioned before. She blinked at Alma.

"Uh—I can stitch in a straight line."

"That's what we need! We're hemming it right now anyway."

Here was hoping that Genevieve wouldn't do any damage to a handmade Amish quilt. Goodness! These quilts sold at auctions for over a thousand dollars, and if there was a stretch of stitching that was sloppy, she'd feel terrible.

"I'll show you how to do the stitches," Alma said. "We'll just say you need to know how to sew before you get married."

Genevieve chuckled. Life was certainly different for the Amish, but it was an excuse that the others would accept.

The women were gathered in the sitting room where a quilting frame had been set up. They sat on kitchen chairs around it, sewing baskets next to their chairs. All four women looked up in surprise when Genevieve came into the room.

"You remember my friend, Genevieve," Alma

said. "She's learning how to sew so she's ready for her own husband."

The women laughed and exchanged a few knowing looks. Alma shot her a smile, left the room and came back with an extra chair. Genevieve quickly took it from her. Having a pregnant woman carry furniture seemed ill-mannered at the very least.

"You can sit by me," Alma said.

Genevieve carried the chair over to the spot Alma indicated. It was by the window, and directly between Alma and Sarah. Sarah sat poker-straight in front of a section of quilt, a needle and thread held aloft in one hand.

"Hello," Genevieve murmured.

"Hello," Sarah replied. The entire room fell silent and Genevieve looked over at Alma.

"I saw Genevieve almost beat her young man in a foot race today," Alma said, a sparkle in her eye.

"I'm not sure I had much chance at beating him," Genevieve said.

"Oh, it was close!" Alma said, and she launched into the story. As she talked, the women started to relax more, laughing together at the funny bits. Alma was quite the storyteller, and a simple two-mile run had turned into an epic race that left a man staring in admiration.

"Well, he's obviously in love with you," Sarah said.

"Is it…obvious?" Genevieve asked hesitantly.

"It is," Constance confirmed with a knowing little smile. "In our community, if you see a man looking at a woman the way your boyfriend looks at you, there's normally celery growing."

Genevieve glanced at Alma for translation.

"We make celery soup for our wedding dinners," Alma said. "It's tradition. So when you've got a wedding come up, you plant a lot of celery that spring."

"Right." Genevieve chuckled. "We don't move quite that quickly."

In fact, she and Scott weren't moving in that direction at all. They were friends...perhaps even less than that now that he'd likely be her direct commander.

"That's a shame," Sarah said. "I like our way of doing things. People get married, start families... It's efficient. Isn't it, Lily?"

Lily had been silent all this time, sitting at her corner of the quilt. She looked up from her needle.

"Very," she said.

"There won't be celery soup at her wedding— too early in the gardening season—but it'll be a lovely wedding all the same," Miriam said. "We'll all work together to make it special. This is her quilt."

"I'm helping with your wedding quilt?" Genevieve asked, putting a hand over her heart. "I'm so honored, Lily."

Lily smiled then, and blushed, turning back to her stitching.

"You know, I was curious about something," Genevieve said. "I was at the pawn shop in town and I found out that the owner was born Amish! I had no idea."

From the corner of Genevieve's eye, she saw Constance blanch.

"Paul Miller," Miriam replied with a nod. "*Yah*, he was born Amish. We went to school together."

"What happened?" Genevieve asked. "Why did he leave?"

"Why does anyone leave?" Alma murmured. "He lost the faith."

"He never really believed in our life," Miriam said. "He was a rebellious boy from his youth. Always doing things his own way and trying to shock his *mamm* and *daet*."

Genevieve glanced around the circle. Constance still looked rather pale, and she eyed Genevieve warily. Genevieve gave her a reassuring smile. Miriam looked rather prim and matter-of-fact. Alma had that motherly, sad look on her face. Sarah was focused on hemming a corner, her bottom lip caught between her teeth, but it was Lily who caught Genevieve's eye. Her jaw was tense, her lips pressed together, and her eyes flickered toward Genevieve a couple of times. Then she abruptly stood up.

"I'll just be a moment," she said, and hurried across the wood floor, her running shoes squeaking, as she headed out of the room and up the stairs. The washroom, maybe?

Genevieve winced. "Was it something I said? Does she know him?"

"He's a few years older than she is," Miriam said, shaking her head. "She can't know much of him."

Constance frowned. "Her brother was friends with him. She knew him."

"Right... Jake and Paul were good pals, weren't they," Miriam said thoughtfully.

"So what of this Paul Miller?" Genevieve asked. "Do you have anything to do with him now?"

"Us?" Sarah looked up from her work. "I don't think I've actually seen him since Linda Yoder's funeral."

"Linda Yoder—wait, Paul was at the funeral?" Genevieve asked. "She was the embroiderer, wasn't she?"

"*Yah*, that's her. She was Paul's great-aunt," Alma said.

Huh. Genevieve tucked that little detail away. Paul hadn't mentioned any personal connection to that piece of embroidery. Was it possible that his interest in it was personal and not professional?

Overhead, the toilet flushed and the squeak of those running shoes came back down the stairs.

"I don't think Lily likes him, though," Constance said quickly, her voice low. "So let's not talk about Paul. She's nervous enough about her wedding without poking at her nerves with this chatter."

And Constance, who'd been selling her household items to Paul at a much-increased return had effectively shut down this line of conversation.

When Genevieve met the plump woman's gaze, Constance's face flushed.

"We need to finish this quilt tonight, ladies," Sarah cut in. "We'd best get stitching."

Alma handed her a needle to thread. It looked like her sewing lesson was about to start.

Constance had been Genevieve's number-one suspect since seeing her in the pawn shop, but Lily had just popped onto the map. That was a guilty look if Genevieve had ever seen one. But why on earth would the young little bride-to-be steal an expensive heirloom from one of her closest friends? Was it spite because of Alma's handsome young husband? Or might something else have driven the girl to steal?

If Gen had to put her money on one of them, as of tonight, it was Lily.

SCOTT SAT AT the small kitchen table with a mug of tea in front of him. Benjie lay at his feet. Technically, he should be in the kennel. Bonding like this should only happen with his handler, but the dog had eyed him so forlornly that Scott had gone back to get him and brought him inside. Just for a bit. He'd put him in the kennel before bed.

Before Genevieve had left, they'd shared a quick dinner of Amish cooking that he'd bought at the Amish market. Now, he found himself eyeing the door, waiting for her return.

He had to stop this. Had to stop missing her when she wasn't around. That was dangerous ground. Scott bent over and stroked Benjie's head. The dog looked up at him, gave him a gentle lick, and then laid back down at his feet.

Scott took a sip of tea and the sound of a car coming into the drive outside made him straighten. He went to the window—it was Gen's cruiser. She got out of the car, and looked up, catching him watching for her. He gave her a sheepish wave and she smiled and waved back.

Well, he looked like a fool now. She was a Pennsylvania State trooper. She could take care of herself. She was strong, tough, smart, and incredibly capable. But something inside him still wanted to stand between her and danger. He sighed.

The side door opened and Genevieve entered. She stepped out of her low-heeled dress shoes and carried them hooked on two fingers. She gave him a tired smile.

"So, I have a definite suspect," Genevieve said. "I just don't know why she'd do it."

"Yeah? Which one?"

"Lily. The young one who's getting married in a couple of weeks."

"Really? So you think this might be for spite?"

"Maybe." She sighed. "But she doesn't seem spiteful. They're making her a wedding quilt—by hand, all of them together. And she's stayed good friends with Alma. I'm not sure Lily could hide spite for that long, you know?"

"So what made you think it was her?" he asked.

"I brought up the fact that the pawn shop owner

used to be Amish. The women all knew him. Lily got pretty worked up. Left the room. Constance said that Lily doesn't like him, and we shouldn't upset her."

"We aren't going near Paul, though," Scott said.

"I know." She put a hand up. "I won't. But he's involved. And I wanted to know who was connected to him. All we need is to know which woman took it. That's it. The watch might be gone already, but Alma needs to know who took it and why. That's as far as this needs to go."

Scott nodded. "Okay. So...that's it?"

"That master embroiderer who passed away— Linda Yoder? That was Paul's great-aunt."

"Really." It was getting more complicated now. "He didn't mention that when he saw the embroidery."

"It could be innocent enough. He might not have been sure. He might have had a complicated relationship with her...hard to tell. But it's worth noting," she replied then sighed. "Anyway, when Lily came back from the bathroom, everyone clammed up and wouldn't say another word about him. Not a word."

"Huh."

"So there's some history there, I think."

Scott sighed. "Do you think you'll be able to figure this out?"

She shrugged. "I think so. Paul is the only way to unload that watch, and keeping it would only make the thief more likely to be found out. I really think there's a connection there."

"There probably is," he agreed. "But if we won't get anyone to press charges…"

Genevieve sighed. "I know."

"Did you want some tea?" he asked.

Genevieve looked like she was about to say yes then shook her head. "I'd better not. I'm going to turn in."

"Okay," he said. He wished she'd accepted, though.

"Good night, Scott." Her voice was soft and it lingered like a touch. She headed out of the kitchen, leaving him alone at the table with his steaming mug of tea.

He missed being partners with her. Those days where they'd spend entire shifts together, and then some. When they'd talk about anything, and they had each other's backs. There was no hierarchy to get between them.

But sometimes a promotion came with sacrifices.

"Come on, Benjie," he said, putting down his mug and standing. "Let's get you back to the kennel for bed. You've got a big day tomorrow."

THE NEXT MORNING, after a shared breakfast of cold cereal, Genevieve headed out for a run and Scott got ready for work. Vince was coming this morning, and he needed to focus.

Ironically, the Genevieve problem had been

solved. They both knew where things stood, and she was determined to respect his new position. Good enough, right? He'd succeeded in saving Gen's job. She seemed to be getting the hang of following his orders.

This should feel better.

He looked out the window as she jogged down the drive, and as she disappeared from view, a cruiser pulled in. That would be Vince. Good timing. He needed this space from Gen to get his head in order. This was supposed to be easier!

"Vince, how are you?" Scott called as he stepped outside. He shook the trooper's hand.

"Scott, good to see you."

"How is your newest…daughter, right?"

"Sophie. She's great. Growing like a weed already and sleeping about six hours at a time. Which is amazing for a newborn. And my wife is doing well, too. The boys are just tickled to have a baby sister."

"That's great. It sounds like you've had some quality time with your family."

"I have. But I'm happy to be back at work, too. How's Benjie doing?"

"Benjie has really improved. He's doing the obstacle course like a pro, he's obeying orders and meeting all the metrics we need to see to send him back out. So let's do a few exercises with you and him together, and see where we're at."

Vince was a stalky, muscular cop with a kind face. He was good with kids, and whenever they needed to send a cop into an elementary school, they tended to send Vince. Being a dad, he seemed to know how to talk to them.

"So, your wife is doing well, you said?" Scott asked.

"She is. Actually, just before Sophie was born, Sonya and I celebrated our tenth anniversary."

"Nice!" Scott shot him a smile. "Congratulations! What did you do?"

"We watched *PAW Patrol* with the kids. She wasn't up to going out, being so pregnant," Vince chuckled. "But I got her a new laptop she really wanted. She wants us to take a trip to Germany next summer. Sophie will be easier to travel with then, and we can see some family over there."

"Family?" Scott shot him a curious look. "I knew your last name was German, but I didn't know you had such close family connections."

"Yeah, my brother is working in Berlin. My dad immigrated to the US when he was eighteen. My grandparents were out there, but they've since passed away. I've got cousins and aunts and uncles…"

"Do you…speak the language?" Scott asked.

"Yah, ich will." Vince shot him a grin.

"Wow. I had no idea. We've got a K9 from a German service dog school that only listens to perfectly pronounced German. He's a snob that way. Won't accept a command with an American accent."

"Yeah?" Vince chuckled. "That's kind of funny.

So you need a handler for him who speaks German."

"Yeah, that's the plan. We're looking."

But first, Benjie's situation with Vince had to work out. It would be easier to find another German-speaking trooper for Konig than it would be to find a home that could accommodate Benjie. Vince had to be Benjie's solution.

"How was Benjie with the kids? Was he stressed at all?" Scott asked.

"No, he liked the boys better than he liked me." Vince sighed. "He was really resisting bonding with me, I think. I've missed having him around, though. Hopefully, he's missed me, too."

Scott hoped so, as well.

"Well, let's head out to the kennel. He'll have had his breakfast by now and Ava gave him a bath this morning, so he should be glad to see you."

They headed over to the kennel building, and when they got inside, Ava had just finished drying Benjie off. Benjie saw them and Scott stepped back to let the dog get reacquainted with Vince.

"Come here, boy!" Vince called.

Benjie trotted over, gave Vince a sniff, accepted a pet, and then moved to Scott's side. He sat down next to Scott, ears high and alert. Shoot. He was acting like Scott was his handler, not Vince.

"I told you before that I trained Benjie when he was a puppy," Scott said.

"Come on, Benjie," Vince said enthusiastically. "Let's go do some obstacles! Come on!"

Benjie looked up at Scott, and Scott could see the confusion and disappointment in the dog's eyes. He thought he'd come home, back with Scott where it all had started. He was clearly unimpressed that Vince was there.

Scott clipped a lead onto his collar and handed it over to Vince.

"Go on, Benjie," he said quietly.

"Bath time, Konig," Ava said cheerfully. She opened his kennel and Konig stretched and came out. "Then after that, we'll take you for a nice long walk…"

The dog just looked at her—no recognition of the words *bath* or *walk*. He let Ava pet him, though, and leaned into her touch. He knew who his friends were, that was for sure.

"Hold on," Vince said. "Let me translate for him. *Konig, zuerst ein bad. Dann ein spaziergang.* Okay?"

Konig's eyes lit up and his tongue lolled happily. He slipped out of Ava's hands and headed straight for Vince, looking up at him hopefully.

"Zuerst ein bad," Vince said, and he pointed over to the sink and hoses. *"Zuerst ein bad. Yah?"* He reached down and pet Konig's head affectionately. "I told him first he has to take a bath and then he can go for a walk."

"Thanks," Ava said, patting the stairs that led up to the counter and the big washtub. Konig trotted over obediently, climbed the stairs and then stepped down into the tub.

"Thanks," Scott said, watching the dog thought-fully for a moment.

They headed outside and first let Benjie do a couple of runs through the obstacle course on his own. Scott and Vince leaned against the rail, watch-ing him run.

"He's fast and smart," Vince said. "But he just won't bond. You have to have seen it, Scott."

"I do, I do…" Scott sighed. "Look, here's the thing. This is Benjie's last chance. If he can't make it work with you, we have to pull him from the field and try to find him a home. That's a smart, fast K9 wasted."

Vince nodded. "I do get it. But in five minutes, I felt more of a connection with Konig than I've ever gotten from Benjie. And trust me, I've tried. He went everywhere with me. He was my buddy. But he just…resisted the bond, you know? But with you? He's very bonded to you."

Scott knew exactly what Vince was talking about.

"I didn't mean for that to happen," Scott said. "My highest priority is getting him back out into the field with you."

"I know, man," Vince said. "But if a connection just isn't happening…"

"Let's not give up yet," Scott said. "First of all, we'll work with him together, and then you'll work with him alone. I'll have Ava and some other train-ers do more work with Benjie, and I'll step back and work with Konig and the pups. We might be able to turn this around yet. Benjie wants it to be like old times. He wants to be my dog—I see that clearly. But that's not an option."

It stung to say it out loud. He knew Benjie just wanted to be his dog. Heck, he knew that if he became a K9 trooper instead of a commander, he'd have a good dog he could count on. That bond was strong, and Benjie had obviously chosen him with all of his canine heart. But that wasn't the direction that Scott was moving.

CHAPTER FOURTEEN

"You seem quieter today," Darlene said. She sat in one of the comfy white chairs next to the window. Outside, clouds had blotted out the sun, the earlier sparkle of the morning having evaporated.

It had been a good run. Genevieve had gone for three miles, according to her smartwatch. She hadn't been pushing it in her runs the last year or more, and it was time to start doing that again. Scott would make her a better trooper—she could see that already.

Darlene steepled her fingers in front of her lips, her ivory bracelets settling down at her forearms. She wore a flowy red kaftan today, and she fixed Genevieve with a mild, expectant look.

"I suppose so," Genevieve said. She'd changed out of her running shorts into jeans and fitted T- shirt. She expected to be busy this afternoon with dog training and other duties. "I've been doing some thinking."

"Anything you'd like to share with me?" Darlene asked.

"Well, I've realized that whatever the reasons I

was coddled in this job, the fact remains that by not going out there and getting the experience, I'm not as qualified as other troopers who've been around as long. And regardless of who is to blame for that, I'm the one who needs to fix it."

"Ah." Darlene nodded. "That's very wise."

"So, I intend to do that," she said. "I'm going to put the time in, and I'm going to keep asking for more breadth in my assignments so I can gain the experience."

"Good for you."

"I'm going to ask for a change in partner, too," she added. "Roy is close to retirement, and he's earned a quieter workload. I need more experience, and I'm not going to get it with him."

"Hmm." Darlene lowered her hands to her lap and tipped her head to one side.

"You disagree?"

"I'm not here to agree or disagree. I'm here to help you sort it all out."

Smooth, but Genevieve could tell Darlene didn't quite agree with that. It didn't matter. This was her career, not someone else's.

"Anyway," Genevieve said. "I've realized that while I've been frustrated because I haven't been given more interesting assignments, the reason for that might be that I don't have the experience yet to be successful with them. So, I'm going to stop being upset about that and I'm going to put my energy into fixing it."

"Do you feel less confident in your abilities?" Darlene asked.

"A little." Genevieve sighed. "I thought I was perfectly capable and only being held back due to an excess of worry. But if I'm too inexperienced, then maybe it isn't personal. Maybe it's...the right call."

"Until you get more experience, at least," Darlene said.

"Yes. Until I get more experience."

"That's quite a breakthrough," Darlene said. "How does it feel?"

"Humbling," she replied. "Five years ago, Sergeant Simpson was my partner, but he's not my partner anymore. He's my SO, and that's been hard to make my peace with."

"How is your relationship with him now?" Darlene asked.

"Good. He's an excellent commander. I respect him, and I'm glad I got the chance to see him again."

"But, personally...how is your relationship with him?" Darlene asked. "Because, yes, there is the proper police hierarchy, and the respect due our senior officers, but there are friendships, too."

Right. She'd mentioned being just about in love with a former partner, hadn't she? Hopefully, Darlene wasn't connecting the dots here.

"Well, I'm not sure how that friendship will work now," Genevieve said. "It's more complicated. He has career ambitions and so do I. Being pals again might have to wait until we're both a bit higher in our careers."

"And how do you feel about that?"

Genevieve gave the older woman a wry smile.

"I know, I know," Darlene said. "That's a very therapist question to ask. But it's important. We can rationally know where things stand, but we have to emotionally deal with it, too. So how does it feel? Right now. In this moment?"

"It feels…" Genevieve searched around inside herself and suddenly a lump rose in her throat. She wanted to simply accept how things were. Power on through it. But it wasn't going to be so easy, was it? "It feels lonely."

Darlene nodded. "It certainly can be."

"But I have no right to that," Genevieve said. "Scott and I hadn't even seen each other in five years. Seeing him now is reminding me of what our friendship used to be. I suppose I'm grieving the loss of my friend all over again, and I hate that. I've grieved this once. That's enough, isn't it?"

"Maybe it's not," Darlene said.

"You're not helpful, Darlene," she chuckled.

The older woman smiled. "Grief can come back. It's wily that way. We'd like to deal with something once and set it aside forever, but that's not how emotions work. That's also not how growth and wisdom work. Every time we deal with a particular grief, we come at it from a different angle. We learn something new. We get a little deeper into it. We walk away wiser."

"So what do you suggest?" Genevieve asked. "I thought it would be better to avoid Scott and just power on through this."

"I think it would be better to take advantage of this time with your old partner," Darlene said. "Talk. Compare notes. Maybe dig into it together a little bit. You were his friend as much as he was yours. But I think it's better to use this time to the fullest so that when you do go back to your station, you've dealt with more of it. It's hard now, but it'll be easier later."

"But he's my SO now."

"Yes."

"Is that appropriate?" she asked.

"You're a state trooper, Genevieve, but you're a person, too. Just like he's a sergeant and a person. If he wants to keep things strictly professional, then you'll have to abide by that. But maybe he'll be willing to talk more. You never know. All you can do is ask and respect his answer."

"I might give it a try," she murmured.

Maybe Darlene was right and it would be good to settle out as much of their old friendship as they could now, before he was her direct boss. There was limited time, and her success in the rest of her career depended on their ability to work together effectively.

THE KITCHEN AT the K9 Training Center was stocked with Amish-made frozen dinners. There were a few options to choose from: cabbage rolls, pickle-potato soup, and roast beef and potatoes in the freezer. In the fridge, there were submarine sandwiches, all wrapped up with the best before date stamped on the top. There was fresh fruit, too, and some cut veggies for snacking.

"We eat really well here," Wendy said as she circled around her desk, purse on her shoulder. "That's one thing I love about this position. They keep the fridge stocked with Amish food they order from local businesses, and it's free for anyone who's working."

"This is a pretty good selection," Genevieve said, casting a smile over her shoulder. "Are the submarine sandwiches any good?"

"The best," Wendy said. "But I'm heading out. If I don't get away from my desk, I just end up working through lunch."

"Where do you go?" Gen asked.

"I drive down the road, park, and call my husband. We have a standing lunch date."

"That's sweet." Genevieve smiled. "Have fun."

"I always do!" Wendy grinned back as she headed for the door.

Genevieve picked up her phone and texted Scott.

I'm getting myself a ham and cheese sub from the fridge. Want me to bring you anything?

She paused. That was probably a tad too friendly—at least for her own attempt to keep things on the professional side. So she added Sir.

A moment later, she got a reply.

I'll have what you're having. I'm in the kennel building. Thanks, Gen.

She gathered up two wrapped subs, two plastic cups of fruit salad, a bag of baby carrots and a couple of bottles of juice, dropped them in a shopping bag and headed for the door. Outside, the wind had picked up and the scent of soil and electricity was in the air—the promise of rain. Over the rolling Amish pasture, she could see a smudge of gray under the clouds—a downpour in process, far in the distance.

The wind was moist and cool, a welcome change from the earlier heat, but she shivered all the same. As she approached the long, low building that housed the kennels, Scott opened the door. He was in shirtsleeves, too, but he didn't show any signs of minding the chill in the air.

"Hey," Scott said, as she eased past him, out of the wind and into the shelter of the kennels. "So, I'm 'sir' now, am I?"

"You're my boss. That's what I call my commander at South Kingston," she replied. "When you take over there, I'll call you sir, too. I thought we should get used to it so we don't giggle or something when other people are around."

Scott burst out laughing and pulled the door shut. "I don't giggle. I might laugh in a very manly way, but I do not giggle."

"I don't know…" She shot him a teasing grin. "I've heard you giggle before."

A flash of lightning lit up the sky outside the windows. A moment later, there was a boom of thunder. The puppies were yipping from their enclosure, and she spotted Benjie and Konig lying together on some stuffed beds under a window, both of their noses turned toward the glass. Benjie looked over at Scott, a forlorn expression on his furry face.

Genevieve knew that Benjie was trained with sudden bangs and loud noises, so a storm was nothing for him. But his stare held silent accusation.

"Benjie's mad at you?" she asked softly.

He sighed. "You can see it, too, huh? Yeah… I had him working with Vince. He knows he's got to go back. He's not pleased with me."

"They understand more than we think sometimes," she said.

"True," he agreed. "But there isn't much I can do, is there?"

Another crack of lightning lit up the window. The older dogs stayed where they were, as if on guard, noses twitching. The puppies, however, had set up a little howl.

Scott nodded toward the puppy room. "We've got puppies to comfort, too. Bring the food. We'll eat in there."

WHEN THEY'D FINISHED EATING, Scott sat next to Genevieve on the floor, two puppies snuggled on his lap, a third in Genevieve's arms, and a fourth lying prone between them. Rain pattered on the roof and thunder rumbled overhead, but sitting on the floor with puppy breath warming his fingers, it felt like late evening—the only light coming from those overhead and not from the windows, which were streaming with rainwater and darkened by angry clouds.

They'd be getting some much-needed rain in these parts. It had been dry lately, and the farmers had been watching the skies. There would be plenty of happy Amish with a good downpour today.

"How did it go with Vince?" Genevieve asked.

"Not as well as I'd hoped," Scott replied. "He'll come back in a couple of days, and we'll try again. Benjie is pretty determined to be my dog, it seems."

Genevieve nodded. "He's holding a grudge."

"I know."

"He loves you."

"He's not mine, though," Scott said. "I can't help that. I mean…"

Did he wish that he could just keep Benjie? Of course! But that wouldn't be good for Benjie—he was a dog who was happiest with a job. Waiting for hours on end for his owner to get home? No, that wasn't the life for a trained K9. Benjie needed to feel useful, and he needed to bond with Vince.

There were a lot of things Scott wanted right now that weren't going to happen—like being able to have Gen in his life again the way she used to be. But that wasn't happening, either, was it? Sometimes a guy's heart could yearn until it broke, but that didn't change facts.

And maybe a dog's heart could do the same.

A crack of lightning lit the hallway and then a boom of thunder rattled windowpanes. Genevieve popped her last baby carrot into her mouth and paused in the act of biting down as the echo of thunder rumbled on past them. Then she crunched.

The puppies starting to whine and Scott pulled them all a little closer.

"It's okay," he said quietly. "Thunder happens, guys."

Gen shot him a smile. "This is like puppy preschool."

"Yep." He chuckled. "They just need comfort. They need to know that loud noises are okay, and if we aren't alarmed, they don't need to be, either."

"Like the first time you go into a firing range," she said. "Do you remember how loud it was?"

"Yeah…" He scratched a pup's fluffy rump. "You and I used to do target practice together. Who do you shoot with now?"

"I go alone." He looked at her and she shrugged. "I'm a big girl."

"You could go with your partner."

"He's had enough of me after a long day, trust me there."

"Other friends on the force?"

She was quiet for a moment. "I like the noise-canceling headphones and the solitude. Just me and the target. I can think."

There was nothing wrong with that, but something shining deep in her eyes when she'd said it made the scene sound lonely.

"You've changed a bit," he said.

She smiled faintly. "That happens, Scott."

He'd missed out on five years of Genevieve's evolution, and he found himself wishing that he hadn't. Actually, he found himself wishing that they could go shooting together. She wouldn't be lonely then, would she?

Another boom shook the building and the puppies put up another whine. Scott pet the dogs within reach, and Genevieve pulled another pup up against her chest and kissed the top of her head.

"Just a storm, little one," she murmured. "Just a storm…"

Her gaze softened as she pressed her cheek against the dog's head, and another puppy came scrambling up, wanting in on the snuggles. She gathered him into her arms, too, and she laughed softly.

The click of dog toenails echoed through the hallway, and Scott saw Benjie and Konig standing in the doorway. He gently displaced his lapful of puppies and pushed himself to his feet to open the baby gate. A puppy started to whine as the older dogs came in, and Benjie walked over to the pup and looked down at it. They seemed to communicate silently, because the puppy stopped whining, and lay down on the floor.

The lights suddenly flickered and then went out, leaving them in darkness. The only light was the grayish beam coming from the open door, and the puppies starting yipping. He could hear their little toenails scraping on the floor as they circled.

"It's okay, guys," Scott said, keeping his voice calm and pleasant. "That happens, too."

He couldn't make out anything in the darkness, his eyes needing time to adjust, and he suddenly felt Gen's hand brush against his side.

"There you are," she breathed.

He chuckled. "Hi. Nervous?"

"No." She laughed softly. "Is there a generator or something?"

"Yeah, if the electricity doesn't come back on, it'll kick in after five minutes."

"If we were Amish, this wouldn't affect us at all," she said.

Her voice was soft and close, and he couldn't help but think that if they were Amish, life would be a whole lot simpler. If two people felt something for each other, the community would get in there and push and nudge them right into a wedding. There was something kind of sweet about that—people who cared about making sure people who belonged together got together.

Scott started to move toward the door, but a puppy was in his path. In fact, he had puppies pressing up against his legs from all sides.

"I'm hemmed in," he said.

"Me, too…"

Genevieve's hand was still on his side, and he put his hand over hers. Then he shuffled closer to her. He wasn't sure why he did it—instinct, maybe?

Another boom of thunder made his heart tremble in his chest, and he felt Genevieve flinch. He ran his hand down her arm and tugged her closer still. She collided with his chest and he felt her breath tickle his lips.

"Sorry," he whispered.

"That's okay…"

He couldn't see her in the darkness, and he reached up to touch her cheek. She was so close, and all he could think about was where her lips might be. If she were anyone else, he'd be giving orders, getting a plan moving to turn the lights back on, but she wasn't anyone else, and how much he'd missed her suddenly crashed down around him with the strength of that howling storm outside.

"I'm trying really hard to keep this professional," he breathed. "But it's not going well."

"Then don't try."

And against all of his training, against all of his promises to himself, and every instinct for his own career, he moved his head toward hers until he felt her nose against his. She tipped her chin and her lips brushed against his. He knew he should pull back, because if he did this now—

Oh, heck…

He slid his hand into her hair and his lips came down onto hers as another peal of thunder shook the building. It might as well have been that kiss that shook the very ground under his feet, because everything was changing in that moment. His own reserve was crumbling, and a long-repressed aching for Genevieve thundered through his veins. It was like his heart was cracking open and all of those emotions he'd cataloged and pushed aside had come flooding back in.

Her lips were warm and soft, and he could feel her hands balling up his shirt at his sides. This was what he'd wanted for years...this was what he'd run from! She was everything he'd ever wanted in a woman, and this kiss hammered that home.

Genevieve pulled back just as the overhead lights flickered once and then came on. He stared into her wide blue eyes. She looked as shocked as he felt. A kiss in the darkness was one thing, but in the light, he suddenly realized what he'd done. With security camera proof.

What *they'd* done. Because she'd most definitely kissed him back.

"Wow..." he breathed.

"Scott..."

"I didn't exactly plan that," he whispered.

"Me, neither."

Thunder rumbled again and lightning lit up the outside.

"Should we talk about it?" he asked. Because he didn't know what any of it meant, but he was pretty sure he owed her a conversation at the very least. And maybe he was hoping that she'd tell him what it meant.

"No," she said. "I don't want to talk anymore. I've had enough talking."

He had, too. So much conversation. So much discussion. So much trying to nail down what they were and how they felt. A kiss was simple and to the point. That had been exactly what he was feeling—inconvenient as that might be.

Before he could say anything else—give her one more shred of an excuse to stay—Genevieve turned. She hurriedly pulled the baby gate aside and headed out of the puppy enclosure and for the front door. He followed her, and as she erupted into the storm, the wind and rain immediately drenched her. A pup had wandered after him— the one that had been on his lap—and he bent down and picked it up in his arms. Gen didn't turn around—just plunged on ahead toward the house.

Then he shut the door and looked down to find Benjie at his side. Benjie gazed up at him with that loyal look of love, and he had to wonder what he'd done to earn such devotion from this K9.

"So, you forgive me now, huh?" he said quietly.

Benjie would be happier if he could just bond with his handler. And Scott would be happier if he could let Genevieve go, but that kiss had both liberated and nailed him down in some way he couldn't quite explain yet.

The puppy in his arms licked his chin, and he smiled ruefully. Yes, Scott was truly foolish, but he didn't really regret that kiss. Not yet. It had been too long coming.

CHAPTER FIFTEEN

GENEVIEVE STOOD IN the bedroom, a rivulet of water making its way down her back. She shivered and peeled off her T-shirt. The rain had subsided to a gentle patter, the wind had died down and the lightning and thunder had moved on. She grabbed a towel for her hair and then worked on getting her wet jeans off.

She'd kissed Scott! And…she'd meant it. That was the part that left her feeling shaky. She'd accepted that she'd once had a crush on him, but today she'd crossed every line she'd sworn she'd never cross, and kissed him. To make it worse, she was feeling territorial over this man. Scott was not hers, but she was now forced to admit that she really wished he could be.

Genevieve shut her eyes, looking for calm.

"What is wrong with me?"

Genevieve took a hot shower and then dressed in a fresh pair of yoga pants and another T-shirt, and left her room.

Wendy spotted her on her way down the stairs

with her wet clothes. She was just tucking her purse under her desk.

"Did you get caught in that storm?" Wendy asked, her gaze landing on Genevieve's sodden ball of clothes.

"Afraid so," Genevieve said with a weak smile.

"The laundry machines are downstairs," the older woman said. "Feel free to do as much as you need to do. I didn't pull the dog blankets out of the dryer yet, so you could leave those in a basket on top, if you don't mind."

Genevieve smiled her thanks and headed down the narrow staircase into the finished basement below, flicking the light switch on her way. She put her clothes into the washing machine and started a load. She heard the door behind her at the top of the stairs open and turned, expecting to see Wendy.

Scott stood in the rectangle of light and he gave her a cautious wave.

"Oh, Benjie, you good boy!" Wendy's voice filtered down from upstairs.

Genevieve smiled. "He's stealing hearts, is he?"

Somehow it was easier to talk about Benjie than to talk about the elephant in the room.

"Yeah…" Scott descended the stairs, leaving the door behind him open. He stopped across the room and leaned back on a table. He was giving her space.

To keep her hands busy, she opened the dryer

and pulled out a blanket. She folded it up, put it on top of the dryer, and grabbed the next one.

"I know you don't want to, but we should probably talk about that…" he said.

She looked up and found Scott's gaze locked on her. He looked uncertain.

"Nope." She forced a smile. "I don't think so. That kiss didn't happen."

"You sure about that?" He smiled without humor. "Because I'm going to have trouble thinking about anything else…"

So was she, for that matter! That kiss had tumbled her emotions right upside down, but emotions could not rule—not if she wanted to keep her job, or if he wanted to keep moving in the right direction. It was one kiss. That was all.

"Scott, if I would like to stay employed, and if you would like to get your promotion, that kiss didn't happen," she said slowly. "We both have a whole lot to lose."

"And you don't want to even talk about it?" he asked.

"No." She forced herself to stare into his eyes and smoothed her expression. She did not want to talk about it. What good could come from that? Darlene might think that talking it out would be a benefit, but she had no idea how deeply Genevieve felt for this man. Breaking that seal was a terrible idea.

"Okay…" Scott looked away as he nodded. She'd hurt him—she could see that plainly.

"Scott, I don't think we dare," she said softly. "It was one kiss. We can just…not do that again."

"Can we?" He looked up again and eyed her with a look so filled with longing that her breath caught.

"Yes," she said, sounding much surer than she felt. "Of course, we can. We're adults. We eat our vegetables, go on runs, do paperwork, pay taxes. We can do the right thing here."

He grimaced. "So, this would be right next to broccoli and taxes, huh?"

She felt the smile tickle her lips. "Nestled right between."

"Okay." He nodded. "We don't talk about it and we don't do it again."

She pulled another blanket from the dryer, shook it out, and started to fold it.

"We're keeping this professional, then?" he asked. "Keeping it to work?"

"That's probably safest." Genevieve put the blanket on top of the last one and pulled the third and last blanket from the dryer.

"Fine. Then on the professional front, I need you to take Benjie into town today—just the two of you. Walk him around. Give him some orders. Maybe we can get him used to the idea that other troopers will be in his life. What do you say?"

Strictly business, but she could see the softness in his expression. This was a good idea, both for Benjie, who needed time away from Scott, and for Genevieve—for the exact same reason. She and

Benjie had that in common—they'd both fallen for the wrong cop.

"I can do that," she said.

"I appreciate it." He pressed his lips together, and for a moment, their eyes held. He looked like he wanted to cross the room, come closer, but he didn't.

"Scott, are you trying to get me out of here for a bit?" she asked softly.

"No, no…" He winced. "Gen, none of this is your problem. None of it, okay? I know we aren't talking about this, but I'm responsible. And I won't make anything uncomfortable for you. I promise you that. I really do need the help with Benjie. I feel like I'm failing with him, and he's going to be the one to suffer."

"I'll head out, then," she said. "Time to get Benjie used to other troopers. Do you want me in uniform for this?"

"It couldn't hurt," he replied. "Just to give him the whole experience."

And maybe she wanted that uniform again, too. Life felt safer behind it—the authority of the Pennsylvania State Police grays—but, somehow, so did her heart.

A HALF HOUR LATER, Genevieve was behind the wheel of her cruiser, in uniform, and with Benjie next to her in the passenger seat. He sat up straight and whined once as she pulled out of the drive.

"You're with me today, buddy," Genevieve said.

Benjie turned around and looked out the back window. Yeah, he was missing Scott. This dog had definitely bonded with Scott over anyone else. That wasn't helpful in a service dog, though. Not when Scott wasn't his handler.

Genevieve started at a flower shop and walked Benjie through it at a close heel. She walked him down a busy sidewalk, and she stopped at a bench, letting him sit and watch squirrels run up and down a tree. He behaved beautifully and listened to all her commands.

An Amish girl asked if she could pet Benjie and Genevieve told her no, explaining that Benjie, as a working dog, needed to keep his focus.

"Benjie is a police officer," she explained. "If you wouldn't rub a trooper on the belly, then don't do the same to a K9 dog, either."

The girl laughed at that, but she understood.

While Genevieve took Benjie through town, her mind kept going back to Scott and that kiss. She couldn't banish it from her mind, and she didn't really want to. The truth was, he had never been far from her thoughts, even during that five-year silence. But she'd have to get used to seeing him every day and treating him like he was just her boss.

That wasn't going to be easy, and it would probably be smarter to simply move to a different law enforcement agency and start over. But Scott was right—the Pennsylvania State Police was top-notch. With no disrespect to city cops, she'd be stepping down if she left.

Genevieve turned onto the waterfront walkway and only realized the way she'd come when she spotted the rushing deluge of the Conestoga Creek. The water was higher since the rainfall yesterday, and it frothed and gushed past the banks in a muddy torrent. Some moveable fences with Town of Strausfeld labels across the top of them had been put up along the riverbank to keep people back. The river could be dangerous at high-flood stage.

Genevieve walked Benjie along the sidewalk and ahead she could see the gaudy sign for the pawn shop. Benjie started to pull in that direction and Genevieve tugged him to heel.

"I'm the one in charge, Benjie," she said. "Behave."

She'd promised Scott that she'd stay clear of the pawn shop owner, but then she spotted someone she recognized approaching the door. It was Alma.

"Alma?" Genevieve called.

The woman turned—she looked pale and upset.

"Are you all right?" Genevieve asked. They'd stopped in front of the door.

"I just came by to have a word with Paul," Alma said. "This morning when I was at the bank, I saw him talking with a teenage girl in our community, and I didn't like how familiar he was being."

"What did he do?"

"Oh, just being a little too attentive, if you know what I mean."

Genevieve's hackles went up. "How old is the girl?"

"Eighteen. So she's grown, but she still needs her community. I was going to step inside and tell Paul to leave her alone or else I'll report him to the girl's family." Alma put a hand on her belly.

"Isn't this something your husband should be doing?" Genevieve asked. A pregnant woman confronting a man like Paul didn't seem like a good idea.

"I'm the one who's here," Alma replied. "Maybe it's my maternal instinct now, but I'm not leaving before I give him a piece of my mind." She hesitated. "You wouldn't mind stepping in with me, would you?"

That wasn't a bad idea. Genevieve nodded. "Sure."

Genevieve held Benjie in a close heel at her side. Benjie trotted along perfectly, his tail low, his ears high, and on full alert. She pulled open the door, the bell jangling overhead, and Alma stepped ahead of her into an empty shop. The door swung shut behind them.

There seemed to be some new sports equipment that had been put out in the most prominent spot on the first shelf—cleats in various sizes, some football pads. Genevieve saw movement in the back room, and Paul emerged. He started at the sight of them, then immediately slowed. He was intentionally calming himself.

"Hi, there," he said. "What can I do for you?"

Alma shot Genevieve a less confident look.

"Go ahead," Genevieve murmured.

"Paul, I saw you talking with Amanda Beiler this morning," Alma said.

"Oh, yeah." Paul crossed his arms.

"I… I…" Alma sucked in a breath. "I don't like how familiar you were with her. She's young. And you're far too old to be flirting with a girl her age."

"I wasn't flirting," Paul said. "I said hello."

Alma moistened her lips. "I just want you to know that if you start giving her any special attention, I'll be reporting you to her family."

"I didn't do anything! I said hello. We chatted."

"You know very well what I'm talking about," Alma returned.

Genevieve sauntered along the front cabinet, letting her eyes roam over the cheap jewelry, bringing her far enough to the other side of the store that she could see past Paul and into the back room. She could see something lying on the table—it shone golden, but that was all she could make out.

"Look, Alma, I'm not trying to start anything up with Amanda Beiler. I'll admit she's grown up into a nice-looking woman, but—"

"Then let it stop at that," Alma snapped. "You know what, I'm going to talk to her father and brothers, and if you're so innocent in giving her attention, that shouldn't bother you in the least, should it?"

"There's no need for that," he said, softening his tone. "Alma, you misunderstood…"

"Paul, I did not misunderstand anything," Alma said firmly. "Now, you stay clear of her."

Alma turned then and cast Genevieve a grateful look. "I'd best get home to my husband now."

Genevieve gave her a nod, and Alma headed out the door.

Good—Alma had sensed something amiss with Paul and wasn't letting him get away with anything. Some people needed a little extra community supervision. Genevieve looked into the back room again at the item lying on the towel inside.

If she was going to follow orders, she should leave, but somehow she couldn't do that. She was already there, and she had a strong suspicion that Joseph's stolen watch was on that table.

"What's that, Paul?" she asked.

"Nothing." He pulled the door shut behind him and shot her a challenging glare. He was obviously in a bad mood now from being told off by Alma.

"Would you mind showing it to me?" she asked.

"Why?"

"Is it a watch?" she asked.

"No. It's not."

"Then why not show me?"

"Do you have a warrant?" he countered.

"No, I'm just a curious citizen, looking at what you've got to offer."

"That isn't for sale. So never mind, then," he replied. "I think it's time you left, ma'am."

Genevieve raised her eyebrows at him. Was he really kicking a police officer out of his establishment? He didn't waver, and Benjie next to her had stilled. She knew that feeling—Benjie was focused in on Paul, sensing danger, no doubt.

"Why is that, Paul?" she asked, her voice low.

"Because I don't like the fact that you came in here accusing me of doing something wrong with that girl," he snapped back. He then circled around the front of the cabinet, standing too close and blocking her line of view with his body. He smelled musty, like he needed a shower. "And I have a business to take care of."

Paul looked down at Benjie and the dog gave a low growl.

"Hold," she said softly. Benjie stilled.

"I didn't accuse you of anything. Alma had a conversation with you. That had nothing to do with me."

"You were obviously standing there on guard," he snapped.

"Did she need protecting?" Genevieve asked.

Paul's expression darkened. "No, she didn't. But I don't like how your dog is eyeing me right now, either."

Alma had sensed something menacing in Paul, and so had Benjie. Frankly, so did Genevieve. Paul was too shaken up to hide his true colors.

"He's a trained service dog. You have nothing to worry about," she replied calmly.

"It would be a lawsuit if he bit me," Paul said. "Just pointing that out. I haven't done anything and you don't have a warrant. I know my rights." He took a step closer to her, obviously trying to intimidate. When she didn't move, Paul put a hand on her shoulder and gave her a shove. That was all Benjie needed. The dog leaped, caught Paul's wrist and the man went down with a cry of pain.

Great. Now she had to do something, but putting hands on a police officer was an offence. Up until that touch, he'd been within his rights. But when he'd touched her, it was over.

Genevieve bent over Paul and pulled out a set of cuffs.

"Release," she commanded, and Benjie let go of Paul's wrist. He hadn't broken the skin, but there were indentations where his teeth had been.

"Well done, buddy," she said, casting the dog an approving look. That was a perfect takedown, including the pressure he'd applied with his jaws. She was impressed.

Still…she'd have a whole lot of explaining to do.

Genevieve cinched the handcuffs and pulled Paul to his feet. Then she took out her phone and dialed Scott's number.

"Hello?" His voice was soft, deep. Now was not the time for that.

"I've just cuffed Paul Miller," she said, suppressing a grimace. "You might want to get down here."

"ARE YOU CHARGING me with anything?"

Scott could hear Paul's rising voice as he got out of his cruiser outside the pawn shop. A few people had gathered on the sidewalk, peering inside the shop—Amish and English alike. They didn't even turn until he came up behind them.

"Excuse me, please," Scott said.

A man started and stepped back, and two Amish women stared at him in mute surprise. They stepped back, too. As Scott entered the store, he pulled the door shut after him and flipped the sign to Closed. That would have to do for now.

Paul sat on a large spool of some sort of cable, his hands cuffed behind him. He looked more angry than anything. But then, so was Scott. He'd told Gen to leave the pawn store owner alone, and she'd known his reasons. Without anyone willing to press charges, it wasn't worth jeopardizing a community contact who would help them with other investigations. If he was angry with the cops now, Paul wouldn't be in any hurry to help them in the future. But Scott wouldn't question Gen in front of him. He knew her well enough that she might have a very good reason for this... At least, she'd better!

Genevieve met his glance easily enough when he walked in. She stood with her legs akimbo, her arms crossed over her chest. Just like old times... Benjie joyfully bounded to his feet and came running up to Scott.

"Her dog attacked me!" Paul said loudly. "I think I'm bleeding!"

"There's no broken skin," Genevieve replied calmly. "I checked."

"Attacked?" Scott asked, keeping his tone neutral.

"He's vicious! He attacked! That dog's not safe!"

Benjie sat there, a sharp eye on Paul, and Genevieve, too. Benjie was in work mode, and there was no way he'd attacked. Took down, perhaps, but that wouldn't be an attack.

Scott moved a few yards away from Paul and Genevieve followed him. Her face was a professional mask, but he noticed that she fiddled with her belt in the way that said she was stressed. He lowered his voice for her ears only.

"What happened?" he asked.

"Alma wanted to say something to Paul about how he was talking with a young woman in their community. She didn't like it, and she asked if I'd step in with her. She wanted the protection," she said. "So I did."

"What girl?" Scott asked. If Paul was crossing any lines with young women, he'd personally make sure it stopped.

"Her name is Amanda Beiler. It sounds like Alma suspects he was hitting on her, or something. She didn't like it. Paul got his hackles up, too. But Alma said her piece and then left."

"So how come Paul is cuffed?" he asked.

"I saw something that shone like gold in the back room," she said. "I know you told me to leave him alone, but if the watch is here, I wanted to intercept it before he sold it off. I asked about the item, he got belligerent and put a hand on my shoulder and pushed me."

"Did he now…" Scott's own anger rose at that

little detail. So not only was Paul putting the Amish community on edge, but Paul figured he could put hands on Genevieve, too? That was assault.

"Benjie waited until he made contact," Gen went on. "He jumped, caught him by his wrist and took him down—without breaking any skin." She shot the dog a fond look. "He also released on my command. He's a good dog."

"Yeah, he is…" Scott muttered. It sounded like Benjie had done exactly what he was supposed to do. That was heartening. "Did you get a look at the item in the back yet?"

"I was waiting on you." She looked at him and he could read the uncertainty there. She wasn't as certain as she'd appeared, and somehow that softened him.

"Paul's been secured this whole time?" he asked.

Genevieve nodded.

"Then we have cause to take a peek around the store. I'll see what's there." He wasn't sending her back. He'd do it himself.

Scott headed around the counter.

"Is there anything in the back room I should be aware of?" he asked Paul.

"Like what? A vicious attack dog?"

"Are you alone? Is there anyone else back there?"

"No one, just me—and you two," Paul said irritably.

Scott noticed that Benjie was set to follow him, and Scott let him. Paul wasn't going anywhere, and if he tried, Gen was capable of stopping him.

Scott eased the door open and looked into the room. It was a small room, with a counter facing the door. Lying on the counter, on top of a dingy-looking hand towel, lay a gold-faced watch with a leather band. He bent to get a closer look.

Written in all caps around the top of the face was "A. Lange & Söhne." Scott pulled a glove out of his back pocket and used it to pick up the watch.

"So, it looks like the watch showed up," Scott said, coming outside.

Paul heaved a sigh. "It's not stolen."

"One very much like this is missing, and was taken from a private residence," Scott replied.

"The owner brought it here!" Paul snapped. "Joseph Hertz, right?"

Scott looked at the man in surprise.

"Yeah—" Paul rolled his eyes. "I'm not a fool. The man brought it in himself last night. He wants to sell it—find a buyer who can pay what it's worth. That's not easy, you know."

"It takes connections," Scott said.

"Sure does. But I didn't steal anything," Paul said. "Bring him in. He'll tell you the truth. Joseph Hertz brought me that watch and asked me to get a price for it. We grew up together, and he knows he can trust me!"

Scott looked over at Genevieve. The chances that the man was lying were slim. They could verify his story too easily for it to get him anywhere. Besides, dislike him as he did, Scott could hear the ring of truth in Paul's voice.

"We will check up on that," Genevieve said.

"Please do!" Paul retorted. "Now, what about these cuffs?"

"You laid hands on a police officer," Scott said. "One in uniform, to boot. So there's no confusion about her role here."

"I shouldn't have done that." Paul lowered his voice and faced Scott. "I was wrong. I was angry. I apologize, and I will never do such a stupid thing again. You have my word. Ask anyone around here—I'm trustworthy."

He was not, but if they took Paul in now, they'd never figure out what had really happened with that watch. He had a feeling that Joseph Hertz would confirm the story, and any lines of communication with the Amish would be severed. They'd clam up. He'd been against investigating the stolen watch any further before, but now he was inclined to dig deeper. Gen had been right—there was something very wrong here. He should have listened to her earlier.

"It's not my pity you're looking for, Paul," Scott said curtly. "It's Trooper Austin's."

"Trooper Austin..." Paul turned toward her. "I understand what I did was over the line. But your dog certainly set me straight. I assure you that I will never do such a foolish thing again. And I'm asking you, respectfully, to give me a warning and let me off with only that. If you'd be so kind. Please."

Gen looked over at Scott and he angled his head toward the door. They stepped aside together.

"My first instinct? Throw the book at him for laying a finger on you," Scott said, his voice low. "But you were right before. There's more going on here, and everything is about to close down. If we let him go with a warning, we can keep an eye on him and see what he's really up to. But it's your call."

"Mine?" Gen raised her eyebrows and chewed on one side of her cheek. "Okay… I want to get this guy on more than a shove. Let's let him walk and see what else we can get him on."

They headed back to Paul.

Genevieve crossed her arms over her chest. "How much can we expect from you in terms of cooperation in the future?"

"Oh, a hundred percent! I'm your guy. I'll help you out any way I can. I mean I'm a law-abiding citizen here, and I have no desire to thwart the law."

Genevieve stepped forward, put a hand on the man's shoulder and bent to undo the cuffs. They came off with a click and she pocketed them.

Paul rose to his feet, rubbing his wrist with one hand.

"Paul," Scott said, his voice low, "I'm going to give you a piece of advice, and I hope you follow it."

Paul blinked at him.

"If you ever even think of laying a hand on another officer again, you will be dealing with me personally, and I will be slapping you with every single charge that will stick. I will stand over those charges and make sure you face every single one. I'll be at every hearing. I'll be at every court appearance. Do you understand me?"

Paul swallowed then nodded. "Clear as a bell."

"Good." He tapped his leg and Benjie fell in beside him. "I'm going to have a chat with Joseph Hertz, and if his story doesn't match yours exactly, I'll be back here with a warrant."

Paul swallowed hard. "It'll match. But talk to him alone. He wife doesn't know."

As they took their leave, Scott let out a slow breath. The looky-loos had dispersed and he noticed a wide-eyed Amish woman across the street watching them. It wasn't Alma Hertz, either. He knew that woman—thin, small, quite young…

"That's Lily Huyard," Genevieve said softly.

Right. She was one of the women who'd been at Alma's place when the watch went missing.

"Where's your cruiser?" he asked Gen.

"Parked over on 13th Street, by the dry cleaner," she replied.

He knew the area. "I'll drive you back over there."

"Thanks." Genevieve eyed him uncertainly. "How mad are you?"

"I haven't decided yet," he said. His heart was still going faster than it should.

He unlocked his cruiser and let Benjie into the back, then he and Gen got in. For a moment, they just sat in the stuffy quiet as the AC started to cool the inside of the vehicle again.

"Joseph didn't steal his own watch," Genevieve said. "He couldn't have. He wasn't home when it went missing."

She was thinking about that missing watch. He was thinking about how they were going to work things once he was her boss. Dammit, she was never going to be just another trooper, was she? She'd always be special. He'd always be prioritizing her—even if she hated it.

And that didn't help either of them in the least.

CHAPTER SIXTEEN

As PROMISED, Scott dropped Genevieve off at her car, and once she was alone in her vehicle, she let out a shaky sigh. Joseph hadn't stolen his own watch. Would he corroborate Paul's story, or had the man just lied to their faces? There was more to this tale, and she needed to find out.

But Scott was mad. She knew him well enough to know what that silence meant. He hadn't said a word to her until he'd dropped her off, and all he'd said was, "Meet me in my office in an hour."

That was it.

She'd disobeyed direct orders from her superior officer, and that realization was sitting heavy in her stomach. She'd expected her friend to understand her motivation, but her boss? If this was her current commander at South Kingston Station, would she expect him to understand?

Genevieve drove back to the K9 Training Center and stood in the kitchen for a few minutes, looking out the window over the obstacle course. It was empty, and she could see Ava leading the puppies

outside in a training exercise that involved something in her hand that they could smell.

"You okay?" Wendy asked, opening the fridge
and pulling out a bottle of water.

Startled, Genevieve looked over. "Yeah. I'm
good."

"You look spooked," Wendy said with a faint
smile. "I saw Scott powering in here like a thunder cloud. Is that about you?"

"Yep." She sighed.

Wendy winced. "Sorry, sweetie. He's in his office already if you want to go talk to him."

Genevieve looked at her watch. She still had ten
minutes until the hour was up, but what was she
going to do, just stand there and worry?

"I might as well," she said.

Genevieve headed back through the foyer and
down the hall toward the commander's office. The
door was shut and she tapped on it.

"Come in." His voice was muffled, low, solemn.

She opened the door and stepped inside, pulling
it shut behind her. Scott sat at the desk, his expression grim. She had reasons for what she'd done, but
she hadn't had to ask about the item in the back
room. She could have simply told Scott about it
and let him decide the next move. Instead, she'd
acted on her own—against direct orders. Was this
her third strike? It very well could be, by the look
on Scott's face.

"Are you firing me?" she asked. If he was firing her, let him do it now. They didn't need to draw it out.

"No." But he didn't seem surprised by the question, which meant it had crossed his mind. "Have a seat, Gen."

She slid into a chair opposite his desk, but looking at Scott sitting behind that desk, he wasn't her old friend anymore. He was a different man now—more experienced, with more authority, and unwavering.

"You disobeyed a direct order," Scott said.

"I did, but going into the shop was only to give Alma some protection while she said her piece," she said. "Then Paul started acting cagey. I asked a few questions, and he acted cagier. I know I should have left, and if he'd just been a bit politer, I probably would have. Then he came at me, and Benjie took care of the rest."

Scott pressed his lips together.

"And for what it's worth, I'm glad you finally saw what I saw. There's more going on there. I know Paul is up to something, and that watch was stolen—even if Joseph somehow got it back in the meantime. Until this makes sense, I'm not going to be able to let go of it."

"I get it. You've got this desire to pick out the injustice and fix it. But it's not always possible."

"We can talk to Joseph," she said. "It isn't like there's not more threads to follow."

"I know," he replied. "I'll talk to Joseph myself."

Genevieve eyed Scott warily. She could see a

glimmer of her friend in the man behind the desk, but he had his defenses up. "I'm sorry. If he hadn't put his hands on me—"

"You don't have to apologize for someone else's behavior." Scott shook his head slowly and he deflated a little. "I realized something when I found out he'd pushed you. I felt a blinding rage."

Genevieve blinked at him.

"I'm serious," he said. "I was glad that Benjie took him down. But I realized that I had a different emotional response when it came to you."

"What are you saying?" she asked softly.

"I'm saying you're special." He sighed and rubbed a broad hand over his eyes. "And you shouldn't be. You need a commander who's going to give you an equal shake. You need someone who will champion you, send you out and see your strengths, not react like some protective wolf when you're crossed!"

Maybe she liked him feeling that way. Because Scott wasn't holding her back. He just wanted to, and those instincts were coming from a different place inside Scott. She'd touched his heart.

"Why couldn't you just follow orders?" he asked softly. He pushed himself up from his seat and walked over to the bookshelf. "You weren't here to dig into local thefts. You were here to prove you could follow orders. This isn't going to be an easy one to explain."

"Fire me," she said.

"No."

"Why not?" she demanded. "If I were any other trooper, I'd be fired on the spot. This is my third strike, isn't it? So fire me!"

"No!" He turned again, his eyes filled with fire. "And do you know why? Because you deserve better!"

"Maybe I don't!" She stood up, too, and met him in the center of the room.

"Trust me, you do. I'm not doing you any favors here."

"We can make this work," she said. "You're a good leader."

"But I can't be your SO."

"Why not?" she demanded.

"Because I'm in love with you!" He grimaced as if he regretted the words as soon as they were out, then he gave her a look filled with such agony that her heart hammered to a stop. "That was always my problem, Gen. I felt too much. I wanted to take care of you, to protect you, to listen to every thought that crossed your mind. I wanted to be your answer... I thought my emotions had just edged over the line, but it was more than that. I was in love with you back then, and seeing you again hasn't fixed the problem. If anything... I love you more this time around."

"Scott..." she breathed. Her best friend, her closest partner, the man she'd never been able to let go...loved her? It sure did explain her own racing heart right now.

"It's okay. You don't have to say anything. And

I know I'm fully in the wrong for even telling you about it, but—"

She closed the distance between them and pressed her lips against his. His arms folded around her and she leaned into his kiss, treasuring every moment of it. He loved her...and maybe it was all kinds of unprofessional, but hearing it had filled her heart to the brim.

When she pulled back, he stared at her. He no longer looked worried, just beaten.

"I'm sorry," he said dismally.

Genevieve stepped out of his arms then and felt her throat close off with emotion. "At least you didn't forget me. I couldn't bear that."

"Forget you? I thought about nothing but you for five years!"

"Good," she said, lifting her chin.

"So...what does this mean?" he asked. "I shouldn't have said anything, but...is there any way we can work together still? Am I crazy for even asking that?"

And while she'd just been arguing that they could, knowing he loved her and not being able to do anything about it would be a special kind of torture. She wished this didn't matter, but it did.

Genevieve shook her head. "We can't."

Scott let out a shaky breath, his eyes moving over her shoulder as if he could find answers around the room somewhere. Then his gaze came back to her face.

"It's not quite so simple... The commissioner

made it clear I can't transfer you out. He said you have to make it work at South Kingston Station, or nothing." He swallowed. "Look, I'll do my best to treat you like everyone else."

As if that were possible. Now she'd have to pretend she felt nothing for him, too? She wasn't that good of an actress.

She shook her head. "I'm not lying to everyone and I'm not going to have some secret, tawdry relationship with my SO."

"Of course not," he said. "I would never ask that of you. I'm not asking you to pursue anything with me. I know how inappropriate that is. I can get my feelings under control. How I feel about you is *not* your problem. I mean that."

His voice was low and earnest. Just regular old Scott, the man she'd known so well, and fallen for so completely. It was like the years had melted away, and it was just Genevieve and her partner, opening their hearts and saying it like they felt it. Why hadn't they done this years ago?

"And what about how I feel about you?" she asked, her voice shaking.

"How…do you feel about me?" he asked cautiously.

She almost couldn't believe that he didn't know already. He'd spent this much time with her and he had no idea?

"I love you, you frustrating man!" she said. "Okay? I love you, too."

Scott scrubbed a hand through his hair and stared at Genevieve, her words taking a moment to land.

"Wait, what?" he said. It sounded foolish coming out of his mouth, but he really needed the confirmation here.

"I love you, too," she whispered.

He caught her hand and tugged her in closer. Tears sparkled in her blue eyes and he dipped his head down and caught her lips with his. Every time he kissed her, it was like a wild relief. He slipped an arm around her slim waist, inhaling the scent of her. She smelled like springtime, and the aroma of her perfume knocked at that part of his heart that held the bouquet of lilacs and fresh-baked bread. She was like the comfort of home and the excitement of vacation all rolled up into one. She filled every part of his aching heart. He pulled back, and she let her hand linger on his biceps.

"It can't work, though, can it?" she asked miserably.

"Not with me as your boss, it can't," he admitted. "Obviously, I'd get myself fired if I started something up with you. That would be wildly unprofessional on my part. And I have to tell you, if you were mine, I'd be wanting to protect you. I couldn't help it. Because if anything happened to you…" He shook his head. "And your whole problem has been men holding you back. I can't be that guy."

"Yeah…" Tears sparkled in her eyes.

Genevieve pulled out of his arms and suddenly they felt empty.

"And you've worked too hard to get here. You deserve this position, Scott. The troopers deserve you, too. They'll love and respect you."

"And you?" he asked.

She was silent, and for a moment, he wasn't sure if she'd even answer. Then she said, "I'll hand in my resignation."

"No! You've worked as hard as I have."

"True. But I'm not just handing it in. I'm asking you for that letter of reference," she said. "I need a job with another police force, and a glowing reference from you should do it."

She was asking for that fresh start, that clean slate, that chance to gain the experience she needed to move forward in her career in law enforcement. She was asking for the ability to move on, the move away from the Penn State Police, and away from him. She deserved all of it.

"Will you be close by?" he asked.

"I've got to get away from my father's reach," she said. "So, no. It'll have to be another state."

A lump stuck in his throat and he blinked back the mist in his eyes.

"We only just found each other again…" he said.

She nodded. "I don't know what else to do. I'm not going to give up being a cop, and neither of us wants to hide a relationship. But we can't work together. Like you said, the commissioner won't let me transfer, and you've worked too hard to give up this opportunity."

There really was no other option, was there?

He'd known five years ago that he'd let his feelings go too far, and here he was, entangled with Gen again. At least this time he'd been able to tell her how he felt. Maybe it would make getting over her easier. And then again, he doubted it.

"Are you sure you want to leave?" he asked. "Because I can rein this in. I can…keep it strictly professional. I can. We can try, at least."

He'd have to, and for her sake, he'd smother his feelings under a load of hard work and duty.

"I've been thinking about leaving since I lost my temper with Tom. I had good reasons to leave for another force—well-thought-out and they made sense then. I didn't know I'd feel this way two weeks ago, but I don't think my plan should change. You have a future here. I don't. It's okay. Nothing has actually changed."

Was it as simple as sticking to their previous plans? Because nothing felt simple anymore, and his heart felt raw.

"If it's what you want," he said.

She nodded. "Will you give me the letter of recommendation?"

"It'll be my first act as commander of South Kingston Station," he said. "You'll have it. I'll make sure they'd be crazy not to hire you on the spot." He tried to smile, but wasn't sure he managed it.

Genevieve nodded, but her lips wobbled and she

didn't say anything else. She turned for the door and every atom in his being screamed at him to go after her.

But he didn't.

Because what was he supposed to say? What was he supposed to do? He'd known from the start that his feelings for her were all wrong. And that would have to be his burden to bear.

He rammed that pain down as far as it would go and let out a shaky breath. He was no better, no smarter, than any other guy who'd fallen in love with Genevieve Austin. But he'd loved her more, and more truly—he knew that for a fact.

It would just be harder to get over her.

THAT NIGHT, Scott went out with the dogs. Konig ran ahead, but Benjie stuck close—putting his nose into Scott's palm. He must have sensed something was wrong. Scott looked down at the German shepherd, his heart heavy.

Vince was coming by in an hour or so to try a few more exercises with Benjie, but Scott was going to have to be pragmatic here. Vince and Konig seemed like an excellent team, and it was Scott's job to make the right choices for both the dogs and the handlers. If Benjie wasn't going to be a match for Vince, it was up to Scott to make that call. And he'd have to have his own personal pain hidden by the time Vince arrived, too.

But right now, what he wanted to do was go take a long walk in the woods, away from everyone else, anyone who might see his heartbreak, and get it all under control before he came back. Not that that could happen in one hike. This was going to be a long process, and he could blame himself for falling for her again, but he'd never had a choice in that. Not the first time—because heaven knew he'd fought it!—and certainly not this time around.

Genevieve just filled a certain part of his heart with no effort of her own. And he knew his competition was fierce for her. But more than that, he knew that, in the long term, they'd never make each other happy. They couldn't.

Unless, once she was part of some city police force, he called her up and took her out for dinner? Even if he had to fly out to do it. Would that be setting himself up for more pain? Probably. He should listen to the universe and get over her. Again. Although, how successful he'd been in getting over her the first time was still up for debate, seeing the state he was in now.

"I keep making the wrong calls when it matters most, Benjie," he said quietly. "I fall for the wrong woman, and even the wrong dog, huh?" He ruffled Benjie's head.

Even with Benjie, he'd held him in the program too long. He should have cut his losses and taken Benjie out when he'd still had a chance at finding a good home. And with Gen, he needed to do the same thing—cut his losses. He knew she couldn't be the one for him, no matter how much he loved her. So, he needed to stop dragging this out.

He needed to do better this time.

Konig stopped before he got to the forest and looked back at Scott. A man stood by the fence that separated the Hertz pasture next door. It was Joseph. He had his blue shirtsleeves rolled up, and he lifted his hat in greeting and leaned against a fence post, watching Scott.

Joseph wanted to say hello, apparently. Scott would much rather carry on into the woods, but it would be rude. Especially after they'd been involved in the Hertz's personal business. Besides, he'd planned to see Joseph today anyway. He needed to see if Paul had been lying. With a sigh, he headed over in the Amish man's direction.

"How are you doing?" Joseph called.

Konig fell in beside Scott, and when he reached the fence, Joseph squatted down and said a few words to the dog in German. Konig just about turned into a puddle of affection for the man.

"I just wanted to tell you not to worry about the watch anymore," Joseph said, standing up again.

"I saw one very much like the one you lost at the pawn broker," Scott said.

Joseph's face colored. *"Yah."*

"Joseph, did you hide your own watch, and your wife misunderstood, or something?" Scott asked. "Things happen sometimes."

"No, no," Joseph said. "My wife wasn't mistaken. It was taken from our home, all right, but...the person who took it returned it."

Scott eyed the man curiously. "Care to tell me more?"

"It was Lily Huyard."

"Really?" Scott asked. So Gen's hunch had been correct.

Joseph shrugged. "She handed it to me, apologized profusely, and said that she would take any consequences that came to her. With the watch back, I said I saw no reason to report her. And she said we would have to wait and see as she was in *Gott*'s hands."

Scott blew out a breath. "I'm glad you have it back… I'm just curious about why she took it."

"She wouldn't say," Joseph replied. "And it felt wrong of me to press her, especially since she'd done the right thing in returning it."

"So why was it at the pawn shop?" Scott asked.

"Well…with the watch missing, and my wife not knowing it was back again, I thought maybe I could use the money from the watch to pay off some of my debts. A few are resting rather heavily these days, especially with a baby coming. I wanted to keep that watch, but I always knew it was a kind of nest egg—a just-in-case bit of wealth that could be used when I needed it most. I'm building my own family now, and paying off the last of this land will be of greater use to my *kinner* than some shiny bauble they can never wear because it's too fancy, anyway."

"That's very practical," Scott said. "I'm glad it worked out."

Joseph nodded. "Thank you for your help, all the same. I won't keep you."

"Can I give you a piece of advice?" Scott asked. Joseph paused.

"Tell your wife everything now—before she hears from someone else. She needs to know what happened, or she'll never be able to trust her friends fully again. Besides, I have a feeling this one is going to get out, and anything to do with another woman needs to be out in the open. Trust me there. She'll understand just fine with it coming from you."

"*Yah*, I'll do that," Joseph agreed. "That's wise council."

As Scott headed down the trail toward the woods, he paused and then looked back at the house.

Blast it. He wanted to know what had happened with Lily Huyard. Why on earth had the girl stolen an expensive watch and then returned it? With her wedding coming up, her family would have paid for all of those expenses. And her new husband would take care of future expenses. Why would she do it?

He pulled out his phone and shot a text to Genevieve. This could be his last gift to her—solving her mystery.

I thought you might want to know. It was Lily who took the watch. She returned it to Joseph, who took it the pawn shop himself to sell.

A moment later, she replied.

Lily? But why?

No idea, he typed. Did you want to talk to her and clear this up?

Thank you, Scott. There was a pause. I'm going to miss you so much.

Tears pricked his eyes and he tapped back.

Me, too, Gen.

It didn't encompass a fraction of what he was feeling, but texting never could. He'd miss her desperately, and she might be the reason he never would settle down with another woman. Gen was the kind of woman who hooked a guy's heart and left him ruined for anyone else.

CHAPTER SEVENTEEN

ALMA INSISTED THAT they take the buggy to Lily's parents' farm. She said a buggy was just less aggressive than a police cruiser, and Genevieve had to admit that she was probably right. Before they'd left, Genevieve got out of uniform and into jeans and a blouse. The last things she needed to do was to panic an entire household.

"I just don't know why she'd do this!" Alma said, flicking the reins. The buggy bumped over a deep crack in the road, and overhead, a branch scraped along the roof.

"It's very unlike her," Alma went on. "But no matter who it was, I was going to be shocked." Alma glanced over at Genevieve and she frowned. "Are you all right?"

"Me? I'm fine," Gen said.

"No, you aren't. It's all over your face, Genevieve. You look so sad. We'll set it straight, you know. And I want you to assure her straight off that you aren't here to arrest her."

Genevieve nodded. "I'll be sure to tell her."

"But it isn't Lily that has you looking like your

heart is split in two," Alma said. "I'm willing to believe it's your handsome beau."

This young woman sure was insightful. Genevieve sighed. "We told each other how we felt, and realized it can't work."

"But…what?" Alma squinted at her and then put her attention back onto the road.

"It's complicated. It has to do with jobs, and who is whose boss, and all sorts of work drama," Genevieve said. "The end of the matter is, he's worked very hard to get an important promotion, and with him feeling as he does about me, I can't work under him."

"You can't let him be your boss?" Alma asked.

"Exactly."

Alma shook her head. "You know, we Amish let the men be the boss and we don't mind at all. You can't take it so personally. It's just a division of jobs, really. It works well."

"It seems simpler here," Gen said. She wouldn't be able to explain it in a way that Alma would be able to appreciate anyway.

"It is a simple life," Alma agreed. "And a happy one. Do you want my advice?"

"Sure." What could it hurt at this point? It wasn't like Genevieve had any answers of her own.

"I say, marry him now," Alma said. "It'll shake out."

Genevieve smiled in spite of herself. "You don't know how much I wish I could."

Alma gave her a sympathetic smile. "Men are complicated, aren't they?"

"Incredibly," Genevieve agreed. And that would have to cover it.

The Huyard farm was about a fifteen-minute buggy ride from Alma's place, and Alma was an expert with those reins. When they rumbled into the Huyard drive, Genevieve saw an orchard spread out—rows upon rows of leafy trees. If Genevieve had to guess, she'd say that this Amish family did fairly well. The house was freshly painted, there was a large stable, two buggies visible, and a teenage boy was washing one of them with a bucket of soapy water and a sponge. This didn't seem like a family struggling with finances.

"They're a good family," Alma said, as if reading her mind. "Lily's father is the bishop, you know."

"So, they're well respected."

"Very." Alma reined in, and she leaned out of the buggy to wave at the boy. She called something in Pennsylvania Dutch, and the boy pointed toward the house. Alma looked over at Genevieve. "Lily's inside."

Genevieve hopped out of the buggy and watched as Alma tied her horse to a hitching post. Then they headed up to the side door of the house. Lily opened the door before they got to it and gave them a wary look.

"Hi, Lily," Alma said. "Can we come in?"

Lily looked behind her then shook her head. "Can we talk outside? It's a full kitchen."

"Sure," Alma replied, taking a step back. She dropped her gaze. There was a distance between these two young women now, and it was palpable.

Lily asked something in Pennsylvania Dutch and cast a look toward Genevieve.

"Genevieve and I have become friends, but it started out when I asked her to help me find Joseph's watch. I asked her to come with me today," Alma said. "This isn't official, though. I just wanted to know about the watch, not involve police in any way, and she respected that. She's promised that it will stay that way, too. Right, Genevieve?"

"Of course," Genevieve said. "I just wanted to know what was behind what you did. You don't seem like the type to just take something, and it didn't feel right to me."

"I'm not a thief." Lily's lip quivered. "I did take some things…but that's not who I am! It's not."

"What happened?" Alma asked.

"I gave it back, didn't I?" Lily pressed.

"You did, and I thank you for that," Alma replied.

"Did you also take a piece of embroidery done by Linda Yoder?" Genevieve asked.

Lily froze.

"The dogs found it buried in the woods," Genevieve added.

"I went back and it was gone…" Lily rubbed her hands over her face. "I had to do it. One of Linda's nieces had the piece of embroidery, and it was just in a drawer. I didn't think she'd miss it, and Paul said if I didn't steal it, he'd tell my fiancé about things I did during my *Rumspringa*. I went to some parties with Paul back then, and he introduced me to some people…and I wasn't behaving well." Tears leaked down her cheeks. "I stopped going. I did! I was ashamed of myself, and I stopped, but it was too late, because Paul had pictures of me…"

Genevieve's pulse sped up. "Sweetie, what kinds of pictures?" She tried to keep her voice calm, but if Paul was doing what she thought he was doing…

"Just me with other boys. Sitting too close. Or with…beer in my hand. In one picture, I was sitting on a boy's lap."

Okay, that could have been a lot worse, but Lily cast Alma a dismal look.

"In our community, that's a big deal," Alma said softly.

"And Paul said he'd tell your fiancé about this if you didn't bring him expensive items he could sell…"

"*Yah.*" Lily nodded. "He said he'd ruin my wedding! So I thought I had to!"

"But something stopped you," Genevieve said.

"My conscience stopped me," she said. "It was after I took the watch. He'd told me to take anything that looked like it was worth something, and if I didn't bring enough, he'd hand over those pictures. So, when I saw the watch, I thought I could take just one thing and it would be done. It would be big enough that he'd leave me alone. But I just couldn't hand the watch over to him. I'd stolen it, and I was so guilty. But on top of that, I was thinking that if I behave even worse in order to get married, then Paul will have even more power over me for the rest of my life. Sometimes you have to face things. And when you do wrong, you have to apologize and make restitution, and until you do both, it's not over. So, I decided that I'd make things right, and I'd tell my fiancé the worst. And if he didn't marry me, then…that was my punishment to bear."

"Oh, Lily!" Alma put her arms around the girl. "Did you tell him?"

Lily nodded.

"And what did he say?"

"He was upset. But he said he did some dumb things in his *Rumspringa*, too, that he didn't want anyone to hear about. And so did his sisters. And he thinks his sisters still deserve good husbands, so…he said it made no difference, and we'd still get married."

"I'm really glad to hear that," Genevieve said. "Lily, you do deserve a happy life with a good man. Okay? From what I've heard, you're a really good woman. I mean that. Don't let Paul shame you. And don't shame yourself for having been young. Young people make mistakes, and they have to learn as they go. That's totally normal. So forgive yourself, too, if you wished you'd behaved differently. Going forward you will, okay?"

Lily nodded and wiped her eyes. *"Danke."*

"But here's the thing," Genevieve said. "I know you like to take care of things inside your community, but what Paul did was very wrong. He targeted a teenaged girl. How old were you…seventeen? That's the *Rumspringa* year, right?"

"*Yah*, seventeen."

"Okay, so he targeted a teenaged girl, put her in unsafe, precarious situations and took pictures of her. Then he used those pictures to blackmail her into stealing for him. There are a lot of laws broken, but more than that, he'll do this again to the other girls in your community. Alma noticed him giving some extra attention to another young woman, and it makes me wonder if he's up to the same thing with her. It certainly felt off to Alma."

"*Yah*, it felt creepy," Alma said. "I didn't like it."

"The thing is, once these predatory men find something that works, they don't stop. If he isn't caught and made to pay for his actions, then he'll keep it up. Because he's got a nice side that he shows, right? He helps some women who are desperate. He makes a show of being compassionate. So that helps him hide."

Lily's face had paled.

"Did you give him anything that you'd stolen?" Genevieve asked. "I just need to know to protect you."

Lily nodded. "Some farrier tools from my father's shed."

Genevieve nodded. "Okay, that's not so bad. But if we want to protect other girls from this man, then you'd need to press charges against him. I can help you with that, every step of the way."

"I don't know…" Lily breathed. "I just want to get married…"

"I know," Genevieve said. "I guess the other option is to spread the word far and wide in your community that Paul Miller can't be trusted—that he takes advantage of girls and he lies, lies, lies. That might help protect some girls, too."

Lily was silent and she twisted her apron around her finger.

"I'd need my *daet*'s permission," Lily said after a moment. "He's the bishop, so even if my fiancé agreed, my *daet* would have to agree, too."

"It sounds like there will have to be some quiet, private conversations with your family and your fiancé…soon your husband," Genevieve said. "It's okay to do it that way. It's okay to talk it out, be very sure, and get the support and advice from the people who love you most."

Lily brightened a little. "It will take a few days."

"That's okay," Genevieve said gently. "You take the time you need. And when you're ready, you can call me at this phone number, and I'll help you with the rest." She pulled out a business card and handed it to Lily.

Lily looked down at the number. "I'll talk to them tonight. I'll call you in a day or two. Is that all right?"

"That's perfectly all right." Good. She was tough—Genevieve had known that from the start.

It was time to let her use that strength to protect herself and her community, and put that predator where he belonged.

In a way, Genevieve envied Lily that strong, united, protective community. And yet, Genevieve had a strong, wealthy and protective father—there were two sides to every coin, weren't there?

Maybe it was time to have another chat with her dad… This time about a more personal matter. Genevieve was heartbroken, and in times like these, her dad's support was like a whirlwind. Maybe she needed that whirlwind now.

WHEN GENEVIEVE RETURNED to the K9 training facility, she pulled out her computer and wrote a short email giving her resignation.

Dear Sir,
I am submitting my resignation effective immediately. I would like to thank the Pennsylvania State Police for my years of service, for the training and the support. I leave with only good memories of my time working with the state's best officers.

She sent it to Scott and Commissioner Taylor both. It was done.

Then she dialed her father's number.

"Genevieve?" Her father's voice was curt, a little worried.

"Hi, Dad." Her voice trembled. "I just quit my job…"

"Oh, Genny… Whose butt do I need to kick? Just tell me!"

She couldn't help but laugh through her tears. "No one's. It's kind of complicated…"

Somehow it helped to lay it out before the one man she knew would love her no matter what she did. Fresh starts hurt sometimes, but they could hurt a little less with some support around her.

SCOTT STOOD BACK fifty yards, watching Vince work with Benjie. The man was patient—he was a very good K9 officer. He cared about the dogs, he knew how to work with them, and he put in the time. But again and again, Scott watched as Benjie failed to respond to commands.

And Benjie knew those commands. Wait. Hold. Stay. Gun. Crawl. Get them. Down. Retrieve… All those commands were life or death for a K9 partnership out in the field, and Benjie knew them. He did them perfectly with Scott.

Just not with Vince.

Konig sat at Scott's side, patiently panting as they waited. Finally, Vince came back across the field, Benjie at his side.

"I don't know what to do," Vince said. "Are you seeing anything I'm doing wrong?"

"Nothing. It's not you," Scott said.

He looked sadly down at Benjie, and the dog looked up at him with an open-mouthed grin on his fool face. He didn't know what was in the balances here, did he? He was just a dog who'd chosen the wrong guy.

"Try it again with Konig," Scott said, passing over the page of his commands in German. "I want to see how you do with him."

"Konig, kommen," Vince said, and Konig jumped forward happily. *"Fuss."*

Konig fell in at a close heel to Vince, his attention on his handler like a pro. Scott could feel it in his gut—those two were a perfect match.

He looked down at Benjie, and Benjie stared up at him with such love in his canine face that it brought a lump to his throat. He squatted and gave the dog an affectionate rub behind the ears.

"You really love me, huh?" he said softly.

Benjie gave him a lick across the chin.

"Blast it…" he muttered.

His phone rang and Scott stood and picked up the call. It was from the commissioner.

"Hi, Scott," Commissioner Taylor said. "I just received Genevieve Austin's resignation letter. I need to know what happened before I proceed with anything."

Scott's heart hammered to a stop. She'd sent it in already? Was this really over?

"Sir, here's where it stands. She's a good officer and she's smart. She's compassionate, but she's also tough. She's got what it takes to be a huge asset to the state police, and I won't be the one to hold her back."

"Okay… That's no help if she's not working for us, though."

Scott looked out over the field to where Vince had Konig running drills. The dog was alert, keen, completely focused on Vince's commands, and dang, could that dog run fast.

"She doesn't need to quit. Reject her resignation. I'm going to respectfully decline the command position at South Kingston Station." Even as the words came out of his mouth, he knew his life was unalterably changing. He was turning down a huge advance in his career so that Gen could get a fair shake. He was going to step back and let someone else move forward, all because he couldn't do this at the expense of the woman he loved.

What would his father say about it? He realized in a rush that he didn't care. This wasn't about his father, or about anyone's else's grudging respect. This was about being true to himself. He'd accept the consequences.

"Are you serious?"

"Yeah… I am." Scott sighed.

"Are you looking for another command position, then?" the commissioner asked.

"Actually…" It was tempting. Very tempting. But then he looked down at Benjie. "No, sir. I'm going to step back down and apply for K9 duty again. There's a dog here that needs me."

"A dog…"

"He's one special dog, sir. I also had a chance to work with Gen again and remember what it was like to have a partner. I miss it. I want to work with Benjie—have my K9 partner and work in the field."

Benjie looked up at him, his tail softly thumping the grass. Scott couldn't just leave him to be shuttled around to other people who'd never really fill his heart. Benjie was his...whether he'd wanted a dog of his own or not. And working here at the training center, or out in the field, he and Benjie could stay together. Benjie would have his way.

"You say that Genevieve deserves another chance, but you won't work with her," the commissioner said. "That doesn't sound promising to me."

"She's excellent. She's got what it takes, and she's adjusted her attitude about authority. I'm sure of that. I'll stake my reputation on it."

"Strong words. Why won't you work with her yourself?"

Did he really have to confess this? It looked like he'd have to.

"Because I'm in love with her," he replied. "I have been for years. And that's not fair to put her into that situation."

"If you two are dating, you know you'll have to report it to Human Resources," the commissioner said.

"Understood. We aren't dating. But she deserves this chance to simply do the job. She's a quality officer, sir. I'll vouch for that."

"All right, Scott. I know you would never make a decision like this lightly. I'll have to respect that."

"Thank you, sir. Can I ask one favor?"

"You can ask, but no promises."

"Would you reject Genevieve's resignation?"

"I can't do that, but I can have a talk with her and ask her to reconsider," the commissioner said. "In fact, as one of your last acts as acting commander at the K9, why don't you let her know that, before I accept her resignation, I really want to talk to her?"

"Thank you, sir." And he meant that with every fiber of his being.

When Scott hung up, his gaze moved out to the field where Vince had stopped the drills to reward the dog with pets and scratches. Konig had never looked happier, and when Vince looked over, he gave a thumbs-up.

"The heart wants what the heart wants, huh, Benjie?" Scott said ruefully.

Whatever happened now, at least Scott knew he was being true to his. But what Scott hoped in the deepest part of his heart was that he and Gen would have something to report to Human Resources, after all. What were the odds that Gen would take a chance on the partner she never forgot?

CHAPTER EIGHTEEN

GENEVIEVE CARRIED HER bag down the stairs. Having handed in her resignation, there was no point in staying there any longer. It was time to regather her thoughts and make new plans.

Wendy looked up from her desk in surprise.

"You're not due to leave yet," she said.

"I know. I'm…checking myself out."

Wendy arched an eyebrow. "They won't like that."

"I know." Genevieve gave her a nod. "It was nice to meet you, Wendy. I hope I'll see you again under better circumstances."

"You, too," Wendy said weakly, her eyes following Genevieve as she headed for the door.

So much had changed since Genevieve had arrived at the puppy school. A week ago, the thought of leaving this way would have made her sick. It would have felt like failure. But now? She knew what she had to do, and it was high time she got to it.

Besides, she'd told Scott how she'd felt about him and that had unblocked some part of her heart that she'd kept hidden away. And now that everything was out in the daylight, even her options looked different.

She headed out the front door and spotted Scott leaning against the railing of the porch, his phone in his hand. Benjie sat at his feet, looking happy to be next to his favorite human. Scott looked up at her.

"There you are," he said. There was a certain tenderness in his voice that she knew was reserved for her alone, and it brought a lump to her throat. She'd miss this man so much.

"I was packing up," she said, trying to sound tougher than she felt. "I'm leaving now."

He waggled his phone at her, and she could see an email open on it. "I've been told to pass on that the commissioner doesn't want to accept your resignation. He wants a chance to talk you out of it."

"Scott…"

"I'm serious. You can't just quit."

Was he really going to make this harder on her than it already was?

"I might need to talk to Tom myself and explain, but it won't change things."

"Gen…" He shook his head, his dark gaze catching hers. "I turned down the promotion."

Genevieve heart seemed to stop as she stared at him. "What?"

"I turned it down. I talked to the commissioner an hour ago, and I told him that you're an excellent trooper, that your attitude has adjusted, and that you're an asset to the state police. You deserve a proper shot, and I won't stand in your way."

"But what will you do?" she asked.

"K9. Benjie needs me. I think Konig and Vince are a better match. For one thing, Vince's German is better than anyone else's around here."

"So…just like that?" she asked.

"No, not just like that." Scott crossed the porch, his boots thunking against the wooden boards. "It was a much harder choice to make, but it's the right one."

"For Benjie?" she asked.

"For me." His voice dropped and he caught her hand. "Gen, I'm not going to be your SO anymore. Equal footing—that's what we needed, right?"

"You're doing all of this for me?" she whispered.

"I'm actually doing it to be true to myself," he said. "I realized that I was pushing for commander to impress my old man, but working with you made me see that what I really want is to be in the field. But I was hoping that if we didn't have that pesky boss situation in the way, and if your way was clear to move on in your career the way you deserve, that you might consider me a partner again…"

"Technically, Benjie will be your partner," she said with a low laugh.

"I'm trying to be cute here," Scott said with a smile touching his lips. "I'm talking partner, boyfriend…and eventually, if you'll have me… more…"

"More?" she breathed.

"I love you. I know you better than anyone, and there's no other woman I want. I'm not pressuring you. You want time? You got it. If you want to reject me completely, I'll find a way to get over it. But, yeah, if you feel what I'm feeling, then I'm in this for the long haul. All the way."

"Scott..."

He moved in closer and tugged her against him, lowering his lips over hers.

Her eyes fluttered shut and she leaned into his warm arms. When they pulled back, she said, "What about the security cameras?"

Scott looked up, his cheeks reddened. "I forgot about them. Sorry. But what do you say? Will you give me a chance?"

"With which one?" she asked, a smile toying at her lips. Because she knew he was hers now—well and completely hers. "Are you looking to be my partner? Boyfriend? Awfully serious boyfriend? More than that, even?"

She was teasing, but Scott caught her eye and grinned.

"Are you really calling my bluff, Austin?" he asked. "All right. I'll prove how serious I am about you. Marry me."

She stared at him. "Do you mean that?"

"A hundred percent. Marry me. I'll sign any prenup your dad wants me to sign. But be mine, Genevieve..."

The laughter evaporated and tears welled in her eyes. "If you really mean it—"

Was this actually happening? Was Scott asking her to be his wife? She tried to tamp down the soaring hope in her heart, but she didn't manage it.

"I do really mean it." He tugged her in close again. "What do you say?"

Scott Simpson proposing marriage...it was almost unbelievable, but after this week together, it wasn't. She knew how much she loved him, and she knew how much he loved her. They'd just been two star-crossed fools running away from the deepest love they'd ever known.

"I say yes!" she said.

Scott pulled her into another kiss, and muted from behind the glass, Genevieve heard the whoop of delight from Wendy, who'd apparently been at the window, listening to all of it.

She'd marry him, and she'd have her best friend at her side and in her heart for the rest of her life.

She didn't pull back until she felt Benjie's snout push between them, and then she laughed and pet the dog's head affectionately.

"And Benjie makes three," she said with a glistening smile.

* * * * *

If you loved this book,
be sure to check out Patricia Johns's
The Butternut Amish B&B miniseries:

Her Amish Country Valentine
A Single Dad In Amish Country
A Boy's Amish Christmas

Available now at Harlequin.com!

HARLEQUIN
Reader Service

Enjoyed your book?

Try the perfect subscription for Romance readers and get more great books like this delivered right to your door.

See why over 10+ million readers have tried Harlequin Reader Service.

Start with a Free Welcome Collection with free books and a gift—valued over $20.

Choose any series in print or ebook. See website for details and order today:

TryReaderService.com/subscriptions